MURDE

MISCHIEF

WG Eggleton

Cover design by Ann Nolan, freelance artist residing in Victoria BC, Canada

Note for Librarians: A cataloguing record for this book is available from Library and Archives Canada at www.collectionscanada.ca/amicus/index-e.html
ISBN 1-4251-0664-1

Printed in Victoria, BC, Canada. Printed on paper with minimum 30% recycled fibre. Trafford's print shop runs on "green energy" from solar, wind and other environmentally-friendly power sources.

Offices in Canada, USA, Ireland and UK

Book sales for North America and international:
Trafford Publishing, 6E–2333 Government St.,
Victoria, BC V8T 4P4 CANADA
phone 250 383 6864 (toll-free 1 888 232 4444)
fax 250 383 6804; email to orders@trafford.com
Book sales in Europe:
Trafford Publishing (UK) Limited, 9 Park End Street, 2nd Floor
Oxford, UK OX1 1HH UNITED KINGDOM
phone 44 (0)1865 722 113 (local rate 0845 230 9601)
facsimile 44 (0)1865 722 868; info.uk@trafford.com
Order online at:
trafford.com/06-2422

10 9 8 7 6 5 4 3 2

1

"I'M GOING TO kill her!" Shirley Foster declared and then waited. Waited for nothing. Most mornings in this kitchen, a kitchen geared for laughter and fun, did not start with discussions of murder. She looked across the room to the glassed-in breakfast nook and waited to see if any reaction would come from its sole occupant. She hadn't really expected a reply but that wasn't going to slow her down. Picking up her juice and cereal, she moved out of the kitchen area and took her spot at the breakfast table.

"I'm going to kill her!" she repeated. "That's all there is to it. Next time she starts waving her cigarettes around I'm going to kill her!" With that resolution the pretty young woman picked up her spoon and turned her full attention to a bowl of oatmeal and apples.

"You are not going to kill her," finally came the reply from behind the Victoria Times-Colonist newspaper that was waving in the air across from her. "You do not murder someone because they smoke."

Shirley's face made a brief grimace as she looked over at the tall lanky man, her husband, who was already putting down his paper.

"Don't be tedious, Stephen! Of course, I'm not killing her

because she smokes; I'm killing her because she's Cynthia. That in itself should be enough. You'd know that if you'd been listening at all. The smoking is just the final straw. Besides, do you think she even cares about smoking? That's what makes it so annoying. She probably doesn't even like smoking. She just cares about power, about being above the rules. I bet she didn't even smoke before it was illegal and only does it now to piss me off. And it's working! But I've had it and I'm telling you the next time, the very next time I'm going to kill her. Not because she smokes but because I hate her!"

Shirley was a petite blonde in her late twenties and although she was the mother of two young boys many thought she needed maternal supervision herself. This impression was partially created by her fluttery dramatics. The delicate features on her animated face only served to reinforce it. However, on closer attention one could see a firm chin and a cold unwavering glance in her dark blue eyes. There was fierce determination and an unflinching will behind Shirley's energy. Few people became aware of this and those that did very often were taken unpleasantly by surprise.

Her husband, Stephen, knew his wife and enjoyed her. As he knew her roles were but a diversion, her enthusiasm and her games entertained him. A tall brown-haired man of thirty odd years with a calm, natural manner, he was neither attractive nor unattractive. His movements were relaxed and unhurried, as was his life. That was how he liked it. Shirley brought excitement to him, just the right amount and just the right kind.

"You are not going to kill her and you do not hate her."

"I do hate her! I do!" Shirley insisted firmly.

At this outburst, the Fosters' two young sons bounded down the stairs from the bedrooms and into the kitchen area demanding, "Who does mommy hate? You said hating wasn't nice?" Not waiting for an answer, a competition quickly broke out.

"I hate Bobby Thompson."

"No, you don't – I do!"

"I do so. I can hate anyone I want. I hate lots of people. I hate you!"

"Mom!"

Stephen folded his newspaper and rose from their breakfast table. It was time to bring things back to the real world. "You do not hate Bobby Thompson or anyone else. Neither does your mother. She is playacting, pretending. Now get your things and get in the car or you'll have to walk to school because I'm leaving now." The youngsters went screaming down the stairs towards the front part of the house going nowhere slowly and nowhere quietly.

"I do hate her and I am going to kill her," Shirley stated once more.

"Alright," Stephen replied. "Hate her if you must. But don't kill her. We don't want you to lose your job."

"Maybe I could just make her disappear," said Shirley thinking of new angles.

"That's it," Stephen agreed. "Change yourself into a witch and make her disappear."

"You're humouring me."

"Yes, I am," Stephen said as he bent to lightly kiss his wife before he left for the day's work. "See you tonight and try not to murder anyone."

Shirley now was left in an empty family home, a quiet family home. She took what remained of her orange juice, went through the sliding patio doors and settled into one of the chairs on the back deck. This was her favourite spot and this was her favourite time of day. This was when she dreamed or not, but it was always when she planned and she schemed. Stephen was right she did need her job. But she wondered, she wondered.

*   *   *   *   *

In a three-story stucco apartment building at the corner of Douglas Road and Battery St, Victoria there was little similarity to the Fosters' morning. This was where Doris Webster lived, and like Shirley Foster, she worked at the CIBC located on the corner of Cook and Fairfield Road. And that is where the similarity ended. She did know Cynthia Harmon and her cigarettes but Doris would never have wanted to kill her, or would she? No one knew what Miss Webster, as she was known, thought, wanted or did. One wondered if Miss Webster thought, wanted, or did anything.

Doris's home was half a block from Mile 0 where the Trans Canada highway officially begins and ends. Here Dallas Road, which is part of the scenic ocean drive, and Douglas Street, which takes you downtown, meet at the southwest corner of Beacon Hill Park. This the principle park of Victoria was set aside way back in the 1860's as green space. In the 1890's it became a municipal park and with its meandering pathways, formal gardens and wildflower meadows it remains a favourite area to wander for both locales and tourists. But not for Doris – there was no one to go walking with and Doris would never walk in the park alone.

Yet here across the street from the entrance to the Park was where Doris Webster lived or rather resided. It was an attractive clean neighbourhood and her building fit right in. Its gardens were always tended, the two-toned stucco regularly cared for, the big flat wood frame windows continually cleaned. It looked the way you'd expect the tenants to look – tidy and old.

Doris Webster was fifty-five years old, an old fifty-five year old. A big square matronly woman with short cropped gray hair. She had never married. In fact, she had remained with her invalid parents till their demise fifteen years earlier. She was then faced, at the age of forty, to learn to live alone and to earn that living. Change had never been welcomed by Doris and this had been an exceptionally hard time for her. She had had to move from her parents' home to an apartment. She'd found this building with tenants her parents' age. That made it feel like home and safe. The building had a secure front entrance from Dallas Road to a traditional apartment building. As well, along the Battery Street side, there were units like little townhouses with private entrances. The openness of the townhouses did not appeal to Doris and she had moved into a front corner apartment on the second floor.

She had had to get a job. Somehow, she never knew exactly how, Doris was hired by the CIBC. Doris had had to move and had had to find a job. She did both of these with much pain and never intended to move again. From that time until now, routine and repetition had been her comforts and of course, her memories, especially the memories of her father. He continued to be her support and her comfort. What would her day be without her morning talks with her father?

Doris rose each morning promptly at six. Her drapes were opened wide to the sights of the park. The bed was made. The overstuffed apartment tidied, although with all the clutter one could never tell. Laundry sorted, ironing done and Doris dressed and breakfasted. Minor events that in Doris's world were major events. Then to talk – a cup of tea, a chair, and a nice long chat with her father; well her father's picture to be precise. This was what Doris enjoyed.

"I do not like that Cynthia Harmon. No, I do not. She is an evil woman. She wants to make trouble for me. She has Mr. Manders blinded. He thinks she is so important and always so right. She isn't you know. She lies to him and she flirts with him! A real little flirt, I wouldn't say tramp but some people would I'm sure. It's Miss Harmon this and Miss Harmon that. Now she is telling me Mr. Manders isn't satisfied with my work; that Mr. Manders thinks maybe I'm too old, too inflexible. Mr. Manders says maybe I should retire. Mr. Manders says all these things but not to me! No, I only hear from Miss Harmon, the great Miss Cynthia Harmon. And who are the Harmons anyway? No family that you or Mother would have cared to have in our home. She wants to make trouble that's what she is like. She has already had that nice little Julia Cheung fired. Now she wants to make trouble for me. I know it. I don't like it. I wish she would go away, just go away!"

The clock on Doris' buffet bonged eight o'clock and the morning talk had to end. It was time to run. The Number 5 bus would be here too soon. She was just around the corner from the bus stop but it still always seemed too far. Why was she always late? Why was she always rushed? Always rushed, too much to do, too much to think about and Cynthia Harmon. Yes, Cynthia Harmon.

*   *   *   *   *

West of Victoria along highway 14 (better known as the Island highway) are the Western Communities – View Royal, Colwood, The Highlands, Langford and Metchosin. It was here in the community of Colwood that Mike Baker, employee of the CIBC Cook and Fairfield branch, lived with his family. Each morning started with Mike feeding his young daughter her breakfast while his wife showered. It was a happy way to start the day and recently truly happy times were rare.

Mike was an attractive young man. As is said, he was tall, dark, and handsome. Lately though his dark good looks weren't as noticeable as the lack of sleep, the obvious strain, the worry. He had married Linda two years ago. They had bought a townhouse in the Oak Dell complex on Mount View road. It was not a large complex, just 23 townhouses in a square facing a courtyard. Actually it was a parking lot and Mike always wondered why it hadn't been made into a children's park. Still it was a pretty complex. The townhouses were not exactly identical. There were lots of windows and corners, which gave them the feel of a house rather than of an apartment. The attractive, two story, blue siding with light beige stucco units, each with a garage, were ideal starter homes for new families. The one disadvantage was the distance from town and the ugly commute to work but that distance had made the price more reasonable. Even so, with both Mike and his wife Linda working, they could just afford it. Then the baby had come. Little Erica, she was their blessing, their little miracle. But she had taken her toll. One of the reasons they had selected this home and area was because it would be a good place to raise children. But not right away, once they were settled. The baby had been a surprise, financially a big surprise. Linda had not been healthy. Her work had stopped very soon after conception and the medical expenses started soon after that. They were coping but only just. The home was one of love but also one of tension.

The kitchen still had the basic builder paint on the walls. The curtains were simple horizontal blinds from Canada Tire. The character of the room came not from the decoration but from the clutter. There were appliances, dishes, baby dishes, bottles, and assorted odds and sods on the counters. Then there were toys, toys everywhere.

It was here that Mike sat feeding his young daughter. Erica giggled and played and had food going everywhere. Mike carried on, he was used to this meal being a playtime. Linda entered and poured herself a coffee. She was a pleasant looking young woman. She would never be considered strikingly attractive. She looked like a gentle, happy young woman who only wanted to be with her small family and that was what she was. Her light brown hair, cut short for easy care, was still wet from the shower. Without makeup and in casual slacks, Linda looked even younger than she was. Today, she also looked hesitant.

Sitting beside Mike and reaching for Erica's hand, she started to talk.

"I think I might be able to get my job back at the store."

"No, you stay with Erica; we'll manage," Mike answered.

"It would be a help and I want to help. I don't like you working so hard," his wife replied.

"I don't work hard," laughed Mike without any real humour. "I'm an assistant, basically the office manager's assistant, old Cynthia's gopher. You know how much time it takes. I seldom work past five, no weekends, virtually no overtime. I could do with some overtime if I could get paid for it."

"Why wouldn't you get paid?" asked Linda, confused. "If you work it...."

"Any overtime has to be submitted separately to be paid," Mike explained. "And Cynthia has to approve it. She won't. It doesn't look good on the budget! I could work it but she wouldn't pay me any extra for it."

"That's not fair," Linda insisted.

"It's the way it is," Mike said. "It doesn't really matter though because there isn't really a need to work extra time. Sometimes we're busy and sometimes there are problems. I'm not one of the straight-off-the-street whiz kids though, so I know what's what. It's not a big deal. I've worked in all the jobs and been doing this for a while. I'm good at it. So it's not hard."

"Okay, maybe not working hard. But you are worrying. I want to help," Linda continued.

"You do help. You help with Erica. When I'm away I know she's being taken care of properly. I never have to worry about that."

"I want to help with the money," Linda persisted.

"Say you did go back to work," answered Mike, bringing logic to bear. "What about Erica? We would have to pay someone to look after her. There would be the additional travel expense for you to get to and from work. Not to mention to and from wherever we had to take Erica. Considering your clothes for working, your lunch money, and all the other little things, we wouldn't be any further ahead."

"But what are we going to do?" asked Linda, desperation starting to be heard in her voice.

"It's not really as bad as that," replied Mike. "We have to hang on until my next promotion that's all. The next move has a real nice jump in salary. That would settle us down enough to catch up. We would still have to be careful for a bit. But we wouldn't be going backwards."

"Is there a chance for a promotion?" she asked.

"There's always a chance," he said. "They'd have to move Cynthia. If they did move Cynthia, there's a possibility I might or might not get the job. They might transfer someone in."

"Oh, Mike, no!"

"It doesn't matter. First, Cynthia would have to leave and why would she? She has it good. Does next to no work, has Manders wrapped around her finger. Why leave? 'Course something sudden could happen, something she didn't planned on." This last was said more to himself.

"What do you mean? What are you talking about?" asked his wife, sensing a change in her husband.

"Oh, nothing," Mike quickly replied. Smiling gently at her, he added, "It's just if something unexpected happened it's likely I would get the position. They wouldn't want to take the time to bring someone in from another location."

"Oh," said Linda, still not sure she understood what was going on in her husband's head.

There wasn't anything more to say but there was plenty for Mike to think about and lots of time to do so. He walked along the quiet country street to Sooke Road. There he stood with the other commuters waiting for the bus that would take them through the Colwood Crawl into Victoria. The Crawl was the affectionate, or not, term for the snail's pace traffic that made its way from Colwood, past car lots, shops and a couple of neighbourhood pubs, to the Trans Canada highway. There the traffic headed into Victoria, still crowded and still not fast but better than the Crawl. Each day the commute was an irritant and an added stress to Mike's already stressful life. Today, however, he didn't notice any of it, he walked as in a fog and just kept thinking, "If something sudden happened."

*　　*　　*　　*　　*

Cynthia Harmon started her day never imagining the amount of discussion she was causing throughout the city. If she had known she would not have minded. For one thing, she was used to it. For another, she was a fighter and a survivor.

She had learnt very early that life was a struggle. Her youth had been spent in Belmont Park, the military housing just off the Colwood junction. You didn't live in Belmont Park without becoming a fighter. You fought to fit in, you fought to be different, and you fought to survive. Her first goal had been to get as far from the military world as possible. Her longer-term goal was to never endure the side affects of poverty again. She intended to have so much money that no one, not even herself, would remember the home she had left.

Her first goal had been reached by marrying at the very first opportunity. The marriage only lasted as long as it took Cynthia to discover that a man married to her was not as profitable as a man married to someone else.

One man after another was one step after another for the completion of her next aim. She no longer had any contact with her family. She had obtained a nice pile of possessions and a comfortable stash of funds. But it was not enough to stop the memories. She had grown to realize it would never be enough. She didn't mind; she now liked the game. She liked the power, the intimidation, and she liked her greed.

At twenty-eight, Cynthia Harmon was a warrior. Her

life was one of control, discipline, and power. She ruled the staff at work. She ruled her lovers. She controlled those who considered themselves her friends. Her life ran according to her wishes and she designed it down to the smallest detail. Cynthia's day started with an early morning swim in the pool of her Windsor Park condominium. After her swim, her grooming procedure began. To an average office worker, this would have been an elaborate production saved for special occasions but Cynthia knew her assets and used them. She had never been a Girl Guide but she did like their motto, "Be Prepared".

To see the finished product, a magazine perfect woman with full blonde hair and green cat eyes, one sensed not only beauty but also money. In fact, Cynthia's world smelt of money. Cynthia lived in a four-storey condominium half a block from the Oak Bay Beach Hotel, the heart of traditional "old money" Victoria. In any other harbour city, this area would be packed with high rise buildings but not Victoria. After a couple of towers were built over James Bay way back in the 60s, the city had quickly passed bylaws prohibiting high rises. The priorities were to prevent the congestion created from such buildings and to protect the view for as many as possible. The priority was not development. Things did not change much in Victoria and the by-laws remained.

Cynthia's front window overlooked the Oak Bay Marina. A marina that year round was fully occupied with sailboats. This was a sailor's dream – a climate where you could sail any and every day of the year.

There had been sailors when Cynthia was growing up navy sailors, military men, living with their families in Belmont Park. Her father. She had left those people, left that world and was determined to fit into the one that she saw around her. The distance from her old life to her new one was much greater than the physical miles she'd traveled. She was never going back, never looking back. She enjoyed how far she'd come and she wanted more. Everything that had happened so far had just been the first step but a pretty good first step.

Inside Cynthia's apartment the picture of elegance continued. Good taste was everywhere. It looked just like a photo layout from a decorating magazine. It was all very obvious that a large number of dollars had been put to work. But somehow it didn't seem real; it was all too new, too protected. Cynthia had not yet managed to attain an air of unconcern for her expensive objects. For anyone aware of Cynthia's paycheck, it would also be clear that Cynthia could ill afford the costly toys she now enjoyed. And Cynthia did enjoy. Each day she rose counting her good fortunes.

Once fully dressed, she had a half-cup of coffee. All stimulants in moderation. She had seen the results of too little moderation with her father and alcohol. She had her half-cup of coffee and no breakfast. To her, it served no purpose but as a delay of the day. It was a time-out in the action.

After her coffee, Cynthia went down to the building's car park and unlocked her new BMW. This was one of her special treats. Just getting into the little car made her smile. She would never forget the look on the face of the man who had accidentally scratched her car door in a parking lot. He would never park beside a silver BMW again. What a fool! Parking too close to her, he had opened his door right into her car while she getting ready to drive away. She had been at her most calm as she got out of the car and walked towards him. He had started to bluster but stopped quickly when he saw the hardness in her face. It ended quickly with another cheque, ostensibly for damages, in Cynthia's hands. No, he would never park near a silver BMW again! She laughed at the memory; but she hadn't laughed then, no sir!

Cynthia was not a person to let the world slip by her. No matter how many thoughts whirled around her head, she took time to cloak herself in as many pleasures, large and small, as possible. That was why she took the same route to and from work each day. This was definitely frowned on by security experts, but she'd like to see someone try to kidnap her! Besides Cynthia had decided on the most aesthetic route and that was the route she took each and every day.

She turned onto Oak Bay Avenue and drove slowly down the row of Tudor shops. Once the car reached Richmond, Cynthia turned left onto the narrow road lined with trees and old well-kept homes. The homes were the reason she drove this street. No two were alike yet all exuded care and privacy. Where Richmond meets Fairfield, the car knew to turn right and to increase its speed. This road was a favorite. In spring, the trees blossomed and the street became a pink postcard. Today, though, was October and Fairfield Road offered a different pleasure. At certain speed, without interference from tourists, the bumps and curves of this street created a gentle but stirring roller coaster ride which brought Cynthia to the bank's parking lot, eager for the day.

Small pleasures? Yes, but Cynthia's main interest in life was taking care of Cynthia and in that no concern was too small. She was self-indulgent, she was self-centered, she also was happy. Not many around her were, which added to her joy.

2

IN THE SERENITY of the Rockland area, the rest of Victoria does not exist. Just east of the downtown core, this prestigious neighbourhood is filled with graceful old estate homes. The world is private, quiet, and lavish. One can't imagine hardship or unhappiness living here. This is where local sculptors have their creations displayed as part of the garden designs. This is, after all, where the Lieutenant Governor's house is.

While Government House itself is closed to the public, the grounds with their 100-year-old gardens are open from dawn to dusk each day. Visitors enjoy the sights and smells of exquisite formal displays and of wild native plantings. They come to admire the gardens and are surprised by one of the most spectacular ocean views in the city.

This was the world of Dave Manders and his wife, Sybil Manders (nee Westcott). The Westcotts were an old family with a great deal of old money. Their house was on Pemberton, a side street of Rockland so even more private and more quiet. This was the Westcotts' family home and although the lands had been sold off, the house remained a single family residence, contrary to many grand old Victoria homes that now were apartments or nursing homes.

It was a majestic three-storey house with a stone wall surrounding the property and providing gateposts to its entrance. The stone continued for the porte cochere, the entrance originally designed for the arrival of carriages. The two stories above the stone were Tudor style in beige and green. Four double chimneys rose from a shake roof. The front windows overlooked an expansive front yard and the rear windows looked over a back garden that was a mini-park. A large English perennial garden surrounded the property lines. Border shrubs and flowering trees were intermixed to add variety of height and colour. This all edged a lawn of thick green grass that would have done any of the local golf courses justice. The centerpiece to all of this was a large concrete fishpond with assorted water plants, fountains and grandfather goldfish. Dave Manders sat in the breakfast room, which overlooked this back garden, but he saw none of it.

Dave Manders had married into this wealth, having had none of his own. His position as manager of the CIBC was due more to his efforts to gain respectability and visibility than to anything else. He had needed that respectability to mix with the people of the life he wanted. More precisely, to mix with the daughters of the people. Marrying money seemed a lot easier and more fun than earning it. He had hit the jackpot when Sybil Westcott agreed to be his wife. Being a bank manager wasn't much but Dave Manders had never had much ambition for work. His ambition was for money and lifestyle. Being a bank manager had been enough to get him Sybil Westcott. He had got what he wanted and he didn't need to do more. He was living the life he wanted with an attractive wife at his side in public and various young women at his side in private. He prided himself on being organized and down-to-earth. He kept what he classified as his real life quite separate from what he referred to as make believe. To a spectator his whole world looked artificial except for Sybil.

Sybil came from a family who not only knew how to live with money but knew how to make it, keep it, and use it. She knew its advantages and she knew its disadvantages. She was a lovely lady; an elegant painting with salon coloured hair that framed an open interested face. She was a trim well-tailored woman whose movements were smooth and gracious. But for all that, to look at Sybil Manders one only saw the grey eyes, which didn't just see you but also understood you, read you. When she softened those eyes you would follow her anywhere, safe and content. When she hardened them, you knew she was to be obeyed.

Dave's morning meal was usually spent alone reading the paper and checking with his broker in Toronto. He had started using a Toronto broker when the Vancouver stock exchange's ethics were in question. That matter settled years ago, but Dave remained with his fellow back east.

Today was not to be an average day. Sybil entered the breakfast room as Dave was still eating. Dave's surprise at seeing her hadn't found its way into words before Sybil spoke.

"I want to talk to you about Cynthia Harmon," Sybil informed him. "I do not make it a policy to interfere with your work or with your favorites. However, I have been receiving complaints regarding her rudeness to several of our oldest family friends. I do not intend to allow a little slip of a girl to bring hard feelings between valued acquaintances and myself. If this continues, these people will simply pull their accounts and disassociate themselves from you. Consequently there will be a strain for me with them. I will not have it. I would suggest you see that Miss Harmon learns some manners."

"There is nothing wrong with Cynthia's manners," Dave replied. "The old fogeys who complained probably deserved to be insulted."

"That is entirely beside the point," replied Sybil. "Not all the complaints were with business either. When you took her to the Union Club for lunch, she ran into Gwen Hamilton in the ladies room. Your Cynthia took the opportunity to extol the virtues of some makeup that covers up the signs of excess drinking. At the Oak Bay Beach Hotel when you took her for drinks, she told Rosemarie Crawford that her husband's suits seemed to be too small for him these days. You seem to be losing your good sense. You usually take them to places where our friends wouldn't run into you. I suggest you are not the one in control of this small endeavor. So either tidy this affair up or I will."

With these final words, Sybil exited as determined as when she entered. Dave was left alone with the overwhelming awareness that this conversation had taken place on a morning when the market was again dropping.

* * * * *

The oldest residential area of Victoria, James Bay, is south of the city core and west of Beacon Hill Park. It is here that the few high-rise buildings that were allowed to be constructed remain. One such building sits half a block from the park on Toronto Street. Built many years ago, it continued to be well maintained, well secured and popular with the owners, particularly absentee owners whose rental incomes were reliable, with no fuss or muss.

It was one of these units that Jim and Judy Morrison had rented five months ago. It was a nice location within an easy walk to downtown, within moments from the duck ponds, the soccer fields and meditation pathways of Beacon Hill Park. It was also just around the corner from the Emily Carr house – where the most famous of Victoria's artists had been born in 1871. On the way to the Emily Carr house was the James Bay pub. This of all the landmarks in the area was where Jim most liked to walk and he liked to walk there frequently.

Inside the suite there was little sign of permanency.

There was a double sleeping bag in the bedroom, a couple of suitcases and scattered clothes. In the kitchen a couple of dirty dishes stood alone on the counter. The dining area was empty of any table or of any chairs. The walls were void of any pictures. The living area however, held a brand-new big-screen colour television and a complete stereo sound system.

Judy was an emaciated pale girl of twenty with long stringy hair. Jim was a small wiry youth with horrific skin. Judy was muttering and hiding at the same time.

"What ya talkin' about?" demanded Jim. "We did it before and nothing happened. We ain't goin' stop now!"

"I can't," Judy whined. "I'm sure Cynthia knows about it."

"So what if she does," he challenged. "She can't stop us."

"But she knows," cried Judy. "I'm sure she knows. And she knows I'm a phony."

"You ain't no phony. You said you'd worked in a bank, now you have!" Jim said laughing at his little joke. "Now say it   say what you're goin' do."

"I can't anymore I tell you."

"Oh yes you can. We only need a bit more," Jim said, trying to smooth her worries.

"I don't think you care for me at all, just for what I can get you," pouted Judy.

"I'm still here, ain't I? I can get better and prettier anytime I want and I coulda left lots of times. But I'm here, ain't I? Ya too dumb to see that?"

This backhanded compliment seemed to be sufficient for Judy whose face became almost pretty as she smiled.

"I guess if you were only interested in money, you would just kill me. I'm worth a lot more dead," she giggled. "We were given a little booklet of our benefits and I'm worth lots if I die. You would get it all because you're my husband. Aren't you?"

"Sure, sure I'm you're husband. Now are we going for it or not?" he demanded.

"Okay, but this is the last time," she said still hesitant. "I'm sure Cynthia won't stand for much more."

"She's nothing," Jim said smugly. "I can handle her."

*   *   *   *   *

In their little Fairfield house Diana Hillis and her sister, Anna, were finishing breakfast and arranging their day. Diana was a thirty-one year old widow with a youthful but sad air. Sad that is except for the glint of humour that lived in her eyes. Once in awhile the corners of her mouth would twitch slightly into a smile and then one would hear her full laughter. That was seldom. Her humour was a private entertainment that she shared with few. No one knew Diana better than her sister and even Anna could not always tell when Diana was making fun. Anna was the younger sister and the more open. No one had to guess what Anna was thinking. Every emotion was written on the vibrant face.

The sisters were happy with their life in the little house. Fairfield was socially between the old money, some say snobbery, of Oak Bay and the blue collar, transient world of James Bay. It was also between the two geographically. Fairfield was on the opposite side of Beacon Hill Park from James Bay. For both sections of town, there was the beauty of the park and also that of Dallas Road with its ocean side scenes.

The Fairfield area was an established neighbourhood that mixed the young and the old, the well off with the middle class, the starting up and the retired. There was a friendliness, a dignity to the area, a respect for your neighbours and the neighbourhood. Here the sisters lived in small beige stucco bungalow on Faithful Street. A modest house with red steps leading to the sheltered entranceway of a front door surrounded by leaded glass windows. They lived peacefully and equally. On occasion one tried to mother the other but not generally. As a rule they were equal. That was why Diana surprised Anna this morning.

"No!" Diana barked so fiercely that Anna jumped.

"Why not? What's the matter?" Anna asked, confused. "I've always come up to the bank to meet you when we have lunch together."

"Not today," replied Diana. " And not again until I let you know it's okay."

"What's okay?" asked Anna. "What is wrong with you today? Going through the change?"

"No, dear," Diana said. "I'm not going through the change. Anyway, not that I've noticed."

"Then what is it?" pried Anna. "Tell little sister all about it. Speak Diana."

"There really isn't anything to tell," she said. "There is something wrong at the office; I can feel it. Something is going to happen and I don't want you there until it's finished."

"Until what's finished?" demanded Anna. "I know, you're redecorating and you want to surprise me!"

"No, nothing so pleasant," Diana answered. " Something unpleasant. I think….." Diana paused knowing what she was going to say would sound foolish. "I think harm is going to be done to someone."

"Are you serious? Look at me so I can see if you're teasing me." Anna knew her sister well and knew her love of teasing, but still could not always tell the serious and the fun. Diana's eyes worked as Anna's lie detector. Today they showed no lies, no teasing.

"What are you talking about? What harm? To who?"

"To whom."

"Never mind that, answer the question."

"I don't know what harm. But I think to Cynthia," Diana said slowly.

"Cynthia! Why would anyone want to hurt her?" asked

Anna. "And what do you mean harm?"

"I think kill her."

"Well I guess that is harm alright!" Anna said. "You're not serious."

"I'm afraid I am," replied Diana. " There is an air about the place that is violent, like death."

"Surely, no one would want to kill her!"

"Well, in fact, I think Shirley would," said Diana. "But then so would a lot of people, that's the problem."

"You've gone off, girl," Anna informed her sister. "Gone right off this time. Why would anyone want to kill Cynthia? And Shirley is way too spinney to kill anyone."

"Shirley is not nearly as spiny as she lets on," she replied. "And as for reasons, there are several. First she's the boss and everyone hates the boss."

"Not enough to kill them!"

"Maybe not. But with a few other annoyances it might be enough for someone. Doris thinks Cynthia wants to fire her. Mike needs the money he would get from Cynthia's job. Something isn't right with Judy either. I don't know how much longer Mr. Manders can take being made a fool of by sinful Cynthia either."

"None of those are reasons for murdering someone," Anna said.

"Not to you and me; but are any reasons sufficient?" asked Diana. "Anyway they might be good enough for someone," she continued. "Also there's that new woman that started while Cynthia was away. Watching them as they were introduced, I'd swear they already knew each other. At least Barbara seemed to recognize Cynthia and it didn't look like she remembered her fondly."

"Do you do any work at that place or just sit watching everyone?" her sister asked.

Diana laughingly replied, "I try to fit in a little work."

"It sounds like everyone in the place wants Cynthia dead except Cynthia," Anna rationalized. "Since you appear to be in earnest, I will indulge your imagination and not come to the bank. By the way, you haven't mentioned your own motives. Do you also have a reason to kill Cynthia?" Anna teased.

"Yes," Diana replied quietly. "I have a reason."

With this remark Diana left the room and left Anna with her mouth hanging open with surprise.

3

NOW AT THE bank, the little silver BMW pulled smoothly into the parking space that Cynthia had designated for herself. Locking her car, she walked slowly towards the bank looking around the parking area. This was part of the morning premises check but it was also a surveying of her domain. Entering the ABM banking vestibule, she was greeted with the usual mess. Actually it wasn't bad today, just receipts and papers overflowing from the waste containers – no signs of drunks or the homeless using it for their "facilities".

Cynthia unlocked the bank's door, leaving the clean up for Mike. Whether it was a little or a lot that needed to be tidied, it was left for Mike. Cynthia did not do housecleaning.

Standing at the entrance, Cynthia ran her eyes around the branch. To her immediate right was the receptionist Pat's desk. The position had had many names (branch steno, manager's secretary, meeter-greeter) over the last few years and at certain times didn't exist at all. It did now though, and regardless of the current title, it was still basically a receptionist and manager's secretary job.

Directly behind the receptionist desk was the manager's office, Dave's office. A smile played on Cynthia's lips as she checked it. Next door and running down the right hand side of the branch were the financial advisers' offices. There were four of them in total, Barbara, Craig, Cecilia and Brian. She liked rattling off the employees' names. Counting the part-time it was a large staff for a branch these days and it was a bit of a game reciting the names as she checked out the premises each morning. Cynthia continued walking down along the offices and moved into the back room where the four support officers worked. Nothing out of the ordinary – then, of course, there never was.

The teller line was at the back of the branch and ran across the banking lobby from the FA's offices to the side counter area. There were three Customer Service Reps as they were now called. Many customers still referred to them as tellers. Then again so did Cynthia.

Behind the teller line was Mike's desk neat as always with nothing left out – and the two vaults. One vault was under timelock and two combinations. It held the cash, securities, and safety deposit boxes. The other, the book vault, had a single combination and no timelock. It only held the records, papers – some very important but nothing negotiable. Cynthia stopped and spun off her combinations on both doors and pulled the book vault door open.

Moving to the left side of the branch, Cynthia passed hers and Shirley's desks. Coming back up towards the branch's front, she walked behind the side counter with its sit-down cubicles for the Personal Banking Reps. On this side of the office, behind the PBR workstations, were Diana and Doris's desks.

Half way down the left wall there was a door that led to the lunchroom, the coat closet, and the washrooms. Cynthia entered and glanced around through all the rooms. Even though she went through this inspection each morning, she did not rush. She conducted the morning review with pride.

After all, she owned this space and everyone in it. Nothing unusual caught her eye. The ABM secure room was the last area she glanced around and then Cynthia returned to her desk. One last thing and the morning check would be completed. An alarm test needed to be completed each morning. Pushing the monitor to test mode, Cynthia went to the nearest alarm button and pushed it. After hearing the confirming beeps, Cynthia reset the alarm, pulled out a cigarette and sat waiting for Mike to arrive.

He stopped each morning to collect the mail from the main post office. It took some time since he didn't drive. That was his decision, drive or not drive, public transport or walk. She didn't care. Cynthia could have easily driven by and picked up the mail but with all the maneuvering it took with the one way streets, she didn't want to and what Cynthia didn't want to do, she didn't do. It remained Mike's task.

Cynthia sat waiting for Mike and for once she actually was thinking about him. He had been telling Dave about the screw-up with the Wilsons' term deposits; he had been blaming her. He was right, it was her mistake. Mike did know the work, Cynthia would give him that. He might know it a little too well for her liking. But if he thought he could get her job by being better at it than she was, he wasn't as clever as he thought. Work was one thing, life was another. In life, Cynthia played for keeps, she didn't like threats, and she didn't give up control. She would have to do something about dear Michael.

Mike finally arrived. He walked directly over to her dropping the day's mail on her desk for opening. Neither spoke. Next, he spun his numbers on the vault door and brought out the necessary files. Cynthia followed him into the vault, carried out just her personal workbasket and returned to her desk. She organized her desk and started opening the mail. Mike finished the rest of the setting up, went back to tidy the ABM vestibule, and then, as was his custom, went off to make coffee.

"Let me guess," Cynthia said sarcastically, "You're going to make coffee."

"I always make the coffee now," replied Mike.

"Of course, because you can't last a further five minutes. You are addicted, definitely addicted. Sure sign you can't take pressure. That will be considered before you are ever offered a management position. But then, one has to have a job before one is promoted."

Mike moved towards the coffee room not answering. He never knew how to answer Cynthia's thinly veiled threats. At first they had seemed harmless; she really didn't have the authority to enforce them. Over the last few months though, Mike had noticed as everyone had, Cynthia's growing power over Mr. Manders. Now her threats worried him. If he didn't get a better position, it was doubtful if they'd be able to keep their house. Without a job, there was no doubt. They would lose their home. Cynthia's voice broke into his thoughts.

"What? What did you say?" asked Mike.

"I want to know about this Barbara Scott who started while I was away. I do the hiring and I didn't hire her. So tell me what happened."

"Nothing happened," replied Mike. "Mr. Manders wanted the position filled, so I filled it." The look on Cynthia's face told Mike that wasn't enough. "At the same time, Barbara brought in an application, just rejoining the work force and dropping her resume around town. It just worked out. It wasn't a big thing."

"You hired her?" asked Cynthia.

"Well, Mr. Manders officially."

"Yes, officially," Cynthia repeated. "Well I guess next time I'll have to leave you a list of what you can and can not do while I'm away." Mike just looked at her waiting.

"Go, go on get your precious coffee. You'll poison yourself with it one of these days. You won't even need anyone's help!" Cynthia called after him. Then to herself, she said, "Now that's a thought!"

Cynthia had watched Mike wrestling with his thoughts and had waited for him to stand up to her. He never did, really. No one ever did. Except for Diana, that is. Damn Diana, her nemesis!

Judy Morrison buzzed at the door and Cynthia rose to let her in. As Cynthia moved to the door, she wondered why the lowest person on the totem pole seemed to always arrive first. She also wondered why Judy was so scared.

"Good morning, Judy," Cynthia said.

"Good morning, Miss Harmon," replied Judy not looking at her.

"I've told you, Judy, just call me Cynthia. You needn't be afraid of me."

"No, ma'am."

"Don't coward so; I'm not going to beat you," snapped Cynthia. "And don't call me ma'am! You're not my maid!" Weakness annoyed Cynthia and whining annoyed her more.

"No, Miss...Cynthia," Judy said as she tried to get away from her.

"Wait a minute," ordered Cynthia. "Is there something bothering you, Judy? You've seemed so nervous and worried this last while."

"No, ma'am...I mean, no."

"Everything alright at home?" Cynthia asked trying for as sympathetic a voice as she could manage.

"Yes."

Giving up on the sugar approach Cynthia returned to her natural tones.

"I don't stand for deceit and slyness. This isn't that big of a branch and you will discover Victoria, for being a city, isn't that big either. I will know all there is to know about whatever you are hiding. Let me just add, it had better have nothing to do with the bank or with me. If it affects the bank in the very slightest, it affects me and nothing disrupts my life. Is that clear?"

"Yes," stammered Judy.

"You sure you have nothing else to say?"

"Yes, I mean No."

"Do you know what you mean?" asked Cynthia unkindly. No answer came from Judy.

"Alright, continue your flight to safety," Cynthia directed. "Although I don't know where you think you're going in this branch that will keep you out of my sight. And remember what I said!"

Judy ran into the back room to hang up her coat and to escape further discussion with Cynthia. Jim had been right. Cynthia didn't know. Judy had also been right. Cynthia would know soon and she would make trouble. What to do, what to do?

Cynthia continued to unlock the door for the arriving staff only until Mike returned with his coffee. After that she left it for him to do.

With the majority of staff present, Mike and Cynthia returned to the main vault and spun the internal cash safe and individual compartment combinations. The individual CSRs cash bags were withdrawn, along with the working supplies of traveler's cheques, engraved forms and bankcards. Adjustments were made with the treasury cash supply – some cash being taken out and some being added. With everything in order the compartments were closed up, combinations spun and time put on the cash vault. There would be no going back in until the end of the day. The workday was ready to start even as the last arrivals made their appearances.

The same ones were late everyday – Doris, Diana. And it looked like Barbara was going to join that club. Dave was later still but that didn't count. By the time he arrived, she was ready for a distraction. She would take him a coffee. Just the two of them in his office, it was the way she liked it.

Doris was always late. She was late and disorganized. She was so concerned and would try to hurry. She hurried everywhere she went and hurried in everything she did. It only made her slower and more disorganized. And it annoyed Cynthia. Everything about Doris annoyed Cynthia. The reason for this fact, Cynthia never bothered to ponder. That Doris annoyed her was sufficient information for Cynthia to remove her.

Barbara was the new Financial Adviser. She had started while Cynthia was on holidays so they had only met last week. Barbara Scott, there was something awfully familiar there. Not the name, something else, something else that was important to remember. Cynthia had interrogated Mike about Barbara not just to poke at his self-confidence but also looking for a clue to what she couldn't quite remember. Barbara was a trim five foot three attractive package, well-groomed, well-dressed with deep silent brown eyes. Cynthia could see why Dave Manders had hired her. She had that look. The look that Cynthia could not achieve with any amount of money. Old school class, Cynthia's natural antithesis. Maybe that's all it was; Cynthia recognized the type. Anyway she needed to be sure. Barbara, Cynthia would see.

Diana was the last to arrive but unlike Doris, she never hurried, never looked guilty. Miss Cool, Cynthia called her under her breath. Cynthia was as conscious of Diana as Cynthia was conscious of anyone. Not that Diana would do anything to her, she was just an irritation. Diana could not be controlled or manipulated. She was also constantly running interference for Cynthia's victims. Now that was not nice!

Cynthia walked over to Doris's desk. That alone was sufficient to unnerve Doris but Cynthia continued anyway. "Late again, Doris," she remarked. "I don't think Mr. Manders will look favourably on that. He does feel we are wasting our money with you, dear. I have been speaking on your behalf but I'm beginning to feel he is right."

Cynthia walked away pleased with the progress of her plan for Doris. Diana seeing the conversations and imagining the body of words walked over to Doris.

"You alright, Doris?" Diana asked. She and Cynthia were the only two people in the bank that called Miss Webster by her Christian name but there was such a difference in the two voices.

"Yes, yes quite alright," Doris replied quietly. "Thank-you."

"Don't worry about Cynthia. She likes to remind herself she's the boss. That's all."

"She's going to fire me," wailed Doris. "I know she is! She keeps saying Mr. Manders wants to fire me, but I know it's really her."

"Never mind, Doris," Diana said trying to soothe her. "What she says Mr. Manders says and what he really says are two different things."

"She lies. She is an evil woman," Doris continued more to herself than to Diana. "God will punish her. He won't allow such evil to hurt me. He'll show me the way. Such evil shouldn't be in his beautiful world."

"Yes, Doris," said Diana trying to get her attention. "Now forget Cynthia and start your filing. Cynthia is not going to hurt you. Try to remember she is only playing a game."

"It is not a nice game," replied Doris as she left to do her filing. "She is evil. She should go away."

Diana returned to her own desk to try and get as much work done as possible before customers started arriving. This was the most productive time of the day. The office was quiet and energies were high. As the day progressed, the noise increased and energies decreased. That is except for Cynthia. Her energy was constantly high.

One of Cynthia's first chores of the day was to plan her lunch and her evening hours. Today on checking her schedule, she noticed no arrangement for lunch and decided it might be a good time to probe Barbara.

All Dave Manders had been able to tell Cynthia about Barbara was that her husband was one Dr. Robert Scott. Mike hadn't been very helpful and the personnel file said little more. School records were from Vancouver. Employment records were sparse with nothing recent. That was not uncommon with women who had taken time to raise their family; but Barbara's file didn't mention any children. There were enough gaps to rouse the curiosity of a disinterested person. To Cynthia it was a challenge with a magnetic pull. It was definitely a good time to quiz Barbara.

"Hi, Barbara," said Cynthia as she wandered into the financial adviser's office. "You busy?"

"Oh, hello," replied Barbara. "Yes, as a matter of fact, I am quite busy."

"Well I won't disturb you. I was wondering if you wanted to have lunch?"

"I'm busy at lunch."

"That's too bad," replied Cynthia sitting down. "What about tomorrow?"

"Sorry."

"You seem to have your time pretty booked for being new in town. Your are new in town, aren't you?" probed Cynthia.

"No," replied Barbara.

"Oh, you're not from out-of-town. That's interesting."

"Is there something you wanted?" asked Barbara. "I am very busy."

"Nothing in particular. You just seem really familiar."

"You seem familiar too. Victoria isn't that big. We've probably passed each other in a store or restaurant sometime," explained Barbara. "It happens all the time."

"Then you don't think we've met?" asked Cynthia.

"No, I'm sure we haven't," replied Barbara quickly.

That was too quick, Cynthia said to herself. Out loud she said, "Well, you're busy and I'm disturbing you. We'll have lunch some other day. We could make it dinner unless you have a family that waits at home every night?"

"Lunch would be better."

"Fine, lunch then. When?" demanded Cynthia.

"What?"

"When are we going to have lunch?" asked Cynthia. "When do I find out all about you?"

"I don't know," hedged Barbara. "I really am very busy."

"Thursday?" asked Cynthia.

"No, I can't. I'm busy."

"Nonsense, you can fit in lunch," stated Cynthia. "Thursday it is."

Without waiting for a reply Cynthia left the office.

4

THE WORKDAY HAD finished like all workdays. No matter how good, no matter how bad, they all finally reach an end. The last customer was served. The folding door that separated the branch lobby and the ABM vestibule was pulled across the entrance and locked.

As soon as the door was shut, the real action started. There was limited time now for the CSRs to balance, the cash and securities to be locked up, and the courier bag put together.

For Diana and the rest of the staff without cash or lock up responsibility it was not so hectic. This was the finishing up time. Time for interruptions was past and all the partially done activities of the day could now be completed. Files would now receive the finishing touches and be sent to head offices either on-line or by paper through the daily courier bag. Tomorrow's diary was reviewed, the day planned and the relevant customer records organized.

With that completed, Diana started packing up her basket for storing in the book vault overnight. Cynthia saw this and as with everything Diana did, it annoyed her.

"Late to arrive and early to leave," remarked Cynthia. "We're not very concerned about our job, are we?"

"You might not be," answered Diana not rising to the bait. "But I am."

"You'd never know it from the hours you keep," snapped Cynthia.

"Those were the hours set when I was hired," replied Diana. "Which was long before Sinful Cynthia made an appearance."

"Don't call me that!"

"Funny," Diana said shrugging. "I thought you liked that name; or is it only with men that you acknowledge that title?"

"You know why I have...why I had that name. It was a long time ago and I'd wish you'd forget it." Cynthia paused and then added, "I have."

"It was a long time ago but I haven't forgotten and you haven't forgotten either. Neither of us will forget as long as the other is around."

"Revenge," screamed Cynthia. "That's what you want. That's why you keep hanging around. Revenge!"

"Of course," smiled Diana. "Besides you are so much fun to torment. You are so easy."

Diana continued past Cynthia into the book vault. On coming back out of the vault, Diana could see Cynthia was still seething. Sensing how close Cynthia was to erupting, Diana decided to push her even further and sweetly added, "Better calm yourself. You are losing control in front of everyone."

Cynthia looked around and smiled. Then she walked closer to Diana and lowered her voice.

"Damn you, Diana! I'll see you in hell!"

"Quite possibly," Diana replied as she walked by on her way to the door. On reaching it she turned back to Cynthia.

"Can you watch an alarm for me, Cynthia?" Diana said smiling. Turning back to the door, she unlocked it and left without waiting for a response and without glancing at her fuming colleague.

Upon Diana's exit, Cynthia whirled around and yelled at Pat, "Lock that damn door!"

Pat rose from her desk and with no apparent rush walked to the offending door, pulled it tight and turned the lock. She then at the same unhurried pace returned to her desk. Never once by look or word did she acknowledge Cynthia.

Cynthia in turn continued to glare at both Pat and the door Diana had just walked through. Shaking that irritation off, she turned back to the rest of the staff.

"Is everyone balanced? Are we ready for locking up? Is the cash checked? Mike get these people moving!"

Mike and the CSRs had paused to listen to the Diana and Cynthia exchange. How could they not? It might be getting quite common, the arguments but they were still interesting. Cynthia's yelling though was not. It also was getting to be a regular event and as such was loosing its effect. The CSRs ignored Cynthia and slowly returned to the business of balancing the day's entries. Mike moved up and down the wickets seeing who was balanced and who wasn't. It was a good day – everyone balanced without problems. Mike moved slowly from wicket to wicket, verifying the cash bundles to the blotters, watching as the cash bags were loaded. Each bag was double locked. One lock Mike had and one the CSR kept. Down the row, one CSR at a time was locked up for the night and their cash ready for the main vault.

Cynthia returned to her desk, lit a cigarette, and, with great flourish, took a deep drag. This was the moment that Shirley, whose desk was opposite Cynthia's, hated.

"If you have to spit in the eyes of justice, totally ignoring the smoking laws, could you at least smoke your cigarettes," sighed Shirley. "Instead of waving them all over the place."

"Oh, does my smoking bother you?" asked Cynthia with artificial wonder.

"I can't breath," sputtered Shirley. "I can't breath. If you don't care about your health, think about mine."

"Don't faint, Shirley," said Cynthia. "Because I'll assume it's another act and I'll leave you lying on the floor."

"You would, you phony Bette Davis," snapped Shirley. "Quit blowing your bloody smoke in my face!"

"Oh, sorry," laughed Cynthia.

"Like hell you're sorry," Shirley said. She rose and glared into Cynthia's eyes, very slowly and very firmly she said, "I'm going to kill you; I'm going to see you dead!" With those words, she went and got her coat. At the door, she stopped and calling to Mike asked him to watch an alarm. She might be in a rage with Cynthia but she was not so out of control to forget the alarm monitoring procedure. It was mandatory when any cash was out. If this was the day someone attempted an end-of-day robbery, it was not going to be her who had been lax on security.

Mike walked over to Cynthia's desk and said, "The cash is ready for lock-up." As Cynthia looked up at him, he added, "I see I have a lot to learn about people management."

"You're getting pretty brave, Mike. You say anything about any of this to anyone and I'll have you fired," Cynthia threatened. "You understand?"

"With instructions that specific, how could I not?" asked Mike.

"You picked a bad time to grow up, Junior!"

"I understand, Cynthia," Mike said no longer feeling so confident. "I'll get the side counter stuff."

"Never mind, I'll get it," Cynthia replied rising from her desk to go to the opposite side of the office. Between the CSR workstations and the FAs offices, there was the double locked cupboard. It was called this because it had two locks and the keys were to be held by two different officers. This cupboard contained the working supplies of money orders, drafts, and travelers' cheques. These were liquid cash, almost the same as cash. Thus for security, they were to be maintained under dual custody never accessible to one person on their own. Cynthia was about to call someone to join her in collecting the supplies for movement into the overnight security vault when she noticed Judy. Judy with both sets of keys was just closing the cupboard door. "What are you doing?" Cynthia barked. Leaving no time for Judy to respond, Cynthia continued, "You aren't supposed to go into that cupboard by yourself. Why do you think it's called, double locked? Two locks, two keys – get it!"

"I was just getting it ready to put away," stammered Judy. "I was trying to help."

"Well don't help," retorted Cynthia. "You probably not smart enough to realize that things can go missing. And now, you'll be my first suspect if they do! Remember that. Now get me the inventory sheets so we can check these things and get everything put away."

A few moments later, Cynthia and Mike had put the cash and engraved forms away. The combinations had been spun off and the time locks set and checked. The outer vault doors were locked, the lights were off and the staff gone. Cynthia breathed a sigh of relief. It had been an annoying day all around but she was looking forward to the evening. She got her coat from the back, picked up her purse and headed to see Dave Manders.

"Our dinner tonight will be the only redeeming feature of an irritating day," remarked Cynthia. "And how was yours?"

"Oh, Fine…. Fine…" mumbled Dave. "About dinner, I'm sorry but something has come up and I won't be able to make it."

"What's the problem?"

"My wife has made plans for us."

"What about me and my plans?" demanded Cynthia. "Your wife can carry on without you; she'll have to make room for us!"

"There is no more us," replied Dave. "My wife is my

wife. We had a good time together but it's run its course. It's over."

"That's your wife talking," said Cynthia. "Who's in charge of your life you or your wife?"

"This is my decision," Dave answered and even he knew he was lying. "It's over. That's the way it has to be."

"I don't think so, Dave," snapped Cynthia with her cold steel flashing.

"There's nothing more to say," Dave said taking out his checkbook. "Perhaps a little token, a momento?"

"Is that how you got rid of the others," Cynthia laughed. "You are so naïve."

"Come on, Cynthia. We are both adults. We both knew what we were getting into," Dave said.

"Oh really," said Cynthia. "I did but you never knew what was going on. You thought you were the great man, Mr. Dave Manders, in control having a little fun, impressing a poor girl with the finer things in life. Well Dave, grow up, you didn't have a clue what was going on. I came here because you have a weakness for younger women who flatter you and you have money to spare. Actually your wife has money to spare and for some reason she lets you have access to it. So just put the thought of tokens away. You have a lot I want and you are going to give it to me. And we are not finished until I say we're finished. Behave yourself and you will enjoy the ride. Be uncooperative and I will make your life an absolute hell. I can and will destroy you. Now since you seem a little distraught, I will pass on dinner tonight. We will dine together tomorrow. Make sure you remember and I think a small gift, a VERY NICE small gift, asking my forgiveness is in order."

With these words, Cynthia left Dave Manders alone stunned. First Sybil and now Cynthia, how was he to manage either of them, let alone both? How could this have happened? When did he lose control? What was he going to tell Sybil? She had been clear, deal with Cynthia or she would. Oh God, he would have to do something about Cynthia.

5

A PHONE RANG in the three-storey silver geometric building that stands at the corner of Quadra and Caledonia. The building was new, modern new, almost art–deco with flat roofs, flat lines, and 90-degree corners in beams that seemed to be everywhere. This was not an art gallery although it looked more like that than what it was. This was the new Victoria Police Headquarters. Inside a phone was ringing.

Detective Sergeant Deck of homicide took the call. He said little, listened closely and then recorded all the information. Only then did he get up and walk over to his supervisor's desk to report the details.

"Sudden illness at the CIBC at Cook and Fairfield reported to Emergency Medical Services. An ambulance crew was dispatched by the 911 operator."

"So?" Detective Inspector Hanlon replied waiting for the rest of the story.

"Yeah, I know. Bankers have a nasty habit of making people ill at the best of times," Deck joked.

"And this has what to do with us?" Detective Inspector Hanlon inquired.

"That's the interesting part. Call came in to 911 at 9:50.

Reportee advised that there had been a sudden out-break of illness among the bank staff. The call was passed to the Ambulance Service and Fire Department who attended. At 10:13 the paramedics requested a member attend as they had arrived to find one person dead. Two uniformed members attended and they are now asking for us because the EMS guys tell them this looks like a mass poisoning. Since this has happened well before lunch it seems unlikely that this is a simple case of food poisoning."

Hanlon watched Deck as he thought about what he'd heard. Deck was a solid man in all senses of the word. Physically he was a big, balding man in his thirties who looked older. Big but never sloppy, he was strong and powerful, football big. That was often useful in their work but Deck was also solid in the reliable sense. They had worked together for quite some time now and Hanlon was comfortable with Deck. Comfortable – a good word. That really was Deck at the core, he was comfortable with life and with himself. Hanlon envied him that.

"Any indication this was a diversion to cover some sort of robbery or some other act in the area? Are there any other places of interest around there?" Hanlon finally asked. Deck knew what he meant and it wasn't tourist spots! These days with all the international flexing, with the electronic crimes, with the new gangs that made the Mafia look like a simple Italian family, police work was not what it used to be. Nothing could ever be taken at face value. Deck knew that old adage if it walks like a duck it was a duck no longer held true. Sometimes, these days, that duck was really a tractor!

"No, nothing in the neighbourhood," replied Deck. "At least, nothing that's come to our attention so far."

"So what do we think we have?" asked Hanlon.

"The uniforms are still talking with the bank manager and they aren't putting forward any potential scenarios yet   sticking strictly to the facts at this point. They did tell me that the manager has been offering some theories. You know, gas in the heating ducts, Asian flu, radiation from the lights and on and on and on. Sounds like the guy's a bit hysterical at the moment. Wonder how he'd react in an armed robbery."

The inspector flashed a tight smile. "Did you get the name of the bank manager?"

"Manders. Dave Manders," the Sergeant replied after scanning his notes.

"Wonder if he has any connection to Sybil Manders?" Hanlon said, more to himself than out loud.

"Well, could be, same last name and all. The name means nothing to me. Is it important?"

Hanlon didn't acknowledge Deck's question. Instead he continued with his own line of thinking and responded with a different question.

"Did they give you any ID on the deceased?'

"Umm, yeah," the Sergeant again consulted his notes "Harmon, Cynthia"

The Inspector leaned back in his chair looking out the office window at the cars heading down Caledonia to the city core. Hanlon still missed the old station down on Fisgard with City Hall, with Chinatown, even with its antique plumbing.

"Cynthia Harmon. Dave Manders. This is getting even more interesting." He shook his head as if to shake loose the memory that he could just vaguely recall. It was there just as a glimpse and the rest would come, he knew, sooner or later. Turning to his subordinate he listed off his orders with the authority that only comes with experience, experience and time.

And as his final instruction, Hanlon said "Find out if Dave and Sybil Manders do have a connection."

"Then it is important."

"Sergeant, you haven't reached your present rank without learning that everything is important until it is proven not to be. Get a rundown on the Harmon woman as well. I imagine that the coroner's office has already been contacted, but call Thomas just in case and ask him to meet us at the scene, assuming that you told the uniforms to not let the ambulance remove the victim…"

Deck looking somewhat sheepish from the tone more than the content of these words drew himself up a little taller.

"They were so instructed. Anything else, sir?"

"Not right now, Sergeant. Meet me downstairs after you call Thomas."

Deck nodded and returned to his desk to make the call. It took very few minutes and then he got up and left the squad room.

Inspector Joseph Hanlon watched him and did not rush. He filled his pipe then lit it in violation of at least a half dozen local and national health laws. He well knew that the police were expected to uphold all laws and to appear upon demand with no delay. He also knew the first twenty-four hours were the most critical in solving a crime. However, Hanlon believed in getting his thoughts in order before arriving at a crime scene and before questioning witnesses so he quietly smoked. One thought was clear: this was no accident. Was this an arbitrary poisoning or a deliberate murder? That was the question. Regardless, this was no accident. There would be no gas in the heating pipes, no radiation. He knew that to be true. Anyone desperate enough to suggest such solutions also knew it. So why was Dave Manders making such suggestions? What was with Dave Manders, Inspector Joseph Hanlon wondered?

He gathered up his tools of the trade; a cell phone, a pager, and for good measure his gun. Nothing like a gun to convey to witnesses the seriousness of his questions – especially for those in shock following a particularly unpleasant event. Death by poison should fall into that category. He put on his coat and walked out of his office.

*   *   *   *   *

Sitting in the Cook and Fairfield bank manager's office waiting for Manders to join them, Hanlon looked closely around the room. This at first glance was a typical office. The right side wall had a window covered, of course, with vertical blinds. The back wall had a typical computer work station with filing cabinets on the sides below and hanging cabinets above. In the left back corner was a full-size cabinet for more files. In the center of the room was the desk and in front of that stood two visitors chairs. It was here that Hanlon and Deck sat waiting for Manders. It was here that Hanlon wondered even more about Mr. Dave Manders.

This was no ordinary bank office. The computer looked like it had never been turned on and there wasn't a piece of paper to be found. The walls were full of pictures of a man that Hanlon assumed was Manders. All the pictures were celebrations. There were award presentations, banquets, and white-tie affairs. In several pictures, one could see the elite of Victoria. The desk and cabinets had no visible bank work on them. Instead, they like the walls were covered with ornaments and fuss. Hanlon didn't doubt it was all very expensive and all very impressive. If you were impressed but such things, which Hanlon wasn't.

"Look at all this junk and these pictures," was Deck's reaction. "All of himself!"

"Not impressed, Sergeant?" Hanlon asked.

Deck's answer was interrupted as the office door opened and the gentleman in question entered and sat down behind his desk. The Inspector watched him and his doubt and curiosity grew. Yes, he wondered about Mr. Manders. Seeing him in the flesh had done nothing to alleviate that.

Hanlon faced a middle-aged man devoid of originality. The light brown hair was stylishly cut and softly blown dry. The clothes were expensive, very expensive, and cut conservatively. All in all, Mr. Manders had the look of a successful young businessman. That was the rub, Dave Manders was not young.

Manders' outward appearance spoke of youth where there was none. Just as he was playing at being young, he was playing at being confident. His hands, the tiny beads of perspiration on his face told the truth. Then there were his eyes, his brown eyes which darted back and forth, trying to avoid making eye contact with the officers and yet, trying not to be obvious about it. After many years of looking for such signs, Hanlon missed none of Dave Manders' distress and fear. But fear of what?

The moment Manders sat down he started to talk. Not waiting for the officers to speak, he started to rant and ramble. He said nothing talking in circles without taking a breath. Deck had been correct. Manders was hysterical, or doing his best to appear so. Something was wrong. First thing though the rambling had to be stopped. It was taking too much valuable time, and it was allowing Manders to control the situation.

"Alright Mr. Manders," interrupted the Inspector. "We'll leave that for the moment. Now tell us step by step what happened this morning."

"Nothing. I, I don't know, I just don't know. I don't understand," wailed the bank manager.

God, thought Sergeant Deck. How could a guy be in his position and be such a wuss?

"Sure you do," Inspector Hanlon said soothingly. "Start at the beginning. When did you arrive at the bank?"

"What? What? Oh yes, I arrived at my usual time."

"Which is?"

"Oh, nine o'clock. But I didn't notice anything. I didn't see anything. I came straight to my office."

"Was the door unlocked. The main bank door. Was it unlocked? Or did you have a key? Or did someone let you in?"

"What?" demanded Dave Manders who suddenly looked like a trapped animal.

Now why should a simple little question like that startle

you so, thought Hanlon. Is that the reason for your hysteria, that you want to control our line of questioning, and you hadn't anticipated that one? What is it that you don't want us to know, Mr. Manders?

Not one of these thoughts showed on Hanlon's face as he slowly led Dave Manders over the course of the morning's events.

Several minutes later, Inspector Hanlon turned to Sergeant Deck who was taking notes.

"Please recap for us, Sergeant."

"Yes sir," answered Deck. "Mr. Manders arrived at 9:00. Either the deceased or the assistant accountant, Mike Baker, unlocked the door. Mr. Manders cannot remember precisely who it was. He went directly to his office. No one came in, and he received only a couple of telephone calls from customers. Just before 10:00 the deceased came into his office and informed him that she had called 911 because of an illness that was affecting various staff members. He stayed in his office and 5 or 10 minutes later he heard a scream, author unknown. Mr. Manders then exited his office and found the deceased slumped over her desk. She was in his opinion already dead. The body was moved to the staff room just before the EMS unit arrived. He is not sure but he believes that the ambulance attendants called for the police as he had returned to his office after moving the deceased."

"Is that information all in accordance with what you have told us Mr. Manders?"

"Yes, I guess so." mumbled Manders.

"Why did you move Miss Harmon's body?"

"What?" stammered a surprised Manders. "Why we were open... open to the public. We couldn't have her lying there in front of all the customers."

"Yes. I was somewhat surprised when the uniformed officers told me that you had strongly objected to closing the doors when they asked you to do so. You do understand that a sudden death of one of your staff members is quite a bit more important than cashing some cheques, don't you?" Hanlon's eyes fairly bore through Manders' when he spoke these words. The tone of his voice was similar to the one used to lecture a naughty child.

"I couldn't do that. We have a duty to our customers. The people in Vancouver have to approve an unusual closing. It could cause panic." Manders sounded like he was indeed a naughty child. "I did call the Vancouver office, and I spoke with the Corporate Security Officer, Richard D'Angelo. He told me that I should have shown some more initiative and locked up the branch right away. And if I had done that without asking first they would have said that was wrong. You can't win with those people. He wanted me to tell you to call him….when you get a chance." He pulled a piece of paper from under the edge of his phone and handed it to Hanlon. On it was D'Angelo's name and number.

The Inspector took it without any acknowledgment. "That will be sufficient for now. We will need to question your staff immediately."

"Yes. Yes, of course," said Manders as a wave of something akin to relief flashed across his face. "They're not all here as you probably already know. Some have gone to the hospital. I let a couple of the ladies go home after the other police officers questioned them because they were so upset. I guess maybe everyone should have stayed…"

"Too late now," interjected Sergeant Deck. "We'll need a list of all of your staff members even those that were not here today. How many in total do you have on staff? We'll want that as soon as possible. The list is to include home addresses and telephone numbers. And include yourself. We want the names of spouses as well."

"Spouses?" Manders stuttered before continuing. "Oh, of course, of course. There are about 20 maybe 25 people on staff as long as nobody has quit in the last day or two. You never know in this business," said Manders as he picked up his telephone and pushed a button. "Who's this?… Where is Pat?... Oh, okay, then get Diana. Tell her that I need   the police want a list of all of the staff with home addresses, phone numbers, and the names of any spouses.......... Oh yes, the emergency contact list should do. Please bring it in right away............ Yes............ Okay." Turning back to the Inspector, he continued, "It won't be but a moment. We have to have a list like that for emergencies."

"Like today?" asked Deck wondering what Manders considered an emergency.

Flustered Manders replied, "Oh, yes...yes, of course...." Manders was relieved from his embarrassment by a knock at the door. A tall brunette dropped a piece of paper on the desk and left the room without a smile, and without taking her eyes off of the two police investigators.

"That's Pat," Manders said pointing to the closing door. "Here you are gentlemen. Anything else?" He was sounding more relieved by the second.

"Somewhere private we can talk to the remaining employees."

"Yes, well there is this office..." Manders said hesitantly.

"You mentioned a staff room," suggested the Inspector.

"Yes. I believe that that is where your Victim Services people are talking to the staff. I'll show you where it is," he replied rising. The panic in his voice and eyes was now completely gone.

"That will be fine but first there is one more question," said the Inspector. He waited a moment to gauge the response this news would elicit. As he had expected the nerves that had vanished when the questions had stopped now returned. Manders slowly sat back down.

"What can you tell us about the deceased?" Hanlon asked.

"Nothing," Manders quickly answered.

"Nothing, Mr. Manders?"

"I, I don't mean nothing. I mean nothing more than any other employee."

"Naturally. I had not inferred anything other than that of course," said Hanlon watching the panic grow. "That's all we want. However, if there is more to be told…"

"No! I mean, of course not. Of course."

"Do you know anything of her family history?"

"No."

"Her background?"

"No. I'm afraid I can't be of much help in that area. All that might be in her personnel file. Mr. D'Angelo told me that you would probably want to see it so I pulled it out of the files."

"Yes, we will want everyone's files Mr. Manders. But for now what you know will be sufficient. How long had Miss Harmon been working here?"

"I couldn't say for sure…"

"An approximation is fine."

"I, I would say about three years, but like I said…"

"It's alright, Mr. Manders, we'll verify all of this. Her position here was what?"

"Customer Service Manager."

"What does a Customer Service Manager do?"

"Well, they're like an office manager. They're responsible for all of the day to day operations, and supervision of the staff except for the financial advisors. I supervise those employees myself."

"Was she in that position the whole time she worked here?"

"No," Manders was beginning to squirm slightly.

"What was her position when she was hired? Did you yourself hire her?"

"Yes, I did. Sort of a secretary," sputtered Manders. "It was more than that. It's kind of hard to explain to someone outside of banking."

"So, would you say she advanced quite quickly?"

"Cynthia was a quick learner."

"I see. Did you know her before she was hired?"

"No. As I said I didn't really know her," full panic burned in Manders eyes as he said this. He suddenly brightened up. "Diana knew her. She was an old friend of Diana's. Yes, I remember now. I, we hired her on Diana's recommendation. Ask her, she can answer your questions."

Making reference to the employee list Sergeant Deck asked, "Is that Diana Hillis?"

"Yes," said Manders with a sigh.

"You have no other information about Miss Harmon?"

"No, nothing," stated Manders firmly. It was the first thing he had said firmly. There was a brief pause and then he started to rise again. He stood up and for the first time, he looked directly at Hanlon. He then moved towards the door and lead the officers out of his office, across the banking hall to the opposite side of the branch and into the combination staff and lunch room.

6

"IBET MANDERS wishes he could have said a lot less than he did," remarked Sergeant Deck to the Inspector once they were alone in the lunchroom – a lunchroom, a staff room and the only meeting room of the branch all rolled into one. Hanlon hadn't been in many back areas of banks (not a common homicide site). The first thing he noticed was how little space was allocated for the staff compared to the main hall for customers or even to Manders' office.

One room, one room trying to be a kitchen and sitting area. Beside the doorway there was a combination bar fridge with four small burner elements on top. Continuing along the rest of that wall, there was a tiny sink filled with dirty cups, glasses and cutlery. To the other side of the sink was a small working area counter. On it there rested an old, old, old microwave, a kettle and a coffee maker. In front of the cooking area, a table and four chairs formed a pseudo dining area. Hanlon took one of these chairs and continued looking around the room.

Against the opposite wall, a god-awful bright orange couch stood and on the wall opposite the doorway, the wall with the fire exit, there were two mismatched overstuffed chairs and a small table. Various and sundry magazines, advertising posters, and newspapers were strewn about and several cardboard boxes were piled in the far corner directly under the fire emergency exit sign, effectively blocking the door. How anyone would ever get out in an emergency was not at all clear.

The deceased's body had been removed. However it was still difficult to tell if the general disorganization was usual or not, because mingled with these items was the refuse from the paramedics who had apparently been using the space to treat the victims.

Plastic wrapping from hypodermic needles and intravenous bags were on one of the couches and the coffee table. There was a lingering aroma of vomit and something chemical, perhaps an antiseptic. Sergeant Deck wrinkled his nose a bit as he looked around. The coroner Thomas had arrived, taken a first look at the deceased and was now talking to the remaining staff. He would shortly be joining them to advise of his preliminary assessment. Until then Hanlon and Deck waited and talked of the interview with Manders.

"He certainly didn't want to tell us anything. Did he?" was Deck's read on the situation.

"That in itself tells us something," replied Hanlon.

'Yeah, tells us that he's scared shitless."

"Perhaps a bit graphic for my tastes," said Hanlon smiling. "But accurate."

"So we know that he's scared. But scared of what?"

"That is the question," Hanlon said pensively. "While we wait for Thomas, why don't you give this D'Angelo guy a call. Here, use my cell phone." He handed the telephone number and his phone to Deck.

The Sergeant took the items and went back out into the banking hall, knowing that the suggestion also said Hanlon wanted a few minutes to himself.

Inspector Hanlon looked over the room a little more closely. Trying to see the room as it would have been before this morning's situation. On the kitchen table was a half-empty box from the Dutch Bakery, some used cutlery, and as in every office the ubiquitous coffee mugs. The room smelled of stale coffee and that aroma did nothing to improve the general atmosphere. It was all very ordinary. All very ordinary except that he and Deck were sitting here waiting for the coroner to say why one person was dead and eight others in the hospital. Hanlon wondered if anything was ever really ordinary. Or was it just an illusion we developed because we cease to see our surroundings until something disrupts us – like death? For Hanlon that was always the hardest and most interesting part of the job, discovering what was real and what was not. The question of reality versus the illusion of reality held no such interest for Sergeant Deck.

"Man, what a mess." Deck announced as he came back into the room.

"D'Angelo?" Hanlon asked.

"He's not in. I left a voice message asking him to call me." With a sweeping gesture around the room, Deck added, "If we find any evidence here it'll be a miracle."

"Possibly, but the forensic folks have surprised us before," replied Hanlon.

"This is where the evidence is. This is the only place where those people ate or drank anything together. They have to have been poisoned here. It makes sense. Probably in the coffee, the easiest thing."

"Let's wait for Thomas."

"I still say it's poison and it was the coffee."

"And you are probably right," said Thomas as he entered the room. Thomas stood just over 6 foot and had a runner's body. He wore wire-rimmed glasses and had long, thick curly blonde hair. His face was unlined and stress free. Deck wondered how Thomas could always look so happy with the work he did. He also wondered how old Thomas was. He could not be as young as he looked but it was hard to believe he was as old as Deck knew he had to be.

"Nice to see you Thomas," said Hanlon, shaking the other's hand. Hanlon had known and worked with the coroner for many years and had none of Deck's questions.

"You too, Joe," replied Thomas. "Messy one here."

"Is it?" asked the Inspector.

"Mass poisoning? Deliberate or accident? Murder or side effect? Suicide perhaps? Who is the intended victim, if there was one? Is anyone faking? Who did this? One person, or a group? Was the motive a fit of rage, simple boredom, or a premeditated retribution for some real or perceived wrong? Lot of questions."

"Yes, Thomas," agreed Hanlon. "Any answers?"

"Not much yet," replied the expert. "All those affected complained of the same symptoms: cramps, nausea, vomiting, diarrhea. The usual signs of almost any kind of poison really, even your everyday food poisoning. It could be any one of many things, or it could be any two of many things. Then again it could be none of many things."

"Let me guess," Hanlon replied. "You don't know."

"Right, Joe, old man," answered Thomas. "The hospital hasn't named the precise poison yet."

"And you are not going to risk taking a guess."

"Right."

"What can you tell us about Cynthia Harmon, the deceased?"

"Young, and pretty from what I saw."

"You would notice," said Deck breaking into the conversation.

"I try to remember that they were people."

"Sorry," said Deck.

"Cynthia Harmon. Tell us what you do know so far," said the Inspector.

"Young and very pretty," Thomas repeated with a smile. "I'll know better after the autopsy. Body shows no external trauma. Witnesses described her symptoms to be the same as the others prior to her collapse. Her death seems to have been very quick, faster than the others' symptoms would suggest."

"All of which means…" asked Hanlon.

"Possibly nothing, Probably something," replied Thomas. "At this point it means more questions. I'll order an autopsy for this afternoon. The lab tests will take a couple of days but the pathologist should have a preliminary opinion as to the cause of death later today. In other words, business as usual."

"That's fine, Thomas," Hanlon said quietly almost as if he had stopped listening. He was no longer looking at Thomas or anything in the room. He seemed to be drifting away almost ready to sleep. Thomas and Deck waited, watching.

"Aw, this one has caught our intrepid inspector's attention, eh Deck?" said Thomas teasingly.

"You're right there," joked Deck in return. "Every time he starts nodding off you know something is going on – don't know what but something."

"So you two have me all figured out, do you?" asked Hanlon. "Do you have what happened here figured out?"

"Not me! That's up to you boys and good luck to you!" said Thomas leaving the room.

After they were again alone, the two detectives sat quietly for several moments until Sergeant Deck broke the silence.

"He sure doesn't like to give straight answers."

"Thomas has been in this line of work for a long time," explained Hanlon. "He knows that any one event can have several explanations."

"I know that sir," replied Deck. "I just never seem to know when he's serious and when he's being funny."

"He likes to keep his mind active," Hanlon said with a smile.

"I don't know about his mind," said Deck. "But he is sure keeps his mouth active with all his talking."

"So you think he told us nothing, Sergeant?"

"Yes, sir," replied Deck hesitantly. "Don't you?"

"No, Deck, I don't. Thomas told us his instincts say do not believe the obvious in this case. Mine agree. Thomas gave us many possibilities to consider. Some or none could prove of use. That is unimportant. Just remember he said that things need not be as they appear, so keep an open mind."

"He said that?" asked Deck.

"He said that," laughed Hanlon. "Never mind. We'd better start."

Deck left to get the staff files and the first employee. Hanlon stayed and let his thoughts wander knowing that eventually the pieces would find their places. For one thing, as a city Victoria was a small town, small and very old.

Victoria had been around since 1843 when James Douglas set up a trading post for the Hudson's Bay company at the southern most tip of Vancouver Island. Surrounded on three sides by water, there wasn't much land for endless expansion. Even now the only places to stretch towards were Sidney (and that too ends quickly with water) or towards the Western Communities and up island. With this physical restriction, Victoria proper had remained compact, just over 300,000 people and probably no more than 6 miles end to end. Still it was a beautiful little city. While parts of it have changed since the 1843 British trading post, there are other parts that one would swear have not. It wasn't just the historical sites, the horse drawn trolleys or the more modern double-decker buses. It was the traditions and the families.

Yes, for a city Victoria was a small town with age-old traditions kept up by old established families, old established families who were very well known. The Chief of Police came from one such family. Sybil Westcott Manders did as well. Hanlon knew the family name and the Chief knew the family. Young and pretty,, Thomas had said. And Manders liked them young and pretty, the Chief had said.

Hanlon had finally remembered when he had heard Dave Manders' and Cynthia Harmon's names. He thought back to that conversation, an unusual conversation. The Chief had just come back from lunch and had needed to vent his anger. Hanlon happened to be waiting for him on a different matter so got to hear it all.

"No longer even discreet," the Chief had exclaimed, pacing his office. "He always liked them young and pretty but now, with this young chit Cynthia Harmon, he's not even discreet! Why does Sybil put up with it? I never did see what she saw in him. She could have married anyone. You should have known Sybil Westcott (as she was then) when I knew her." The chief was losing his anger as he remembered and finally sat behind his desk. "She was so much fun, so full of life, so bright and pretty. Still is really, but we're all older now. Back then we were all a little bit in love with her and she picked Manders. God knows why! The Sybil I knew would never have tolerated a philandering husband."

Hanlon gave his mind a rest to ponder the abstract as he considered why Victoria remained a small town even with its convention center. It was an "everyone knows everything" small town.

Deck returned with the staff files and with the woman who had delivered the staff list to Manders. Hanlon's first impression had been correct – a tall brunette. With more time now, Hanlon looked closer at Pat. She was probably close to 5'10" and she was well formed. That was an odd way to think of a woman. She was neither slim nor fat – well formed, actually the right word was probably muscular. That was the adjective Hanlon settled on: muscular. Not a common word when describing a woman, it was accurate though when describing this woman. Not someone used to being afraid and she wasn't now. He saw no nervous tension in this woman. That was unusual for anyone being interviewed by homicide officers. Hanlon waited a few moments and noticed that this in no way affected her. There was no seeking a connection. This was a self-contained person. As Hanlon filed these reactions away, Pat finally spoke.

"Is this going to take long," she asked. "I've got quite a bit to do."

"We'll try to be as quick as possible," replied Hanlon. So there was some emotion there after all. What was it, a touch of irritation, of anger? Why?

"Please, sit down. Now you are?" he asked.

"Pat Martin," she responded as she took a place on the couch facing Hanlon. Deck remained standing near the doorway.

"Your position?"

"Kind of like a receptionist."

"I see," said Hanlon, as everyone said, and Pat believed him no more than she believed anyone else.

"What can you tell us regarding today's events?"

"Nothing."

"Sergeant Deck's eyebrows rose slightly and Inspector Hanlon remarked, "Nothing was unusual today?"

"No."

Hanlon and Deck waited.

"Well, except for a bunch of people getting sick and Cynthia dying. You already know that though. So nothing else," she responded with the edge of anger becoming a little more visible.

"Everyone arrived at the normal times. The same people opened the doors, made the coffee, bought the pastries?" asked Hanlon.

"Yes, well, no," said Pat. For the first time, Pat seemed to stop and let go of a little of her anger, to think about her answer.

"What was different?"

"We don't usually have pastries."

"Who brought them?"

"Mrs. Manders, I suppose. That's what we thought."

"Is that her habit?"

"At Christmas, holidays, that sort of thing."

"It isn't Christmas."

"Yes, well, that part was odd but as they say, don't look a gift horse in the mouth and the pastries are so good," Pat almost purred and a small smile appeared. "The Dutch Bakery, you know."

"Anything else different."

"No."

"Who let you in today?"

"Mike."

"Mike Baker?" Hanlon confirmed looking at the staff list.

"Yes," she answered.

"Did he also let Mr. Manders in?" asked Hanlon. Then he waited. Pat did not want to answer.

"Why ask me? Ask Mr. Manders," she finally replied.

"We did and now we're asking you," Manders said before repeating the question. "Did Mike Baker also let Mr. Manders in?"

"No," she said after a pause.

"Who did?"

"Cynthia."

"The deceased, Cynthia Harmon?" Hanlon asked, confirming Pat's answer.

"Yes," Pat said flatly.

"Were they as friendly as usual?" asked Hanlon, showing no reaction.

"I don't know what you mean?"

"Were they happy to see each other, did they chat together – friendly, were they as friendly as usual?" Hanlon persisted.

"I never said they were friendly." Pat answered.

"They weren't friendly?" asked Hanlon.

"I didn't say that either."

"So how were they?"

"Look I know what you're getting at." The anger was

back in a flash as Pat continued, "And I didn't think the police were into gossip. I thought you were supposed to be looking for the facts. I don't know what was going on between them. It wasn't any of my business. I didn't notice anything different between them this morning. They were like normal. I don't know anything more than that."

"What about Cynthia Harmon?" asked Hanlon changing the subject slightly.

"She's dead," snapped Pat. "Is that all?"

Pat waited and Hanlon waited and then finally he said, "Yes, for now." Hanlon watched her leave and as she reached the door, he added, "Who makes the coffee each morning?"

"I don't know. It's made when I get to work," she said, closing the door to the banking area behind her.

Deck turned to Hanlon and remarked, "Now what was that about? She sure did her best not to say anything."

"What she didn't say was loud and clear," replied Hanlon.

"Sure was," agreed Deck. "So do you think Manders was having a thing with this Cynthia Harmon?"

Maybe Victoria isn't that small, thought Hanlon.

"No one seems to want to tell us anything," said Deck.

"You shouldn't find that unusual."

"No," agreed Deck. "But it's like they don't want us to even investigate. As if the death is unimportant, best just forgotten."

"You have a point," replied Hanlon. "That is exactly how it is beginning to appear. We've only seen two people, though, so it's a little early to judge."

7

I T WAS AN hour and a half later and nearing noon. The interviews were going quickly, perhaps too quickly. The officers had heard the same story repeated several times. There should be something, some little thing someone had noticed. After all it wasn't a stranger who had died. It was someone who had worked beside them day after day. Time was passing and very little was being said by any of the employees. The same brief story, with nothing new added, kept being relayed over and over again. The officers were getting tired and hungry but they weren't getting any closer to what had happened that morning.

"Well, we've seen almost everyone now," said Deck. "And we still haven't found anyone who seems very upset or even surprised that Cynthia Harmon is dead."

"True, very true," replied Hanlon. "Let's see Diana Hillis. She should be concerned. Manders said he hired the deceased on her request."

"Right," said Deck as he left.

While he was gone, Hanlon scrutinized the personnel file labeled 'Diana Hillis'. It showed the standard history of a long-term employee recording position changes and regular annual raises. The performance reviews said little and there was no record of any extended absences. The file was that of a seasoned, competent, pragmatic worker – someone reliable. Nothing anywhere in the file prepared him for the definitely middle-aged scattered hen that Deck led into the room.

"This is Diana Hillis?" asked Hanlon with obvious surprise.

"Diana told me to come," whined the hen. "Is that alright? Do I stay? What do I do? Diana said to come."

"That's alright, Miss Webster," said Deck soothingly as he got her situated in a chair facing Hanlon.

Hanlon looked at Deck seeing a new side of him. After Deck had calmed the hen, Hanlon gave him a questioning glance that Deck answered.

"This is Doris Webster. Miss Hillis suggested that it might be wise not to keep Miss Webster waiting any longer."

"She did, did she?" remarked Hanlon. Looking at Doris Webster fumbling and fussing he admitted that Miss Hillis was probably correct. Hanlon saw before him the personification of gray – a short, squat woman with gray hair, a gray face, and dull clothes. This was someone who had been old forever and perhaps nervous forever. She certainly was today, fidgeting with her hands even though she had nothing in them and searching the room with clearly scared eyes. Miss Webster was not handling the strain well. Hanlon had met many Miss Websters in his work. One never knew what they would say.

"I didn't do it!" she shrieked. "God was watching out for me. He did it. I knew he would. She was evil! He protected me! I didn't do it!"

Good God, thought Deck. This is getting loonier all the time.

"What didn't you do, Miss Webster?" asked Hanlon.

"I didn't kill that horrible Cynthia Harmon, of course."

"I see."

"God did," she declared. With those words, she sat back

in her chair and seemed to relax for the first time.

"Why did He make the others sick?" asked Hanlon watching her intently.

"God works in mysterious way," was all she would say.

If we're all His creatures, thought Deck, He certainly does.

"You were not surprised by Cynthia's death?" asked Hanlon.

"She had to die," responded Doris again with a wail. "She was an evil, horrid, terrible woman."

"I see," said Hanlon.

I don't, thought Deck.

"I suppose she had no friends," asked Hanlon still probing. "Except for Diana Hillis and Mr. Manders?"

"She had no friends; she deserved no friends." Doris seemed to have calmed down again. She was now very definite.

"Not even Diana Hillis and Mr. Manders."

"Diana Hillis knew Cynthia Harmon from long ago, knew before any of us that she was bad," Doris replied with conviction.

"She was not Cynthia's friend?"

"She is my friend," Doris said with, for the first time, a smile. For some people a smile changes their whole appearance. Doris was one of those. Suddenly she went from a flustered old hen to a naïve artless child. Hanlon noticed the change and it only increased his alertness. For him, children did not automatically translate to innocence. He had been around too long. He had seen too much. He had also seen enough to realize that so far nothing, absolutely nothing was as it seemed in this case.

"I see," was all he said.

I still don't, thought Deck.

"What about Mr. Manders?" asked Hanlon. "He was Cynthia's friend."

"He was blinded. She blinded him with her lies. She was

a flirt. I wouldn't say tramp but others would I'm sure. But he wasn't blinded any longer," Doris said with pleasure.

"He wasn't?"

"No, I saw," she said proudly.

"What did you see?"

"Yesterday they had a fight. Today he tried to avoid her."

"How do you know they had a fight?"

"I heard them. She thought I had left, but I hadn't. I heard them." Again, she sat a little more erect and seemed proud to answer.

"They were arguing," suggested Hanlon.

"Not really arguing," said Doris hesitantly. "Mr. Manders said something was finished. Miss Harmon said it wasn't until she said it was. She was like that. He was to take her to dinner tonight and he was to bring her a present – a BIG present."

So Manders was lying thought Deck. Then looking back at Doris, he wondered, or is she the one lying? The whole thing is screwy, just plain screwy. If Hanlon was having similar thoughts, no one could tell.

"And today," was all he said.

"Oh today, God killed her!" replied Doris without hesitation.

"Before that," said Hanlon without any sign of being fazed.

You've got to admire the old man, thought Deck. It isn't easy getting anything rational from these nuts!

"Before that," repeated Doris lost in thought. "Before that.....you mean Miss Harmon and Mr. Manders today?"

"Yes, that's what I mean," Hanlon said calmly.

"Mike opens the door for everyone you know," said Doris. Hanlon waited. "Except for Mr. Manders. Cynthia always opened the door for him. Today he didn't like that."

"How do you know that?"

"From his face, of course. From his face."

"Anything else happen today?"

"She didn't visit him and she didn't take him any coffee. She always visits him every morning and she always takes him his coffee. Anyway she used to," she added with the beginning of a hysterical giggle.

"I see," said Hanlon.

"So do I," thought Deck, finally.

"To think Mr. Manders would do that to nice Mrs. Manders. She sends us cakes you know. But it'll be okay now. Now that God has killed that wicked woman," said Doris with obvious pleasure.

"Suppose God didn't kill her, Miss Webster," said Hanlon. "Suppose a person killed her."

"If they did, it was God's wishes. God told them to kill her," Doris replied rationally.

"Would God tell you to kill someone, Miss Webster?"

"I didn't do it! I told you! God did!" replied Doris almost bouncing out of her chair as her full hysteria returned.

"Yes, well, that will be all for now, Miss Webster," Hanlon said motioning to Deck to escort her to the door.

Once the door closed, Deck turned to the inspector, "That one is loony!"

"Possibly," said Hanlon.

"Possibly nothing," exclaimed Deck. " She is loony!"

"Enough to poison the whole staff?"

"Sure," Deck said not quite so confidently.

"And kill someone?" asked Hanlon.

"She wanted her dead," Deck said. Then he added, "Manders might have wanted her dead too. My money would be on him."

"So soon?"

"Sure," Deck paused. "But not a mass poisoning. This is crazy! The loony could do the poisoning. The manager could do the killing. Do we have a poisoning, a killing or an accident?"

"That, Sergeant, is the question."

"What do you think is the answer?"

"I'll pass for now. Let's have the next person, Sergeant." The door opened before Deck could get to it and a tiny blond woman suddenly stepped in.

"Miss Hillis?" asked Hanlon hesitantly.

"Shirley Foster," Shirley said offering her hand. "I saw Doris leave and I'm dying of curiosity out there. I suppose that's better than actually dying. Good ol' Cynthia, what a bitch! Not bad to look at, Manders noticed that soon enough. Rotten underneath though. Pure skunk cabbage. And smoke, God! Yesterday, yes it was yesterday; I told my husband I was going to kill her. Couldn't stand her damn cigarettes. I sat right across from her you see and the smoke was horrendous! And now she's dead. Good riddance. I had a perfect view to watch her moan and groan and have her convulsions. Died right in front of me. Never saw anyone die before. Is it always so interesting?"

Hanlon and Deck looked at each other and then back to Shirley. Both men were taking a moment to absorb this new witness. They saw an attractive energetic woman who glowed with enthusiasm. She was small just over 5 foot and a little over 100 pounds but with her energy she seemed to be much bigger. This was a woman who could fill a room. To Deck she seemed to be bouncing on the spot. Hanlon saw shrewdness in her dark blue eyes. This was also a woman who was used to having her own way.

"You were going to kill her?" Hanlon asked.

"That's what I told my husband," Shirley calmly replied.

God, another spinny one, thought Deck.

"And did you?" asked Hanlon not letting Shirley's comment lie.

"Did I what?"

"Kill Cynthia Harmon?" persisted Hanlon.

Shirley laughed, "Now…. What are you a captain, lieutenant?"

"I am Detective Inspector Hanlon," he said introducing himself. "And this is Detective Sergeant Deck."

"Pleased to meet you," replied Shirley.

Shirley quit walking around the little room and took a seat on the orange couch. She looked directly at Hanlon who was still sitting on one of the kitchen table chairs. Deck had settled in one of the overstuffed separate chairs to her left. The three sat in silence each waiting for the other.

"Aren't you going to ask me any questions?" asked Shirley. "What exactly have you been doing today in here? Doesn't the body have to be autopsied or some such thing? Witnesses interrogated. Told not to leave town. All that good stuff. I've been waiting all morning to be interrogated. Is this it?"

Usually we ask the questions, thought Deck.

"These are preliminary interviews, Mrs. Foster," replied Hanlon. "To understand the usual routine and anything that was unusual today."

"You mean other than someone putting poison in the coffee and killing Cynthia?"

"Someone put poison in the coffee?" asked Hanlon.

"Of course," replied Shirley. "Easiest place."

Maybe she's not so spinny, thought Deck.

"You know this really is quite boring," sighed Shirley. "I had real hopes for today. Everyone getting sick. Then Cynthia keeling over right in front of me. But this interview is really very boring. This is as mundane as explaining to people that they are overdrawn."

"This might not be exciting, Mrs. Foster," answered Hanlon. "But we could use your help. We would like you to give us a rundown of this morning's events in order as they happened."

"You must have heard this several times by now," sighed Shirley. Seeing Hanlon was serious with his question, she continued, "Alright, if that's what you want. I arrived at work. Mike opened the door. I took off my coat. I got my basket out of the vault and started my work. You don't care what work, do you?" she glanced at the officers and then continued. "Nothing much happened. Usual things. Cynthia smoked and was irritated because Diana arrived later than Cynthia thinks, thought she should."

"I understood they were friends," interrupted Hanlon.

"Who told you that crap? I bet it was Mr. Manders – he's so obvious!" laughed Shirley.

"Continue, please."

"Cynthia upset Miss Webster. Everything upsets Miss Webster." Deck smiled as Shirley continued. "Cynthia didn't go to see Manders today. That was different. Then Mike started feeling sick. He was first. Cynthia made some remark about him poisoning himself with the amount of coffee that he drinks. He drinks a lot. Probably why he got sick first. Then a few other people got ill. Cynthia started to be concerned, well concerned for her. She phoned wherever and then she died right there. I screamed of course. That's what one is supposed to do, isn't it? Mr. Manders came out and I thought he was going to have a heart attack on the spot. Diana was waiting on a customer but stopped to suggest the body be removed from public display."

"It was Ms Hillis' idea to move the body?" Hanlon interrupted to ask.

"Yes. Mr. Manders and Mike moved Cynthia back here even though Mike could hardly stand up by then. The ambulance came. Then two policemen came. Then you came. Then all the excitement died away. That word keeps coming up. Wait until I tell Stephen. Yesterday morning he told me not to kill anyone. He didn't say that today though."

"Thank-you, Mrs. Foster," said Hanlon. "One or two more questions and then you can go."

"Me telling you everything," moaned Shirley. "I came here to learn from you, not to tell you everything."

"At this point," replied Hanlon. "You probably know more than we do."

"Don't believe that; but if that's to be your approach, go ahead."

"The suggestions you have made, do you have anything to support your ideas?"

"What suggestions; what ideas?" asked Shirley surprised.

"That there was poison in the coffee for one."

"Oh, simple!" said Shirley. "The only people affected were coffee drinkers. The rest of us are fine."

"That is very observant."

"Anything else then?" asked Shirley. "This isn't as much fun as I thought."

"You also said that Cynthia Harmon was killed?"

"So?"

"Not that she died from the poisoning."

"She died from the poisoning alright," agreed Shirley. "But that doesn't mean she wasn't killed."

"Deliberately?"

"Deliberately," said Shirley without any of her usual joking.

"Why?" asked Hanlon.

"She was Cynthia," Shirley stated firmly.

"You feel that is sufficient reason?" Hanlon inquired.

"She's the only one dead, isn't she?" Shirley said by way of a reply.

"So far."

"No one else will die from this morning's little drama," she said quietly and firmly.

"You seem very sure."

Shirley just shrugged. Deck and Hanlon watched her as she gazed around the room deciding her next words. Finally she brought her eyes back to Hanlon's face.

"I think I'll go now. There can't be anything else. I'm not going to tell you I didn't kill her because everyone says that. Besides you won't believe me anyway. This is really very disappointing. You have no idea what happened. You have no idea who killed her. You're not even going to arrest someone."

"We could arrest you if you confessed," answered Hanlon.

"You're just saying that to be nice," laughed Shirley as she rose to leave. As she reached the door, she added, "But I didn't confess."

Turning to Hanlon, Deck asked, "Is it too late to request holidays starting today?"

"Don't tell me," replied Hanlon. "That you find our little inquiry as boring as Mrs. Fisher."

"Not boring, crazy. They all did it."

"No one seems disappointed, that is quite true," Hanlon said as much to himself as to Deck.

"Disappointed! They're overjoyed," replied Deck. Hanlon nodded and turned back to the staff files.

"Let's see this Diana Hillis..." he said.

"You are seeing her," said Diana entering on cue.

A thirtish slender brunette stood calmly before them. Hanlon knew better than to react personally to anyone in a police investigation. First impressions had become trained instincts; well trained and well behaved. Not now. He found this woman much too attractive.

Gentle eyes, Hanlon said to himself. This was a woman that you noticed but also a woman oblivious to her effect. Or was she? She seemed to be laughing at some private joke. But what could she find funny in this situation, he wondered.

"May I sit down?" Diana asked. One of the gentlemen before her had the appearance of a gentle bear, a big balding man probably much younger than he looked. She turned to the other officer and saw him watching her far too intently. He was in some ways average looking, and yet, Diana looked closer. He was probably around 6 feet tall – no glasses, no facial hair. Dark, thick hair, which was starting to show the gray, surrounded a worn, somewhat tired looking face. Interesting he was, and somehow soothing. Soothing? He's a policeman, Diana reminded herself.

"Certainly," said Deck wondering what was with Hanlon. "You are Diana Hillis?"

"Yes," replied Diana taking the place Shirley had so recently vacated. "I believe you have seen everyone else so assumed it was my turn."

She waited. Deck waited.

What is with him now, thought Deck?

"This is Detective Inspector Hanlon and I am Detective Sergeant Deck. We are making preliminary inquiries into this morning's incident. Any assistance would be appreciated."

I hate this, thought Deck. Hanlon is supposed to ask the questions. I keep the notes. He's acting like he's eighty-five and senile!

"Fine," said Diana. "Where do you want to start?"

"Inspector?" asked Deck.

"Yes, Sergeant," Hanlon acknowledged as if waking from a dream. "Yes, umm, now, Miss Hillis, I think we have a basic understanding of the morning routine. Was there anything unusual you noticed this morning?"

"No," Diana said calmly. Hanlon waited but he could tell she was not going to expand on her answer.

"This morning's events then were not unexpected?" he asked probing further.

"Is this sort of thing ever expected, Inspector?" was her non-reply.

What the hell is this now, thought Deck.

"No," responded Hanlon. "And yet no one seems surprised or interested. Except for Mrs. Foster, that is."

"Shirley has an active imagination," said Diana smiling.

"The rest?" asked Hanlon.

"I can't speak for everyone, Inspector."

Is she ever going to answer a question, Deck thought watching Hanlon watch Diana.

"You can speak for yourself," Hanlon stated with

authority. "Were you surprised?"

"No."

"Why not?" Hanlon said. He needed to get this woman to talk. These one-word answers were not enough.

"Nothing specific," Diana answered. "The atmosphere in here was tense; a very violent feel."

God, thought Deck. The first sane one and she reads the air!

"How long had you noticed this?" Hanlon persisted.

"Not long. But as I said it was just a feeling, no reality."

"There often is a reality to our feelings; we sense things with our subconscious that we can't see with our conscious mind."

The old man's finally cracked, Deck decided.

"If you remember anything more specific, please give me a call, " added Hanlon.

"Certainly," replied Diana but didn't move. Everyone sat in silence with their own thoughts or in Deck's case in confusion watching two people who didn't seem to know what to say or ask of each other.

"Just a few more things," Hanlon finally said breaking the silence.

"Yes," Diana replied calmly.

"Who usually makes the coffee?"

"Mike Baker."

"Mrs. Foster seemed quite sure that it had been poisoned this morning."

"Is that a question, Inspector?"

"Curious to your reaction, Miss Hillis," replied Hanlon.

"Shirley is quite bright and does not miss much."

"Does that mean you agree with her?"

"Yes," Diana said without hesitation.

"She also seemed convinced that Miss Harmon's death was not an accident resulting from the poisoning." Hanlon stated.

"My deductions?"

"Please."

What is this, thought Deck. The suspects are unraveling the case for us.

"I agree with Shirley."

"Care to elaborate?"

Diana waited quietly. Hanlon could see her thinking but the thoughts were evasive. Deck saw no point to any of this.

What had they learnt? The victim was poisoned. She had been having an affair with the manager. They had quarreled yesterday. Today she is dead. So, the manager did it. It could be that simple.

"First," Diana said finally answering. "The only people taken ill are coffee drinkers. The rest of us, all who have juice, milk, water or even tea, are fine. Second, Mike, who is here earliest and usually makes the coffee, was the first person to show any symptoms. Third, whatever was in the coffee could not have been lethal. Mike has 5 to 6 cups of coffee before ten o'clock in the morning. If anyone were to die from the coffee in the pot, it would have been Mike not Cynthia. Unless, Mike is the one who poisoned the coffee. But in that case, there was no reason to get rid of the coffee cup."

"What coffee cup?" Hanlon snapped.

Finally Deck thought something that resembles a clue!

"Cynthia's," replied Diana, oblivious to the excitement the answer had caused.

"It's missing?" Hanlon asked calmly.

"Yes."

"Which tells you what?" continued Hanlon.

"Shirley's right," answered Diana. "Cynthia was murdered."

It has finally been said, thought Deck. What they all knew but wouldn't say.

"Go on," said Hanlon.

"My guess," answered Diana, "is that there were two

poisons. One put in the coffee and one used to kill Cynthia. Thus, the effort to remove her cup. It's not out front and Shirley says she looked while back here and it's not here either."

"Reckless, poisoning so many to kill one person," commented Hanlon.

"I don't know," remarked Diana. "I would say too cautious. If she wasn't so concerned about the others' lives, the real victim wouldn't have been so obvious."

"She?" asked Hanlon.

"Or he," said Diana with a shrug.

"Let's assume your theory is correct and that Miss Harmon was the intended victim. We will need some background on her. Now I understand you were a friend of hers?"

Diana started visibly as if she had experienced a sudden stabbing pain. Hanlon watched and waited.

"I knew her," she replied.

"That's all?"

No reply came to the Inspector's question.

"You recommended her for her original position here."

"It is hard to tell, Inspector, which of your remarks are questions and which are not," said Diana with coldness in her voice for the first time.

"Was Miss Harmon hired on your request or your recommendation?"

"You have the records," snapped Diana.

Now what's happening, thought Deck. First Hanlon had seemed to be almost too friendly with Diana Hillis and now they were barely being civil.

"I would like your answer," demanded Hanlon.

"No," Diana finally answered. "She wasn't."

"Yet, the records show that."

"Yes," Diana said flatly.

"Would you care to explain?" Hanlon said and Deck wondered if that was sarcasm in his voice. Sarcasm was not something Hanlon used a lot in interviews but then Deck hadn't seen Hanlon quite like this before.

"No, Inspector. I would not."

"Humour me, Miss Hillis, " Hanlon demanded. In the loud silence Hanlon and Diana sat opposite each other, seeing only each other. Finally, Diana spoke.

"I was away at the time. I have known Cynthia it seems forever. When Cynthia wanted a job here, she used my name. When I got back, she was already settled. For my own reasons, I let it lie."

"What reasons?"

"My reasons."

"Miss Hillis?" asked Hanlon.

"No, Inspector."

Deck watched the test of wills waiting for Hanlon to pounce. To Deck's surprise, he didn't.

"Was this characteristic of Miss Harmon?" asked Hanlon taking a new tack. "To falsify references?"

"Cynthia was totally narcissistic," Diana replied calmly. The tension that had erupted so fast was now gone just as fast. "That is why it is ridiculous to suppose she died from whatever made the others sick. She never drank more than half a cup of coffee at any time. She was very careful of her body, her looks, her marketable items, as it were."

"I see," said Hanlon.

I do too, thought Deck. No one could stand the broad!

"Yet she smoked," continued Hanlon.

"Not really," smiled Diana. "She played at smoking. She probably got more pleasure out of annoying Shirley than she did from the actual cigarettes."

"You did not like her?" asked Hanlon.

"To know her was to hate her," Diana replied flippantly, then returning to a serious tone said, "but that is irrelevant."

"Not if it's murder."

"It's murder," Diana Hillis stated. The three sat in a silence created by the certainty of Diana's words. Finally Hanlon broke the quiet.

"Alright, Miss Hillis, I think that will be all for now. The lab people are out front I believe." Diana nodded and Hanlon continued, "They will be here for a short time more and then we'll all be gone for today."

"Fine, Inspector. I'll let Mr. Manders know."

Quiet filled the room in the moments after Diana left.

"She had a lot to say," said Deck.

"She had a lot she didn't say," replied Hanlon thoughtfully.

"Do you think she's right?"

"It fits, it certainly fits. But is it her logic we heard or her confession?"

"Her?" Deck said surprised.

"I hope not."

"This is a first! The old man falling for a suspect!"

"The old man?"

"Sorry, a nickname. It slipped."

"Well, the old man is not that old. Not so old that there isn't still more for you to learn, Junior."

"Right, sir," Deck replied. After a pause, watching Hanlon going over his private thoughts, Deck added, "Maybe she didn't do it."

"Maybe. But if she did, we have our work cut out for us," Hanlon replied almost sadly.

"I think we do anyway. No one is sorry Miss Harmon is a corpse."

"You're right there," agreed Harmon. "Let's go get something to eat."

8

DECK AND HANLON walked from the bank towards their car without discussion. Quiet was what Hanlon needed and Deck knew it. Deck took his usual place as driver, waited until Hanlon was settled and then pulled the car from its parking spot. When a break came in the traffic, he turned smoothly left onto Cook. Hanlon didn't know where they were heading but food was more Deck's thing than his. Silently and companionably, they drove along Cook towards the park and away from downtown.

Two blocks later, Deck turned right onto Southgate moving towards the north side of Beacon Hill Park. It didn't look like anything from this side. It wasn't until they left the residential area that the pasture-like field even became visible to their left. As the road curved up a slight hill, the pasture changed into a rocky knoll. Hanlon started to see arbutus trees. Then suddenly there on their left at the five points corner was the Beacon Hill Park entrance and formal sign. It was like coming into the park from the backside.

Deck turned left onto Douglas, passing the old elementary school that had been there as long as he remembered. They drove towards the water, down a corridor of trees, ponds and flowers. On their left was the park. On their right were elaborate, year-round gardens fronting a series of apartment buildings.

"It's always so quiet here," said Hanlon more to himself. "So old."

"Well now it is established around here," replied Deck. "Like our lunch spot," he added with a laugh as he pulled off Douglas Street and into the small parking lot that served the Beacon Hill Drive-In.

"Established is it?" Hanlon asked. "I'm older than you and it's just plain old! I remember when this place had carhops." They got out of the car and headed towards the drive-in building.

"So you're saying you are an old man, Inspector?" asked Deck watching Hanlon to see how he took the teasing. With no reply, Deck continued, "I've been coming here for years. We used to come as a family when I was a kid, with my parents. I don't remember the carhops but I do remember the combo-burgers, a hot dog and hamburger together. Now they were something! Don't know why they quit making them. That's why I still come here. They're not on the menu anymore but I keep hoping."

"You're an optimist, Deck," replied Hanlon. No longer talking about food or history, he continued, "I've been doing this a long time, maybe too long." Deck didn't answer. At some point in each case, usually at the beginning, Hanlon had this struggle. Deck would wait; the inspector had always come out of it before.

"I'm going to have a double hot dog," Deck said firmly. "It's the closest thing to the combo-burger."

"That's some deduction," Hanlon said smiling. Deck had a way of making things simple. Moving towards the ordering window, Hanlon said, "I'll have a regular cheese burger, fries and a Coke."

They wasted little time over their lunch and before long, were back in the car.

"Let's take the scenic route," said Hanlon.

Deck knew what Hanlon meant. He turned right onto Douglas Street and then quickly left onto Dallas Road following the shoreline towards Oak Bay. Hanlon stared out over the water, seeing first joggers, then children flying kites up above Finlayson point, then tourists driving slowly around Clover Point. Next came the water of Ross Bay. You could see Washington from here, everyone said. He always looked but never knew if he saw it or not. He didn't really care. It was just there and he found the water peaceful. Hanlon watched the passing sights in silence lost in his own thoughts. He awoke to the sound of Deck's voice.

"They have tours there now," Deck was saying.

"Sorry, Sergeant," Hanlon replied. "What did you say?"

"They conduct tours there now," Deck repeated, nodding his head towards his left as they passed the Ross Bay cemetery. "Can you imagine? Going hiking through a cemetery looking at gravestones."

"Ever been down here in a storm?" Deck continued, "With the waves coming right up the breakwater and over the street. Now that's a sight, better than any old tombstones."

Deck turned left at Foul Bay Road leaving the scenic route in order to cut across to Oak Bay Avenue. He drove through the village, past the teashops and other English shops. This was the most British part of Victoria. Deck turned onto Beach Drive and started to slow down looking for Cynthia Harmon's address.

Deck found it directly across the street from the Oak Bay Marina. Pulling up in front of a four-storey white stucco and gray stone building, he remarked, "This isn't half bad."

The gray stone on first glance was decoration, there to offset the glassed-in balconies. On second look, it became clear the stone was for chimneys, chimneys for the condos' fireplaces. A smart, upscale building with simple tailored landscaping, it fit right in with the neighbourhood.

Cynthia Harmon's unit was on the third floor, the front corner of the building with a breathtaking view over the marina. Inside, Hanlon and Deck stood at the window and watched the seagulls circling and the sailboats rocking gently in their slips.

"No, not bad," remarked Deck turning back into the room. "Not bad at all."

Hanlon nodded as he walked around the room touching nothing. He let his eyes do the searching and his experience act as his lie detector. The room looked like a display from an interior-decorating magazine. The furniture was of the latest style and was positioned to create an intimate, yet elegant feel. Costly vases, precise ornaments and striking pictures were the finishing touches.

"Not what you called lived-in," remarked Deck.

"No, Sergeant, it's not," Hanlon agreed. He continued to look around and finally added, "It's all recently obtained."

"Yeah," said Deck. "New."

"New," smiled Hanlon. "And expensive."

"Too expensive for what the bank paid her."

Hanlon nodded and the two men walked through the rest of the unit. The condominium had one of the common open-concept floor plans. Coming through the front door, the living room with its magnificent view window was straight ahead. On the one side, Cynthia had her desk and a little office area. On the other, the front living area included space that served as a dining area. Along the entrance hall and behind the dining area was an open kitchen galley. A small bar separated it from the living and dining area so it was open to the windows and light and yet felt like a separate room. Another hallway took them to two bedrooms and two bathrooms. The unit also had in-suite laundry and storage facilities. Hanlon surveyed it all and acknowledged, as Deck had said, it wasn't half-bad. It also was, as they'd agreed, more than what Cynthia could afford on what the bank would have paid her. Hanlon filed those thoughts away and the officers started their search in earnest.

Hanlon covered the living area, starting with her desk

and the papers it held. Deck, for his part, searched the bedrooms and baths.

Cynthia's belongings were very orderly and as with the living room very stylish, very expensive. Everything was carefully done, reflecting not only her tastes but also her concerns. No drugs, save birth control pills, were in the medicine cabinet. An extensive supply of cosmetics, perfumes, oils and creams filled her cupboards. Clothes, feminine, sensual, and designer labeled, filled in the closets. Nowhere was there a masculine touch and yet everything was suitable as props for a woman to be attractive, seductive.

"Nothing here to contradict what we heard at the bank," said Deck as he left the bedroom. "What did that Miss Hillis call it, 'marketable items'? From the back rooms, it would appear her looks took most of her attention."

"Not according to this," answered Hanlon not looking up from what he was reading.

Deck walked over to where Hanlon was seated at Cynthia's desk and peered over his shoulder. The desktop was covered with a ledger and various bankbooks and they were fully captivating Hanlon's attention. The ledger dated back several years. The bankbooks matched the ledger.

"What did you find?" asked Deck.

"The lady kept very complete records. Taxation would be very impressed but I doubt very much that she declared any of this as income."

"She a hooker?" asked Deck bluntly.

"Closer to blackmail."

"If it is murder, that should give us some suspects."

"It's murder," Hanlon said repeating Diana's words.

"You're sure then," Deck asked, sensing Hanlon was finally ready to talk about the case. Hanlon always did this. First the listening, the absorbing, giving nothing away until he had had time for it to gel in his own mind. Then he would start. Deck was used to Hanlon's style of working and was comfortable to wait, wait until the moment Hanlon did want to talk.

"Yes. That was what Thomas was telling us. Everything fits too neatly. Much too neatly for my tastes. When the autopsy and the hospital reports are in, we've heard what they'll say. It was two poisons."

"You agree with those women at the bank?"

"They were there, they know the people involved."

"And they could have done it themselves."

"I thought you had picked Manders as the villain of this piece?" teased Hanlon.

"I don't know about any 'villain of this piece' jazz," answered Deck. "But I think he's a prime suspect for knocking off this Cynthia Harmon babe."

"And he is," said Hanlon. "His name is the last one in this book."

"Now we're getting somewhere."

"The lady has been active for several years. Started out small and grew and grew. She must have been in her late teens when this book started. Names and more names. Mostly men but an occasional woman."

"Any other that we know?" asked Deck.

"Not that I recognize," answered Hanlon. "But it was a long time ago, names can change."

"What's with names from a long time ago, we have Manders now?" said Deck.

"I also found a marriage license, a couple of birth certificates..."

"A couple?" asked Deck.

"Yes," answered Hanlon. "And a registered change of name."

"Cynthia Harmon?"

"Was Susan Smith, born 31 years ago, married Joey Laberg, no evidence of a divorce," replied Hanlon.

"Interesting, she must have been some piece of work," Deck said before asking, "Whose is the other birth certificate?"

"Samuel Marshall; mother is Susan Laberg, father is

Samuel Marshall."

"I bet those names are in your little book."

"It's not so little and surprisingly they're not," answered Hanlon. "That is, Joey Laberg isn't listed. Neither is Samuel Marshall. Here's a Diana Marshall. The name's entered but no amount, which is odd. All the other entries have amounts or items attached."

"Items?"

"Jewelry, furniture, cars," replied Hanlon. "Cynthia Harmon knew exactly what she was doing." Gathering the legal documents, the ledger and the bankbooks, Hanlon remarked, "Not much in the way of momentos or souvenirs for 31 years."

"There's a photo album in the bedroom," said Deck.

"Let's have a look."

Deck returned with the photo album. Flipping through the pages, the pictures -with the exception of a few group shots – were all of individuals. There were no pictures of Cynthia, neither alone or with others. All the pictures were labeled as to who everyone was. Nothing showed when or where or why the pictures had been taken.

"Funny kind of memories," said Deck. "No vacations, no scenery, nothing showing any fun. Just a bunch of different people." Hanlon flipped through the book with a small frown. Handing the photo album back to Deck, he picked up the ledger.

"Read me some of those names," Hanlon instructed. As Deck read out the names, Hanlon reviewed the names in the ledgers.

"Not family or friends," Hanlon finally said. "Victims." He handed the ledger to Deck.

"God," Deck said virtually speechless as he read through the ledger in more detail.

Hanlon picked up the photo album from where Deck had set it and proceeded to go slowly through each page. Suddenly he stopped and stared at the page before him.

"What?" asked Deck noticing Hanlon's reaction. "What is it?"

Deck moved closer to Hanlon and looked at what had so grabbed Hanlon's attention. It was a picture of a woman. Diana Marshall, it said in big red letters.

"Why that's Diana Hillis!" exclaimed Deck. "Maybe Manders didn't do it."

9

THE TWO POLICEMEN did not take the scenic route back to see Diana Hillis. The silence was grim and Deck knew what Hanlon wanted – to get to Diana Hillis as quickly as possible. Hanlon was not happy. Deck drove back up Oak Bay Avenue straight to Cook Street. Left turn onto Cook and even with the traffic lights, they were back at the bank within very little time.

It was closed. It was still only early afternoon but with one death and a large percentage of the staff at the hospital it was understandable. Hanlon gave no reaction upon finding the bank closed but Deck from experience knew Hanlon's frustration was building. They headed to Diana Hillis's home without delay. Deck checked the file and saw that Diana Hillis did not live that far away. Fortunately, thought Deck. Hanlon started to regain his balance and realized the bank being closed was probably a good thing. Homes could tell the officers a lot about a person. Cynthia's sure had.

Deck continued south on Cook, turning left onto Faithful Street.

"Faithful, huh?" remarked Deck. "Someone wasn't very faithful in this little story."

A bit of a grunt, perhaps in agreement, came from Hanlon as they pulled up in front of a well-kept bungalow. It was one of the little box houses that without care look exactly like the little houses used when playing monopoly. Not this one though. The small front lawn was recently cut; fall flowers interspersed between mature shrubs. Everything showed exceptional care, Hanlon noticed as they walked up red painted steps to a door with leaded glass windows.

They rang the doorbell and inside Anna ran to answer it. To her surprise, two grim officers of the law greeted her with their identification. Her first thoughts were of Diana.

"Diana?" asked Anna with worry evident in her voice.

"We'd like to ask her a few questions," replied Inspector Hanlon.

"Then she's alright?" asked Anna.

"Fine," answered Hanlon flatly.

Except that she might be a murderer, thought Deck. Or was it murderess, such a stupid word he always thought.

"Just a few questions," continued Hanlon.

"She's not home yet," answered Anna.

"We'll wait," Hanlon said deliberately.

Anna led them into a pleasant sitting room as she identified herself as Diana Hillis's sister. The room was comfortable, not overly feminine. Simply furnished, there were a couple of small love seats at right angles to each other with two comfortable chairs opposite the far one. These were nestled in a semi-circle around a large fireplace, which was in the center of the wall to their left. On its far side, a doorway led to the back part of the house, probably the kitchen. The pastel walls, scattered floor cushions and the few plants made the whole room come together in a cozy, relaxed way. Hanlon approved. Warm is how he thought of it. Deck noticed the sharp contrast to Cynthia Harmon's apartment. This was not for show; this was for living.

"What is this about? Did something happen at the bank?" Anna asked as she sat down on the far love seat. Hanlon and Deck took chairs opposite with their backs to the entrance hall.

"Why do you ask?" Hanlon said by way of a reply to Anna's questions.

"Because Diana said something was going to happen. That's why I wasn't to go there until things settled."

"What things?" asked Hanlon.

"I don't know exactly. She said things were really tense." Anna paused for a moment then laughingly added, "She thought someone wanted to kill Cynthia. Isn't that silly?"

Neither Deck nor Hanlon laughed. Neither thought it was silly.

"Not so silly," Hanlon finally said. "Miss Harmon is dead."

"Oh," was all that Anna said. The officers watched as she gave this information some thought. Hanlon could see the family resemblance.

"Oh," she repeated. Anna was obviously the younger and was fairer than Diana. Both looked at the world with deep brown eyes. However where Diana's were deep, dark pools that hid her private thoughts, Anna's were open, light and let all her thoughts dance on the surface.

"Oh," she said again slowly. "That's why you're here."

"Did your sister say why she thought someone wanted to kill Miss Harmon?" Hanlon continued to probe.

Deck watched Hanlon watching Anna. To the average eye Hanlon seemed totally disinterested, but Deck knew Hanlon was missing none of Anna's confusion.

"She was kidding," Anna said nervously. "It was silly things. Shirley wanted to kill her because she smoked; Mike wanted to kill her because he needed her job; Judy wanted to kill her because Cynthia scared her. The new woman was funny too. Barbara something. Supposedly she and Cynthia had just met but Diana didn't think so. That's all. Nothing like a real motive."

Now we have a Judy and a Barbara, thought Deck. Too many suspects.

"And did Diana also have a reason?" asked Hanlon. Both Hanlon and Deck could see the obvious distress Anna felt.

"Diana's known Cynthia forever," replied Anna. "She could have killed her before now."

That doesn't answer the question, thought Deck. Anna waited for the follow-up question but Hanlon surprised her.

"This is a nice little home the two of you have. Neither of you married?"

"No," answered Anna somewhat confused by the change of subject.

"Never?" he said probingly.

"Diana was when she was young," Anna said slowly with an obvious question mark in her voice.

"Tell me about it."

"Why?" asked Anna starting to get very uneasy with the questions.

"Background information," said Hanlon casually.

"You'll have to ask Diana. I don't know that much about it."

"You are her sister," Hanlon pointed out.

"Her younger sister," clarified Anna.

The three sat in silence. Hanlon appeared to be resting. Anna squirmed slightly and looked everywhere in the room but at Hanlon.

"Our father was in the armed forces. We lived in Belmont Park," Anna finally said. "That's where Diana first met Cynthia. They were at school there. When Diana finished school, Dad was transferred to Ontario. I was still in school so I had to move. Diana stayed. She wrote that she was married. She had quietly gone and got married. That's Diana. It wasn't much of a surprise to my parents and me. We had known the guy. He was someone she had gone with in school. Then later she phoned. There had been an accident and her husband had died."

"What was the accident?" continued Hanlon.

Anna frowned and a voice came from the hallway behind her..

"Shouldn't you be asking me those questions, Inspector?"

"Diana, finally!" said Anna jumping up.

Diana came into the room from the doorway beside the fireplace. She was facing the officers and was obviously not pleased to see them there. Anna was very pleased to see her though, and quickly left the room the same way Diana had entered. Diana walked towards Hanlon and Deck stopping in front of the fireplace where she remained standing.

"I am right in assuming it's Cynthia you're investigating and not my husband?" Diana asked.

"And any connection between the two," replied Hanlon seriously.

"I see," answered Diana watching his drowsy eyes, not deceived by them. Was this the man she had thought of as soothing? Now there was something else; anger. Anger, though, was personal and he was a policeman. What was happening here? What had he expected? What had she?

"You've been busy," Diana commented in controlled, neutral tones. She moved towards the side couch and slowly took the spot her sister had vacated.

"And you left a lot out when we talked earlier," Hanlon stated.

"Nothing that wasn't there for you to find, obviously," Diana countered.

Hanlon, although trained to be impartial, did not want to believe in Diana's quilt. Deck had no such problem since Diana was making no effort to appear innocent.

"First: you were married. Second: Cynthia Harmon had changed her name. Third: She was also married. Fourth: She had a son whose father was your husband. Is that true?"

"Yes. I don't know. Yes. I don't know."

"Nothing else," demanded Hanlon.

"What precisely is your question?" snapped Diana.

"One could say you have a motive," Hanlon said.

"One could," answered Diana. "But one would be wrong."

"Would they?"

"Ten years ago maybe I had a reason to wish Cynthia dead. Ten years ago, Inspector."

"Where's the child?" asked Hanlon bluntly.

As a response to these words, Diana rose and left the room.

"Has she gone to get the kid?" asked Deck. Hanlon gave a slight shrug by way of an answer. "She's a funny one, isn't she?" continued Deck. "You'd think she wants us to think she's guilty."

Hanlon gave no reply to this at all. Diana was not eager to cooperate, that was more than obvious. That she was a strong personality was equally obvious. Why did he hope it was just her privacy she was trying to protect? He was getting tired, too tired.

Diana returned holding a short, squat glass with amber liquid splashing over a couple of ice cubes. She lit the fire that was already laid in the fireplace. Settling on cushions close to the fire, she sipped her drink and gazed into Hanlon's eyes. Knowing she was making a decision, Hanlon waited.

"I think it will be easier if I run down that part of Cynthia's biography that I know. After which, since it's been a long strain of a day, I request you leave my house," Diana said. Hanlon made no reply. Diana took a deep breath and exhaled slowly giving herself a few seconds to prepare, and then started to speak.

"I met Susan Smith in high school. She immediately informed everyone she was Cynthia not Susan. So she always was. I never knew if it was her middle name or if it was the role she had chosen to play. I didn't care. You say she changed it, you'd know. At school she studied boys. She was determined to be married to get away from her family, mostly her father. She was quite prepared to do anything to achieve her goal. As a result, she was known as 'Sinful Cynthia'. But that is irrelevant. She managed to find a husband, Joey Laberg. Joey was a nice enough guy. I also married. Her husband was not what she had hoped. I think she decided mine might be better. There had never been much love lost between Cynthia and I. Anyway, her husband left the picture. I don't know the details. He left and then Cynthia claimed to be pregnant with my husband's child. He didn't know if it was his or not but he couldn't believe she would lie. I could."

Diana stopped to take another sip of her drink. The fire had died slightly so she stirred it back to life. Hanlon sat quietly and Deck fidgeted.

"Cynthia went to Vancouver supposedly to be in a group home with 4 or 5 other girls in similar situations. She said the baby did not live. I never thought she was even pregnant. If you say there was a child, then maybe there was. Shortly afterwards my husband died, car accident. I didn't see Cynthia for years. Heard about her around town, that's all. Then about three years ago, I came back from holidays to find Miss Cynthia Harmon as a new employee. And that, gentlemen, is the life and times of Cynthia Harmon as I know it."

"What about the years since her employment?" asked Hanlon.

Diana rubbed her forehead and glanced out the window.

"There are a couple of points I would like clarified," continued Hanlon.

"The years since employment," answered Diana. "I can't help you with. Maybe Dave Manders can. For additional details, there are none. None here anyway." Rising she added, "Now I have things to do as I'm sure you do, so I'll show you to the door."

Inspector Hanlon and Sergeant Deck found themselves on the front steps with the door shut firmly behind them. They both wondered how Diana could have said so much and at the same time tell them nothing more than they already knew.

10

STILL ONLY LATE afternoon, it had already been a long confusing day. For the detectives it was nowhere near over. On checking, Deck discovered that the employees affected by the poisoning had all been released from the hospital. They were presumably at their respective homes and they now needed to be questioned. Neither Hanlon nor Deck expected to learn anything new, but waiting even one day might mean missing some small easily forgotten detail that could just be the key.

Their first stop was the James Bay apartment of Judy Morrison. The Toronto street address was almost directly across the park from Diana Hillis' home. To go through the park was a lovely drive but unfortunately too often also very leisurely.

"I'm going to Dallas Road and back," said Deck, as he turned left onto Cook. "I keep getting behind folks driving so slow through the park the damn walkers were passing us!"

Deck drove around the south corner of the park and turned back onto Douglas Street towards town. Within minutes, he had turned left and pulled in front of a high-rise tower that stood alone and out-of-place. Deck and Hanlon gained access without much ado and knocked on a 14th floor apartment door.

A slight, self-conscious female opened the door. Deck's first thought was that the girl was a junkie. Whatever Hanlon had expected it was not this rabbit of a girl. With some effort the officers made their way into her living area.

It appeared to be sparsely furnished, a typical apartment living room with wall-to-wall carpet. It could have been so much more with its bird's eye view of the park. It wasn't more, it was just sad and empty a big almost empty room, empty of character, of everything that makes a home. The little furnishings there were only increased the gloom of the place.

Hanlon noted the leather couch in one corner and guessed that it probably cost more than his well-worn car. He did need to break down one day and get a new one. Hanlon continued into the room. Turning away from the view window, he found himself face to face with a 50 inch television set, the top of the line home theatre model with surround sound. This not only cost more than his car, it likely cost more than everything in Hanlon's house.

Deck took in all of these same sights. It was all he could do to prevent himself from whistling when he saw the television. He doubted that the junkie-like bank clerk, who sat visibly trembling on the couch, earned enough to purchase even one of the items in the room, let alone everything.

As Hanlon watched Judy, Anna Hillis's words were confirmed. Judy was more than just a little scared of Cynthia. No wonder Cynthia frightened her; everything frightened her from the looks of it. No, frightened wasn't even the correct word, terrified fit the bill much better. This girl was terrified. But why? Was it important?

It took some coaxing. Hanlon gently took her through a series of questions: first her name, who else lived in the apartment, how long she had been at the bank, how long she lived here. All questions meant to be calming and evidently they worked. Now he could move onto questions about the poisoning.

The detectives were able to move past witness accounts to finally hearing a first hand account of the poisoning from one of the people affected, from one of the victims. Although none of this information was going to solve the puzzle before them, it was at least heartening to get the routine work behind them. It had to be done and they never knew what would become important as the investigation unfolds. As the officers wrapped up and headed towards the apartment door to leave, it suddenly burst open and a young man of slight build stood before them.

"What's this? What's going on here?" he demanded aggressively as his eyes darted between the detectives and the girl. Deck was even more certain that this one was on something even if the girl had proven during their questioning to not be stoned as he had first assumed.

"These are the police," said Judy. She emphasized the word 'police'. She also moved away from the young man as if she expected some sort of physical reaction from him when she spoke.

"Ya gotta warrant?" he snapped.

"There's been an accident," stammered the girl as she moved back against the wall edging the living room and away from the three men.

"Jim Morrison?" Hanlon confirmed.

"Yah, so what?" was Jim's reply not moving away from the entrance.

"Your wife was one of several people poisoned at the bank today," explained Hanlon since Judy was unable to, busy as she was trying to hide. "One of her co-workers is dead."

"Cynthia Harmon," added Deck watching Jim like he was a fresh specimen.

"So, the old bitch is dead, eh?" replied Jim sniffing slightly. "Good riddance." Jim finally moved past the officers and into the living area. Not willing to sit down while the detectives were standing, he paced the room and then asked, "What's that got to do with us?"

"Routine questions, that's all," replied Hanlon turning back towards the living room. "We were just leaving as you came in. However, as you seem to be acquainted with Miss Harmon perhaps you can add something to what your wife has already told us." He looked down at the fidgeting, sniffing young man and smiled.

"She has been rather helpful in fact," Hanlon said.

Hanlon watched the bantee rooster. The short, thin, wiry man (barely past being a boy) was strutting and puffing exactly like that miniature fowl. It would be humourous if it weren't so dangerous. Hanlon watched him closely and repeated, "Yes, she has been rather helpful."

With his face flushing a bright shade of pink, the youth shot a hard look at his now ashen-faced wife still hugging the corner wall by the entrance. The look clearly promised retribution as soon as the witnesses left.

"Ya better not have used any of your rubber hoses on my lady," he spat with sarcasm. "I know what our rights are, and you can't be questioning nobody without a lawyer around. What do ya think she could tell ya anyways? She doesn't know nothing about nothing. That bitch, Cynthia," Jim said dragging the name out as long as possible. "Was always raggin' on her," gesturing towards Judy. "And blaming her for everything that went wrong at that place. She practically accused her of stealin' stuff. Like they'd even miss a few hundred..." he stopped mid sentence while his face grew several shades darker than it had already been. He rubbed his nose absently and continued, "See, now ya got me sayin' things that you'd twist around, like I was a criminal or something."

Both Deck and Hanlon smiled at him and said nothing. He didn't like that much.

"You're finished with her, right?" he said as he pointed

a grubby nail bitten finger in his wife's direction. "We got nothin' else to say to you without a lawyer bein' here so you don't pull any of your cop tricks." He stopped pacing and moved towards the detectives. A look of guilty pleasure flashed across his face, as his eyes scanned the home theater unit. When he turned to Hanlon, the look of pleasure was gone and in its place was cocky smugness.

"I think you guys should probably get out of here now," he said.

Hanlon moved towards the door while Deck moved towards Jim. He slowly hooked his thumbs in his belt letting his jacket part to expose both his badge and his holster and took a final small step towards Jim. He looked twice the size of the youth as he leaned in a bit.

"You got a bit of a cold there?" Deck asked. Jim squirmed and tried to look defiant but for the first time he had nothing smart to say. "You know, you look a little familiar to me," Deck continued. "Your name's Jim, right? I can't place you right now, but it will come to me… Sooner rather than later."

Hanlon touched Deck's arm. "Okay, we've got what we came for Sergeant. We still have other people to talk to." He headed for the door. Deck followed him after a slight pause.

As he was about to close the door, Deck stopped and looked at Jim. "We'll need to talk with everyone that works at the bank some more and very soon. I will notice things like bruises. Know what I mean?"

As the door closed he could hear the profanity offered in response. Yes, Jim Morrison had heard, and he understood exactly what Deck had meant.

During the walk to the car the police officers looked at each other.

"I used to deal with slime like that every day when I was on the Drug Squad. Drugs and spousal abuse seem to go together," Deck hissed. "I can almost understand the being hooked on drugs, but why and how that leads them to prey on people close to them I will never understand. Nor can I ever close my eyes to it when I see it happening." Hanlon nodded, he understood this side of Deck.

They both knew the husband of Judy Morrison was going to be of interest to them.

*   *   *   *   *

Deck was still steaming as he turned the car back onto Douglas Street heading towards town.

"What a little weasel," Deck ranted. "You just know we could bust him for something but no, we have to go running all over town for a murderer no one wants found. And damn, it's a shame it wasn't Morrison that did it." Deck continued as he talked himself out of his fury, "Too stupid and too much of a coward to have killed our Miss Cynthia Harmon. Can you picture the two of them together!" Deck chuckled regaining his good humour just as they reached Superior Street. It was here that Superior, Southgate, Douglas and Blanshard Streets all came together. And above the streets was one of Hanlon's favorite signs.

"Night is for sleeping; Day is for resting," Hanlon read aloud. He was never sure what it was supposed to mean, probably just an ad for the hotels on this corner but it always made him smile. Whose life was like that? Not his.

Deck headed along Blanshard across the top part of the city to Fort Street. Taking the one way street to Oak Bay Avenue, they were in the outskirts of the village when they found Davie Street. A video store stood where in a couple blocks would be a teashop or a fine linen store. Just behind the store was a wire fenced construction site. It was immediately past this that Deck parked the car.

Hanlon looked at the house before him. It had seen better times. The old estate home now sat on only a portion of its land. Where there had been grounds there was now the construction site's retaining wall. Today was invading a long ago era that refused to die.

This was the Oak Bay home of Barbara Scott. Barbara was obviously expecting them and led them quickly into a cluttered front room. On second glance, one realized the clutter was antiques, artifacts, and collectibles from around the world. Here Hanlon noticed everything cost more than his car. Barbara introduced the officers to her husband, Dr. Robert Scott, who started to speak before the officers could say anything.

"Tragic," he said. "This type of incident always saddens me."

"Saddens?" asked Hanlon taking a good look at Dr. Robert Scott. At first, Scott had looked tall but that was only when standing next to his petite wife. Of average height and build, he had likely been described as attractive in his youth. Now though he was a man whose shape had taken on an overall puffiness. To Hanlon, Dr. Robert Scott looked like his house – old and past its prime.

"The moral decay of our society, Inspector," Dr. Scott replied. "A simple question of too much tolerance. It should be as the bible says, 'an eye for an eye'. I was not permitted the luxury of understanding when I grew up. That is, not the kind of understanding that removes one's responsibility for one's actions."

"Interesting," said Hanlon.

Another fanatic, thought Deck.

"Please sit down, gentleman," the Doctor said as the gracious host. He himself settled in the only comfortable looking chair in the room. His wife hovered at his side. The officers looked around and took seats directly opposite Barbara and her husband.

"I know many of my profession countenance endless excuses of mental duress," the Doctor was saying. "I do not. There are no gray areas. What is wrong is wrong and deserves, rather requires, punishment. So you see, Inspector,

my wife and I are anxious to help in any way we can."
Hanlon quickly stole a glance at Barbara. Her eyes
did not match her husband's words. Hanlon saw a well-
groomed, petite woman. This was someone many people
would describe as attractive and whom Hanlon would describe as nervous.

"Just a few routine questions," said Hanlon breaking
into the Doctor's dissertation.

"Anything, Inspector," replied the doctor. "The perpetrator must be found and justice done. This is, I assume, no
freak accident?"

"It was no accident."

"I thought not," he continued. "I'm glad my mother
didn't live to see what the world has become."

Good god, how old is this guy? And he's still worried
about his mother? Were there no normal people in this case,
thought Deck.

As a relatively new employee, Barbara was unable to
add or confirm any information regarding the morning's
normal routine. What she did say about the day's events
agreed with what the officers had already heard.

"A couple more questions," said Hanlon. "And that will
be all, for now."

"Of course. As my husband said, our time is your time,"
Barbara had sat on the ottoman near her husband but nothing about her was at ease. Her back remained tight and
straight, her hands still in her lap so tightly clasped they
were turning white. And her eyes, her eyes were wary, very
wary.

"Your personnel file shows no recent employment," said
Hanlon as a question.

"Yes," said Barbara nodding slightly.

"My wife is not strong," said her husband. "When we
married, I insisted she stop working. I advised against going back to work so soon. But she decided that's what she
wanted to do. Now this. I was right obviously."

Now what is he talking about, wondered Deck. Surprisingly to probably anyone except Deck, Hanlon gave no reaction upon hearing these words. Deck knew Hanlon. He would file any questions and he would find his answers in his own way and in his own time.

"The people you worked with," questioned Hanlon. "Anything that might be helpful. Did you know anyone before starting with CIBC?"

"No," answered Barbara quickly.

"You're sure you didn't know, or know of, any of your fellow employees?"

"It's not possible, Inspector," answered Dr. Scott explaining his wife's answer. "They do not and would not frequent the same places we do."

Again her husband's words did not match what Hanlon read in Barbara's eyes. Or was she just embarrassed by her husband being such an obvious snob? Or was Hanlon just imagining things? Was this finally the end? The time when he could no longer distinguish the truth from the lies, a witness's impressions from his own? God, he was tired. There was little more to ask and yet so much more he needed to learn.

Back in the car, Deck turned to him.

"If she did it, the husband is probably the reason. Or maybe he did it himself, all that righteous justice he was spouting!"

"Do you think everyone is guilty?" Hanlon asked.

"First thing you told me," answered Deck. "Believe no one until it is impossible to disbelieve them. Second, given specific circumstances everyone is capable of murder."

"Yes, yes, Sergeant," said Hanlon feeling less tired. "You're a good student."

*　　*　　*　　*　　*

The officers' next and Deck hoped final interview for the

day was out in the Western Communities. They headed back into town and then joined the end of day traffic leaving the city. They drove silently out the Trans Canada Highway past Portage Inlet to the Old Island Hwy. The maps didn't call it old but it was. And to the residents it was the old highway because the Trans Canada was the new Island Highway – it didn't matter if it went across Canada, it went up island. Nor did it matter that it had been around for years, it was new. This was Victoria.

On the way, Deck and Hanlon stopped at the 6-mile pub for a quick bite.

"All these pubs used to be for overnights when it was horse and buggy days," Deck was saying as they ate. "It used to take days to come in to town from the farms. The pubs are all named for the distances from town – you know, the 4-mile in View Royal, this one, and the 17-mile in Sooke. You can do a pub to pub tour all the way out."

"You're getting to be quite the tour guide, Sergeant."

"It's the Mrs.," Deck replied. "She reads the historical sections that come with the Sunday paper."

Back on the road, it was not much longer before they were passing the turn off for Fort Rodd hill, the former navy base that was now a waterfront park and historical site. Deck continued on through Colwood Corners where a series of shops and small malls had replaced the entrance to Belmont Park, the military housing of Cynthia Harmon and Diana Hillis's youth. Hanlon glanced at the closed road and thought of how few miles and how few years the two women had traveled to get to today.

On the left side of Sooke Road, the officers could see the beginning of the Hatley Park and Royal Roads grounds. Originally the estate of James Dunsmuir and then a military college and now a university, the grounds were some of the most renowned in Victoria. Lakes, heritage tress, Japanese gardens and the Dunsmuir castle were just part of the sights. However from the road, Hanlon and Deck saw only the stone fence and inside that trees and some of the housing from Royal Roads military past.

Turning to the right onto Mt. View, Deck found Mike Baker's Colwood townhouse and pulled into the parking area. Looking at the row of identical buildings, Hanlon dreaded the thought of returning to one of these in a power outage.

"Nice places," said Deck.

Linda Baker met them at the door and led them through toys and disarray into the living room where the disorder continued. Among toys and books, laundry and blankets Mike lay on the couch.

Amid the blaring TV, the talking toys, and the vocal child, Hanlon was to ask his questions. Each person's noise must be someone else's music. Mike, Linda, and even Deck seemed perfectly comfortable in this world. For Hanlon, it was painful. Too many years of living alone, he guessed. He cleared off one of the chairs and sat down. Deck, smiling at the baby, remained standing behind him.

"We've looked forward to your assistance, Mr. Baker," said Hanlon. "You should be able to clarify some points for us."

"How's that, Inspector?"

"The first one on the scene, you'd know when everyone arrived, who made the coffee…."

"Excuse me, Inspector," Mike said interrupting. "But you're mistaken."

"About what?" Hanlon asked.

"I wasn't first to arrive. Cynthia was. She always arrived first, to make me feel late. That was her way."

"Please explain," directed Hanlon.

"Cynthia likes, liked to play what is known as 'mind games'. If you know what I mean." As Hanlon did not reply, Mike continued. "Things have been really bad for us this past year. Money is very short. Cynthia liked to make it seem that my dismissal was just a matter of time."

"Cynthia was not a nice person," said Linda.

That is an understatement, thought both Deck and Hanlon.

"It was her way. It wasn't serious," sighed Mike trying to look like a philosopher and only managing to look like a martyr. Linda took the baby who was starting to fuss and left the room, letting Hanlon continue in comparative quiet even with the TV still on in the background.

"So Cynthia was there when you arrived," said Hanlon. "Then what happened?"

"I went to make coffee," Mike answered not noticing the reaction this created. "Cynthia made some dig about the amount of coffee I drink. She always did."

"It was a normal morning," probed Hanlon. "Cynthia appeared to be the same as usual?"

"Yes, yes," paused Mike. "I think so. I'm sorry I can't seem to think of anything."

"So you went and made the coffee," Hanlon started to say.

"No," interrupted Mike.

"You said you did?"

"I WENT to make the coffee, like I always do," Mike explained. "But I couldn't; it was already made."

"That was unusual?"

"Very."

"Who did you think had made it," persisted Hanlon.

"At first, Cynthia," answered Mike. "You know more games. But that didn't seem likely even for her. Then, I thought it must have been whoever brought the cakes."

"Who could that be?"

"Mrs. Manders," Mike said slowly. "Only that doesn't seem likely either."

"Why?" asked Hanlon watching Mike's face intently.

"Well, she's never made the coffee any other time. Also, there was no reason for the cakes."

" So who could have made the coffee," Hanlon said leading Mike again to the main question.

"Anyone with a bank key, I suppose," he answered slowly. "They would have then left and returned at their normal time." Mike paused thoughtfully and then continued, "Why all the questions about the coffee?"

"It appears to be highly probable that that is how the poison was administered."

"Oh, oh I see," Mike said in amazement. "You mean we were poisoned?"

Deck and Hanlon shared the same thought and they knew it. Without showing anything in either of their faces and without looking at each other, they both had had the same single reaction to Mike's words. How could his amazement be real when the other staff had assumed this fact in seconds? They had assumed poison, poison in the coffee; they had assumed murder, murder of Cynthia. Besides wouldn't the hospital staff have mentioned the poison when they treated him? Now Mike Baker sat before them a picture of innocent amazement

"Maybe you could help us with one other little matter," said Hanlon changing the subject.

"Certainly," Mike replied.

"Who would be likely to fill Cynthia's position now?"

"Oh, Inspector," said a shocked Mike, sitting up straighter. "I would have no idea. That would be Regional Office, I mean Vancouver...That would be Regional Office in Vancouver's decision."

"Would you be a possibility?"

"I might," Mike agreed reluctantly. "But there are several other people in the region qualified. It could be any one of them."

"Wouldn't the bank want to fill the position quickly under the circumstances, possibly from within the branch?"

"I wouldn't know, Inspector," Mike said formally.

I bet, thought Deck.

Having no more questions, Hanlon and Deck returned to the quiet of their car for the drive back to town. That's what this job was about, driving and driving and in between an occasional ½ hour interview. It was all legwork. At least driving beat walking, Deck acknowledged, speeding up as he turned onto Sooke road. The return trip would be faster as they were now going against the evening traffic. Once in the rhythm of the ride, Deck started to think out loud.

"This is getting crazier and crazier," he said. "They all did it. Either that or our victim, Miss Harmon, rigged this entire thing as a glorified suicide."

"Isn't that stretching it a bit?" asked Hanlon.

"Why not?" asked Deck. "If the ones that look guilty are really innocent then the one that looks innocent should be guilty. The only one that doesn't look guilty is the victim. All the rest look as guilty as sin, even our young Mr. Baker there crying for our sympathy."

"You think he wants our sympathy?" Hanlon asked with interest.

"Are you kidding," exclaimed Deck. "I'm as sympathetic as the next guy but these martyr performances don't cut it with me. He wants the job and he needs the money. Miss Hillis was right about that."

"Miss Hillis has been right about everything so far," Hanlon said neutrally.

"Nuts," said Deck. "I tell you this case is nuts. It could be any of them. My money's still on Manders, though."

"You're a bulldog, Deck. If Diana Hillis is correct about there being two poisons which seems likely, how did he manage to give it to Cynthia when everyone says they avoided each other all morning?"

"You've got a point there," admitted Deck grudgingly. "Someone managed it, why not him?"

"Why not indeed," replied Hanlon. "You can test your theory further because I think we have enough now to pay Mr. Manders another visit."

Deck almost groaned but caught himself.

*   *   *   *   *

The officers retraced their route back into the city and headed into the Rockland area. Following the gentle curves, Deck located Pemberton and turned left onto this even more private road. Just as the road swerved to the left, they saw it – the Westcott family home.

Deck whistled as he drove through the pillar gates and up the driveway to the covered entrance. Half expecting a butler to greet them, the officers got out of their car, went up to the front door, and rang the chimes.

Once again Deck and Hanlon found themselves in an old family home that came from a history of money. No sign of decay here though, this house was not just surviving, it was flourishing. As they were led into the front parlour of the Manderes' home, Hanlon wondered what made this room so warm while the Scotts' had been so cold. His answer came when Sybil Manders entered the room. Her calm, gracious air was what one felt throughout her home. Hanlon now understood why Sybil Westcott Manders still had a place in the Chief's heart and why he was so disgusted with her husband.

Sybil ensured that both the officers found comfortable seats and then she settled herself beside her husband on an elegant couch. Hanlon watched Manders, noting his reaction to their visit and to Sybil's closeness.

Manders was not comfortable. He was even less comfortable than he had been in his office when the detectives first questioned him. In fact, he didn't even seem to be trying to appear calm any longer. Was it the return of the officers or was it his wife's presence that was unnerving him so much?

"I don't see why you have come here," demanded Manders nervously. "I've told you everything I know."

Sybil Manders interrupted her husband to order tea for the four of them. Or, Hanlon wondered, was it to give her husband a chance to recover some self-control. If that was the case, it did not appear to work.

"I've told you," whined Manders. "I know nothing about this morning's accident. I have little to do with the daily running of the office. I wasn't even out of my office all day."

"You helped Mike Baker move Miss Harmon's body into the staff room," Hanlon reminded him.

"She was already dead by then," defended Manders. "Whatever caused the accident had already happened."

"I think, darling," interrupted his wife delicately. "That you had better stop saying accident."

"What, what do you mean?" barked Manders. The officers waited as eagerly as Manders did for the answer.

"Unless I'm mistaken," answered Sybil smoothly. "Our friend, Police Chief Warner, has often mentioned Detective Inspector Hanlon of homicide."

"What?" stuttered an obviously disturbed Manders. The tea arrived providing a moment's diversion and giving Manders time to think.

Deck and Hanlon silently drank their tea as if that was their only reason for being there. Sybil too sipped her tea. All three sat silently waiting for Manders to sort out his confusion.

"I still don't see how that changes anything," he finally murmured. "I still have nothing further to say. Nothing of use to you."

"We would like to find out a bit more about Cynthia Harmon," said Hanlon.

"Why ask me? She was an employee that's all."

"We need whatever information you can provide as to her friends, her recent activities, anything like that."

"I wouldn't know," insisted Manders. "Why don't you ask Diana Hillis. She knew Cynthia Harmon better than I did."

"She suggested we ask you," Hanlon stated bluntly.

"I have no idea why she would say that," Hanlon fudged.

"I think, Dave," his wife again interrupted sweetly and calmly. "that it is unwise to lie to the police."

"Sybil, do you know what you're saying?" demanded Manders.

"Of course, darling," replied Sybil. "I know you're trying to save me any embarrassment or grief but too many people know you were having an affair with Miss Harmon for you to hide it efficiently. You might as well tell the truth." Smiling at Hanlon, she added, "Besides, I understand Inspector Hanlon is quite talented at recognizing liars."

"Alright," said a downcast Manders. "I did have an affair with Cynthia. But it was over."

"When was it over?" asked Hanlon.

"A few weeks ago."

"Not last night?"

"No," Manders insisted.

"I see," said Hanlon.

So do I, thought Deck. You're lying.

"We understand that you and Miss Harmon had an argument last night. We understood it concerned the ending of your affair."

"No, Inspector," Manders said trying and failing to give the impression of a calm in-control man. "That was a bank matter. Confidential, you know, customers."

Silence filled the room. Everyone knowing there was more to ask and more to say. Sybil finally broke the silence.

"Whether or not," she said in the same smoothing voice. "it was ended is irrelevant. What matters is that love was not an issue."

"I'm sure that's important to you," Hanlon started to say.

"It is important to you, Inspector," Sybil said gently nudging Hanlon to silence. "If love is not involved, then Miss Harmon was in the relationship for personal gain. That being the case a price can easily be arranged. My husband would have to be an idiot, which he is not, to believe that killing her was the only way to end the arrangement."

"You seemed to take this quite in stride," Hanlon observed.

"One sees many greedy people in my world, Inspector. Greener pastures, you know. These matters can usually be arranged for a price. Seldom is that price money. I have several connections and some influence. The proper introductions, the desired invitations, the initial acceptance can all be arranged. It doesn't often last. Do they mind when it doesn't? I don't really think so. Our dreams are often more attractive than the reality once they're achieved. This is not new to you, Inspector. I'm sure you see this in your world as often as I see it in mine."

Hanlon saw many things in his world but never the poise and charm of Sybil Manders that could describe the basest side of people and make it sound as beautiful as cut crystal. There seemed nothing to say or to ask following those words of Sybil's so the officers made ready to leave.

As they moved towards the door, Hanlon turned to Sybil remembering one last point.

"One last question," he said. Manders visibly grimaced until Hanlon looked at Sybil and added, "For you. Did you take a box of Dutch Bakery cakes to the bank office this morning?"

"No, Inspector, I did not," she replied firmly and Hanlon wondered if he was really that good at recognizing liars or not.

Pleasantries were exchanged until the front door was opened and the officers headed down the steps to their car. It could have been mistaken for friends parting after an evening drink. Deck and Hanlon said nothing as they got in their car and headed down the drive. Sybil and Manders moved back inside closing the door behind them. It was then that Sybil turned to her husband.

"I said get rid of her, I did not say kill her."

11

"WELL, IT'S DONE!" Shirley exclaimed when her husband walked through their front door that evening. She had been waiting for him in the cozy front sitting area that formed the left side of the front foyer. She rose from the lightly flowered love seat and moved to Stephen's side.

"That's good," he replied cordially as he bent and gently kissed her. Taking off his coat, he turned his back to her as he opened the closet door.

"What's good?" demanded Shirley.

"Whatever's done," Stephen said without any great concern.

"You never listen to me," Shirley said with just as little concern.

"Nonsense," replied her husband turning back towards her. "I always listen to you. I might not always hear you but then you don't always want me too."

"Listen to me now, hear me as well. Cynthia is dead. Now you know what has been done."

"What?!"

"There you go," replied Shirley as she turned away from the front entrance of their Saanich home and went up the few stairs to the kitchen area. It was a modern house built on multiple levels with lots of stairs and lots of open space. Her husband could hear and see her fine from the front entrance but he still followed close behind. She held his full attention now.

"What do you mean 'Cynthia is dead'?"

"Ah, now you're interested," Shirley said enjoying herself.

"I see. It was a lie. You made your point," Stephen said sitting down on one of the kitchen barstools much more relaxed. "Now what did you want to tell me?"

"You sure you want to know?" Shirley teased. "Actually, I've already told you. Cynthia is dead. I said I would kill her and now she's dead."

"Shirley!" exclaimed her husband.

"Seriously! Cross my heart and hope to die," Shirley said with the appropriate hand gestures. "Not really, of course. Cynthia is dead. Okay, maybe I didn't kill her. Maybe someone did it for me. If you ever listened to the local news, you'd know I'm telling the truth. And it's murder. The police haven't said so yet but I'm sure it is."

Stephen Foster waited in stunned silence for Shirley to continue. But she didn't. Instead she turned back towards the counter. He watched as she calmly moved around the kitchen preparing the family's meal. How could she be so removed, so untouched? Was this real or fantasy? Did she know it was murder? If so, what else did she know?

"How did she die?" he finally asked.

"Poison," his wife said sprinkling seasoning on their salad.

"Here," her husband said as he rose and took the utensils from her hands. "Let me do that. Now sit down and tell me from the beginning what happened."

"The beginning," Shirley repeated. "I don't know the beginning. I suppose Cynthia was born. That would be the beginning. How about just today?"

"Fine."

Stephen Foster was finally told the tale of Cynthia's demise. With Shirley's animated story-telling, the tale was bright, witty and entertaining. Stephen continued to point out that this was not amusing.

"You are so serious, Stephen," Shirley finally said.

"This is serious."

"Nonsense," she said refusing to be distracted from her fun. "Yesterday, I said I wanted her dead and today, poof, she's dead! What fun! One has to watch one's wishes. Maybe someone heard me. I see it all now."

"You see what?" asked her husband cautiously.

"Where were you this morning? What were you doing in the vicinity of Cook and Fairfield?"

"Shirley, stop it!"

"I see, no answer. Then again maybe it was me. Do you think it was me? Kind gentleman looks concerned. A new idea has struck. If I am the murderer, how did I do it? I would have gone to the bank early. I have a key to the door so that's no problem. I would have brought the baked goods as an explanation for being early in case I did run into anyone. I would have made the coffee adding a touch of poison for taste. Probably something simple like weed killer. You always hear weed killer or rat poison – weed killer in books, rat poison in movies. Wonder why? Doesn't matter. Then I would have left the bank and returned again at my normal time. That's the easy part. How would I have got Cynthia to have more poison than everyone else? Maybe I didn't, maybe I used a second poison – something strong. Putting it into her coffee was very risky. It would have been hard to do without being seen. I had the best opportunity since I was sitting closest to her. Maybe someone did see something because if I didn't murder her, someone else did. That means there has to be a murderer. What fun!"

"Shirley." She turned and saw a look in her husband's eyes she had never seen before – fear. He was afraid. But was he afraid for her or of her?

"Be careful," was all he said.

* * * * *

Across town Doris Webster sat on the bus going home. With a start she realized she had missed her stop again. Fumbling with her bags, always too many bags, Doris rang the bell and clumsily got off at the next stop. Looking around her confused, she finally selected a direction and started walking back towards her home. Was this all a normal occurrence? Was there anyone to notice? If there had been someone, would she have appeared the same? Did the day's events show any affect?

Doris entered her apartment, turning on the light before closing the door. She quickly bolted the door. Sighing slightly she dropped her bags, hung up her coat and wandered, lost, around the suite.

Doris finally found herself in the bathroom facing the mirror. She stared as if seeing someone she didn't know. Slowly she washed her hands carefully and very deliberately. Looking back in the mirror, a smile and then a shadow passed quickly across her face. Standing there what did she see? Returning to the other room, she prepared her supper. She did her dishes. All was ordinary. Wasn't it?

"Quite a day," she said, talking to her father's picture. "If only it was over. It's not though. It's only started. You don't know. I forgot. I should put the news on for you. No, no, I don't want to hear it all again, to see it again. No."

For a few moments, Doris sat with her head in her hands.

"She deserved it. She did deserve it. Besides it was God's will. It had to be. Everything is. It was so ugly to see someone die. I never thought it would be so ugly. You didn't look like that. Neither did Mother. I guess it's different when you're older and when you're ready. I never thought it would be like that. Can't change it now. It had to be done. It's the best for everyone. It's done and I'm glad. Please let it be over. All those people watching, asking questions, prying. They don't think I see them. They think I'm blind, blind and old and stupid. A silly old woman, that's what they say about me. I know. I'm not. I know things. I could tell them. I knew about Cynthia Harmon and Mr. Manders' argument. No one else knew. I see things. Silly old woman, indeed I'm not. I know what they never will. I know who killed Cynthia Harmon. What do I do, Father, what do I do? She deserved it. She was a bad person; it's only what had to be done. Have I sinned? I didn't tell. No, Cynthia Harmon needed to be gone. She would have hurt me. She would have hurt lots of people. I've done what I had to do. No one should be punished for destroying evil. If only it was over."

12

AFTER COLLECTING CYNTHIA'S personal belongings, the police departed the branch. Staff hoped things would return, as much as possible, to normal. That was not to be the case. Unusual situations trigger a set of internal procedures and murder was definitely an unusual situation.

The day after the incident a trauma team had arrived in the person of one relatively young therapist. She took over Manders' office leaving him to wander around the branch. One by one, the trauma specialist met with each staff member. How were they feeling? How were they sleeping? Just by showing up, she said the branch had gone through something horrendous and for some of the employees her very presence helped. It didn't for Doris.

"Why she asking all these questions?" Doris was whining to Diana.

"They're just trying to help, Doris," replied Diana. "It's nothing to be upset about. She's just here to help."

"It doesn't help," said Doris stubbornly. "Questions, all these questions. It's over; why can't they just let it be over."

"Because it isn't over," Shirley said firmly as she walked by. "It will never be over until the murderer is caught!"

"Thanks a lot, Shirley," said Diana sarcastically as she turned back to Doris. "She's only here for today. She's leaving this afternoon, Doris, you don't have to talk to her anymore."

Diana was right, the trauma specialist's visit was quick. Very quick compared to the audit team that showed up a couple days later.

An internal audit, which normally took about four days, every year or two was usually an odd combination of stress and casual routine. Everyone always wanted to do well and get passing marks. Yet, it was also always a boring intrusion that got in the way of day-to-day business and waiting on customers. Generally though that's all it was: an interruption for a few days.

Not this time. Within a week of Cynthia's death, an audit team of five people, three men and two women, arrived at the bank like a swat team at their first raid. They were going through everything. It seemed like they were going through everything three and four times. They were going to be staying much longer than previous times. Normally the auditoring officers would use random samplings and delegate the balance listings, the pulling of documents, and various other chores to the general staff. That too was different. No help was wanted, no requests made, no questions asked. No casual conversations were initiated or accepted. Silently and seriously, they went about their business.

They started with the money. They opened every cupboard, every teller's bag, every box of coin. They counted every penny of every Canadian dollar and every piece of every foreign currency in the branch. They didn't actually unroll the coin but otherwise everything was counted in detail. Next came all the engraved forms. Every draft, money order and travelers' cheque held by a CSR or held in the vault was inspected and documented. Bank machine cards, normally checked against a master inventory, were listed in detail. Safety Deposit Box contracts, dormant accounts, especially those over 9 years old, since at that point the funds are required to be sent as unclaimed balances to the government, were all investigated thoroughly. Time sheets, payroll records, staff accounts were all reviewed. The security accesses were all verified – for computers, for individual applications, for the bank door key, for the combinations on the safes. Then they turned to accounts and customer files. Every suspense account and expense line was scrutinized. All customers' loan files, securities and mutual fund files were checked in minute detail.

They went about their business taking whatever files they wanted, removing whatever datasheets interested them, occupying whatever desk was handy, operating any computer they chose. Their presence was felt like never before. If nothing previously had told the staff a death in the bank was not to be taken lightly, the audit team's behaviour did.

There was little laughter in the bank now. One couldn't be flippant while under such scrutiny. No matter how strong the desire, no matter how truthful it might be, Cynthia could not be blamed for any of the errors the audit identified. While privately Cynthia might have been discussed one on one with the therapist, publicly Cynthia's name was not mentioned. There was no discussion of before the death, no discussion of the day, no discussion of the aftermath. It was as if Cynthia Harmon had never existed. It didn't matter whether it was from guilt or from being glad she was gone. On this the staff was united. They chose to ignore Cynthia's entire existence. Conversations instead focussed on the intruders.

"That little twerp with the glasses is driving me nuts!" exclaimed Shirley one day at the morning coffee break. "You look at his little weasel eyes and you can just tell he's mentally deficient."

"Mentally deficient?" asked Diana with a smile. "I suppose you told him of this discovery."

"Of course," replied Shirley. "I couldn't let the poor man – I used that term loosely – live his life under the mistaken impression that he was normal or, heaven forbid, actually bright."

"So you called him a moron?"

"Oh, Mrs. Foster," moaned Doris.

"No, I did not call him a moron. I called him a fool."

"You showed a lot of restraint," Diana said.

"I thought so," remarked Shirley in all seriousness. "I mean really do you know what he was complaining about? My business account files are not exactly in numerical order when in alphabetical order. Now tell me is that or is that not of earth shattering importance?"

"It is," the entire group replied in one mocking voice.

"He's always like that," explained Diana. "Don't you remember him from last audit?"

"He didn't do my area last time. Why is it all the failures end up on the audit?"

"I thought you said that about Human Resources?" Pat reminded her. "I know, it's just whichever department has ticked you off this week!"

"No, it's both of them!" Shirley retorted. "And how can you joke about it, this is serious?!"

"No, it's not, Shirley," Diana interjected. "It's the audit and we go through this every time."

"Well, it doesn't matter," Shirley said not giving up ground. "If he says one more thing I'm telling him to go to hell and I'll tell him how to get there."

"How?" asked Pat.

"Do not pass Go; do not collect two hundred dollars."

"That's not hell; that's jail."

"He can go there first. What do I care?"

"At least he didn't call you a thief," Pat said, now serious.

"He called you a thief?"

"The big dark woman might as well have," Pat replied.

"She wants the postage meter checked, locked, watched and sealed in a glass vault. I don't know. I'm going to make a fortune ripping off free postage!"

"Of course, aren't we all?"

"Don't let them upset you," Diana advised. "It's their job. Answer their questions and continue your work as always and before you know it they'll be gone."

"Are they really looking for thieves?" asked Judy timidly.

"What do you think?" replied Pat rhetorically.

"Don't worry about it," said Diana. "They don't invent anything. If there is nothing for them to find, that is what they will report."

"But do they ever find any...any thieves?" continued Judy.

"On occasion."

"They scare me," said Judy. "Every time they talk to me, they scare me."

"They're a nuisance," stated Pat. As she rose and left the room, she added, "They always are."

"A nuisance!" Shirley called after her. "They are one huge pain in the ass!"

"They serve a purpose but unfortunately always disrupt the routine," remarked Diana. "They'll be gone soon though."

"They scare me too," said Doris.

These individual impressions continued swirling around until the audit finally started making signs of leaving. Usually the audit team left in stages slowly reducing in size until the lead officer was the only one left. This time, however, everyone stayed until the end. The last step, the exit interview, was held with Manders alone in his office behind closed doors. Then just as suddenly as the audit team had arrived, they were gone.

Normally the branch report would be shared with the entire staff. However, since Cynthia's death Manders had become more and more withdrawn and no one was surprised that nothing was said. It was part of a time best forgotten.

For most of the staff this might now be possible. Not for Dave Manders, Shirley Foster, or Diana Hillis. The police had returned to their lives and politely but firmly requested their attendance at the inquest.

Originally delayed to give the police time to investigate the death, a date and time had now been set. Since the investigation was still ongoing, the general assumption was that the inquest would be postponed. That was not to be the case.

One early afternoon, two weeks after Cynthia's death, Dave Manders with his wife, Shirley Foster and her husband, Diana Hillis and her sister found themselves sitting in the Victoria courthouse. The presiding public servant entered with minimum pomp and took his place at the front of the assembly. He was a round man, a man of circles. His body was a circle, his near hairless head a slightly smaller circle, with two even smaller circles for ears and on his face, wired circle glasses. It was quickly apparent he did not go in circles when it came to the court. He clearly and precisely set the ground rules for the morning. An inquest did not have the same formalities as an official trial. However there were still rules and procedures and he was there to see that they were followed. Next he turned to the group of people collected to his right, in the traditional jury area, and instructed them on the purpose of the inquest. It was to determine the cause of death, and if appropriate to make recommendations, in the case of Cynthia Harmon. That was it and the inquest had started.

To establish the events of the day in question in their chronological order, Dave Manders was the first to give evidence. He was, as he had been since Cynthia's death, well dressed, well groomed, and ill at ease.

"I arrived at the bank at approximately 9:00 in the

morning. Everything appeared as normal. I went into my office. I was there alone. I did not leave my office."

Dave Manders recited his testimony without hysteria, without repetition. He recited his testimony exactly as his lawyer had advised. It showed.

"At approximately 10:00 a.m. Cynthia Harmon entered my office and said that she had called the police because several staff members had suddenly been taken ill. Approximately fifteen minutes later I left my office to find Miss Harmon slumped over her desk. She was dead. Her body was moved to the back staff room. The ambulance came and then the police."

His remarks were clear and concise. His manner was calm and should have been confident. It wasn't. The little round presiding coroner asked a couple of clarifying questions and then Dave Manders was released. He was obviously also relieved.

Shirley Foster gave evidence relevant to Cynthia's actual collapse and death. Just as the coaching of Dave Manders had been evident, the lack of coaching was evident in Shirley's case.

"I thought it was going to be another boring day. Then it looked like it was going to be really interesting. Then it returned to being boring. First, Mike got sick. Mike Baker that is. I forgot who was next. Anyway lots of people seemed to be getting ill. Cynthia took it as a personal insult. After her indignation, she finally phoned the police or 911, somebody. She didn't want to but she didn't know what else to do. Neither did anyone else. Then she started to make these gasping sounds. I expected her to turn blue or something but she didn't. Cynthia never was very accommodating. Next she hit the top of her desk. Boom. That was it. Not much, eh?"

The coroner sat in silence staring at this new witness. After a few minutes thought, he gently shook his head and said she could step down.

Diana Hillis had nothing new to add. She had been requested more to confirm Cynthia's identity, her hiring and the other two testimonies. This was done quickly, quietly, and with, what appeared to be, little interest. The coroner listened closely, asked a few probing questions to obtain greater detail. He seemed to find the answers satisfactory and Diana's turn was over.

Additional information was provided by the ambulance attendants, by Constables Demos and Fryer, and by a representative from the hospital. Their evidence confirmed that the various staff members had indeed been poisoned. The poison was arsenic. The final testimony was that of Thomas, the attending coroner. His evidence was short and to the point.

"Death was caused by paral poisoning, paraldehyde to be precise."

"I knew it!" exclaimed Shirley to anyone within hearing. Diana tried to quiet her and glanced over to Hanlon. He was watching her. Deck wasn't. His attention was on Manders who was quickly turning an unpleasant green colour.

There was no denying it now. The verdict was in. The verdict was homicide by person or persons unknown.

13

LATER THAT AFTERNOON, Dave Manders received a call from his wife instructing him to join her at the Empress Hotel for tea. The most British of traditions, tea at the Empress was an event – an event that Dave Manders happened to loathe. And his wife knew it. He pulled his Mercedes sedan into the Empress parking lot and walked towards the side entrance. All the way he fumed. This was so old! Who liked it but the tourists and all Sybil's old biddy friends? Hell, he guessed other people must like it as well because even with the hotel's grand front entrance closed, the tea service continued. Or maybe that's why the entrance had been closed, more room for the damn tea. Just like Sybil to order him here like a footman. Meet me for tea, indeed!

And it had to be the Empress, not a nice little teashop close to home. There were after all several. No, it had to be the Empress. More of a landmark than a hotel, the Empress was so well known it was barely mentioned in the tour books. It was just there. Majestic and stately, she was the Queen Victoria of buildings. With her champion, the provincial Parliament Buildings, they kept the inner harbour safe. This was Victoria. This was history.

Dave didn't know and didn't want to know of Queen

Victoria, of history or of tea. He was still fuming as he entered the front lobby and located Sybil sitting on a floral chaise with tea for two on the table in front of her.

Sybil smiled up at him and as he settled, she poured out his tea.

"You know I hate this," Dave whined. "I don't know what you see in it."

"Don't be petulant, Dave," replied Sybil calmly. "This is a special place for me. My mother and I came here when I was girl. Just the two of us would come and have tea. It was an event and it was special."

"See," she said nodding towards a table across the room. "Just like that child and her mother. Those are moments you remember."

"Did you have those then too?" asked Dave smugly as he gestured to a group of kimono clad tourists proceeding across the room.

"It's just the convention," replied Sybil unruffled. "I believe this room today blends very nicely with yesterday. Now have a sandwich," she said bringing the three-tier serving tray closer to him. "I believe this one is ginger and carrot – very nice. Or there's cream cheese and of course, if you want the traditional, there is cucumber."

"Funny, Sybil," said Dave reaching for the closest.

"This whole area always brings back my childhood," Sybil continued. "The Parliament Buildings at night all lit up. It was fairyland to me. And I remember going to the old Crystal Garden pool to swim. Can you believe what they have done to it? Changing it into a garden and aviary? Do you know they have little monkeys in there now?"

"What are you talking about," Dave said bluntly.

"My life, Dave, my life," Sybil replied. "I have many happy memories of being downtown here." She paused, flattened her voice and continued, "And then there's my adult life with you." Sybil paused to pour each of them more tea and to fix herself a scone with jam.

"Did you ever wonder why I married you?" Sybil asked, jarring her husband with this change in topic.

"What are you talking about now?"

"I always knew why you married me. Money, old money, and what you thought it would give you. You've received exactly the life you envisioned. Haven't you? Except for this little mishap, your life has been very good. But why did I marry you?"

"I'm just a bit testy, Sybil. The inquest and everything and you know I don't like all this pomp. It's nothing, it's nothing," he said trying to make peace.

"No, Dave," Sybil continued. "I brought you here so I could talk to you. I brought you here so you would listen and not make a scene."

"Why are you talking like this, Sybil?" Dave asked. "We've been happy, very happy." His wife shrugged. "Sybil, I love you."

"That is getting to be quite a hackneyed expression," she replied. "Especially from you. How many woman, and girls, have you said that to? Have you ever meant it, I wonder?"

"I love you, Sybil," Dave repeated more quietly.

"You love my money and my family name," Sybil rebuked. "That's all you have ever loved. That, however, doesn't matter. Do you want one of the pastries or are you going to have the berries and cream?"

" Berries and cream?" her husband barked. "Forget the damn tea. What do you mean it doesn't matter? What are you getting at, Sybil?"

"But why did I marry you?" Sybil asked returning to the original question. "My father might be the answer. You seemed suitable to the image of a husband, I suppose, handsome but not in a flashy way, bright but not too bright. Controllable, yes controllable. You were controllable, that was the deciding factor."

"Sybil, darling," Dave said soothingly. "You're upset, same as I am, with the death, the inquest and everything."

"When have I ever been upset by anything you have done?" Sybil demanded coldly. "I do not care, I have never cared enough for you to be upset by you. You are not that important."

"Sybil!"

"Cruel, darling," Sybil answered. "The truth often is. Now that I have your attention, listen carefully. I will not discuss what I am now going to say ever again. I do not care if you killed that girl or not. The police, however, do care. I no longer can afford you."

"What?"

"I said, 'listen'. I did not say 'talk'," she said firmly. Sybil took a deep breath before continuing. "You think this fiasco is over. It isn't. It might never be. That is as things are. Nothing in our lives will change immediately. But in the coming months, I will be travelling more. Slowly we will grow apart. Regrettably, we will be divorced. Within the year, I think. In case you have any schemes, I have already changed my will. Divorce me and you will get a tidy sum. Kill me and you will get nothing."

The two sat quiet for many minutes. They drank their tea and finished the last of the pastries. To an outsider they appeared to be an average married couple relaxed and comfortable together. Dave spoke first.

"Sybil, I don't understand. This is so sudden and it's so drastic. You make it sound, well, final."

"It is final," Sybil answered. "But it's not sudden. Since your first affair, I thought it might come to this. My fears have proved to be correct. You have no backbone. You are weak, too weak. You have crumbled during the whole investigation of Cynthia's death. You have no control in your outside entertainments. You are sloppy and indiscreet. Why someone hasn't tried to blackmail you before now, I don't know. If that occasion arose, what would you do? It doesn't matter. If you have not destroyed yourself this time, then you will in the future. You see, darling, I simply cannot afford you any longer. That's all. No need to talk about it any further."

"I have a meeting this afternoon at the museum," Sybil continued smoothly. "We really do need to do something about the turn of the century village. It is still immensely popular and one of the reasons we have so many visitors. But it is getting on and we do need to keep it refreshed. And space is always an issue."

Sybil continued to talk of her concerns as a member for the Royal British Columbia Museum. Rated as one of the best museums in the world it was constantly evolving and changing. Thanks in a large part to the support of Victoria and Victoria residents like Sybil.

Dave heard none of Sybil's concerns. His only concern was for himself. What was he going to do?

"What, what was that?" Dave said suddenly aware that Sybil was again addressing him.

"I said I'm leaving now. Please be sure to leave the girl a good tip." With that she rose and walked away leaving Dave alone in the Empress having tea.

*   *   *   *   *

In their townhouse, the day's legal events were also on the Bakers' minds. In that, the similarity between the two couples ended.

Linda and Mike sat in their brightly coloured kitchen eating their evening meal of macaroni and cheese. The baby was asleep yet their house was still not quiet. The TV spoke from the living room. The radio played in the kitchen. Clutter surrounded them. It was their home and to them it was relaxing.

"Is that the end then?" asked Linda hopefully. "This inquest today, I mean."

"Yes," her husband answered. "I think so. Unless the police arrest someone, I guess."

"Do you think they will?"

"No."

"Why not?" Linda asked.

"I can't think of any evidence they could find."

"Do you know what they've already found?" Linda asked and Mike nodded.

"If they had anything," Mike explained. "They would have asked us about it the day they questioned us."

"You're so good at figuring things out. I don't know what I'd do without you," she said, believing it.

The conversation moved to other areas as their meal finished. Mike joined Linda in the washing up. Later when they were settled happily alone in their front room, Cynthia's death returned once more to Linda's mind.

"I still can't believe Cynthia's really dead," she said.

"Believe it," Mike answered. "She's gone and won't bother anyone ever again."

"That's not nice to say of the dead."

"It's no worse than lying," he replied. "Which is what I'd be doing if I pretended to be sorry that Cynthia's dead."

"Oh, Mike," Linda sighed.

"It's the truth. No one is sorry. It wasn't pleasant to have someone die in the office, but it's a nicer place to work without her. I just wish they would hurry up and fill her position."

"Do you still think you've got a chance at it, honey?" asked Linda.

"I don't know," Mike answered. "The longer it takes the less likely it seems. I've been thinking it might be time to start thinking of another way of making money."

"Really?"

Mike saw the concern in his wife's eyes and changed his tone to one of self-confidence. With a few words and a few kisses he removed her fears but when she left to make their evening coffee the lines of worry returned to his face. The question was still there. What was he going to do?

*   *   *   *   *

"Why can't we leave?" Judy said, trailing after Jim into the living room. "We can afford it now. We could go anywhere."

"You're so stupid," Jim snapped. "Ya think we're god damn millionaires!" His words denied the top of line computer system the apartment now sported. Otherwise though, there was still no sign of permanence. That is, there were no pictures, no trinkets, nothing personal. It continued to be a partially furnished apartment; a sad partially furnished apartment.

"Can't ya see how it'd look if we left now," Jim continued settling in front the computer and making every attempt to look like he knew what he was doing. "Might as well phone the cops and say, hey come and get us. God, don't ya have any brains!"

"But if someone finds out," Judy stammered.

"No one is going to find out if ya keep quiet," Jim stated. "Would ya quit worryin'? Besides there's nothing to find out. Cynthia is gone, simple."

"The police care who killed Cynthia."

"No one else does," Jim replied. "So what are they goin' discover. Nothing."

"I'm scared," Judy insisted. "What if I say the wrong thing?"

"Don't," ordered Jim.

Judy cowered and showed no sign of being able to obey him.

"It'll be over soon," Jim said. "Then ya won't have to remember any of this ever again."

"How can you be sure?" asked Judy.

"Quit bugging me, I just know okay?" Jim snapped. "It's almost over I tell ya!" Judy left the room and he smiled broadly, pleased with himself. Turning his full attention to the computer screen, he was determined that this time he was going to find those infamous porn sites the guys were always talking about.

* * * * *

In the solitude of their backyard, Diana sat and looked out over her garden. Some of the summer flowers, begonias and two-toned petunias, were still out and now the fall flowers were starting. The purple mums and white asters looked nice with the silver leaves of the dusty miller. The burning bush was starting to turn its fall red and with the evergreen shrubs for constant backdrop it all seemed to come together. It was a picture. For Diana, it was a peaceful picture.

Anna came out from the kitchen onto the back patio to where Diana sat. Her thoughts were not on the garden. They were on the afternoon's inquest.

"I think that detective likes you," Anna remarked.

"Don't be crazy," replied Diana moving to take a dead flower off a petunia plant. "Which detective?"

"Oh sure," Anna teased. "You never noticed. Which one really! The nice looking one, the one you were avoiding at the inquest."

"I should never have let you come. And you're imagining things."

"That's it," Anna said smiling. "Be cool. Act like you don't care. Why don't you try and tell me it's the other one you're interested in?"

"I'm not interested, as you put it, in anyone."

"I'll believe you, but I'm your sister." Anna watched as Diana worked around her garden seemingly unconcerned by the conversation. Anna continued, "I still say he likes you. I can tell by the way that he looks at you. He kept watching you."

"That's because he thinks I'm a murderer," Diana said, returning to unload the weeds and plant trimmings.

"No!"

"Yes!"

"Quit kidding around," Anna said.

"Who's kidding?" asked Diana. "He thinks I killed Cynthia."

"But you didn't," Anna insisted. Diana just shrugged and turned back to the garden. Anna continued, "I know you didn't. You couldn't have."

"It doesn't matter," Diana said. "He thinks I did. He might not be positive but he considers it a strong possibility."

"Then why don't you help him," asked Anna. "Prove to him, he's wrong. You could if you wanted."

"Maybe," Diana conceded. She returned to the house and sat beside her sister on the patio. Then she added, "I'm not sure I want Cynthia's killer caught."

"The person you're concerned with protecting is a murderer!"

"So was Cynthia."

Silence embraced them. Each was trying independently to come to terms with what had been said.

"Forget that," Diana finally said. "It didn't mean anything."

"It sounded like it meant something."

"It didn't," Diana repeated. "I don't know. I didn't expect to feel like this once Cynthia died."

"Like what?" her sister asked.

Numb, was the answer but she didn't say it.

"My sister, the fortune teller," Anna said trying to lighten the moment. "Come on, you couldn't have known any of this would happen."

Diana gave her sister a big smile and got up to go back into the house. Over her shoulder she tossed, "Unless the detective is right!"

"Don't be funny!" Anna yelled following her.

14

THE DAY AFTER the inquest, the clouds rolled over Victoria bringing grayness, gloom and the never-ending rain. As the local phrase goes, there are only two seasons on the West Coast: summer and rain. With this melancholy already in the air, Deck received the second call.

"Yes, yes; I got it," Deck said hanging up the receiver. "Damn!"

Inside the new police station was just as open and airy as the exterior. Very few private rooms or offices existed. One large office without walls or doors held the majority of the members of the Victoria Police department. Even so, the desks were not crowded. Not like at the old station, everyone had been on top of each other there. Hanlon had plenty of space and was a fair distance from Deck. Still, he was close enough to hear Deck's disgust.

"What is it?" asked Hanlon.

"Another death, and guess where," replied Deck.

"Where?"

"The CIBC, Cook and Fairfield branch," answered Deck.

Hanlon gave no immediate response. Should he have expected this?

"Sound familiar?" Deck added.

"Who is the deceased?" was Hanlon's only response. "Didn't say," Sergeant Deck replied. "The coroner's been called; it looks like poison. I suppose that means another murder."

The Inspector didn't answer. This time there was no delay. Deck and Hanlon gathered their things and headed for the car. Hanlon would have liked to know the victim's name. This case was getting to him. It was too personal. Someone was dead, that's all that should matter. Regardless, he would like to have known much more than the call said. No matter, it would take very little time to get to the bank. Victoria was not a big city. He had found himself thinking that many times since Cynthia Harmon's death. It was, he reminded himself, big enough to have two murders in almost the same number of weeks. In the same office at that, he added. As they got to the car, Deck's voice disrupted any further thoughts.

"Manders is going to be flying this time," Deck was saying. "If he got hysterical the first time, what's he going to be like with two corpses? Unless, of course, he is the corpse."

It was a good question. It was a question whose answer would surprise both of them. Deck turned the car onto Quadra and raised his speed. There was a pattern to the lights along Quadra and at just the right speed you could sail through every one of them. Any faster or slower, it was red light after red light after delay. At Fairfield, Deck turned left and started the rolling ride to Cook. Past the hospital, around a curve, through the sheltered quaintness and then suddenly, there was Cook Street and there was the bank. Now they would see how Mr. Manders was handling a second death unless, as Deck said, he was the corpse. He wasn't.

The officers found themselves once again sitting opposite Mr. Manders. This was a different Mr. Manders. The original nervous and reluctant child had been replaced by a calm but confused adult.

"I don't understand this," Manders muttered. "There was no reason to kill this girl. She was a harmless little thing."

"The deceased's name was Judy Morrison, is that correct?" asked Hanlon.

Was that relief in the old man's voice, thought Deck?

"Yes," answered Manders. "Judy Morrison, I can't believe it."

"What can you tell us about her?"

"Nothing really," replied Manders. "That's the truth, Inspector. She was ...well, she wasn't....How can I say this? She wasn't someone you would notice. She was just there. That's why I can't believe someone would kill her."

"We haven't established that yet, Mr. Manders," Hanlon said.

"Oh, I assumed because of the other..."stammered Manders. "You know what I mean."

"Because Cynthia Harmon was murdered you assumed Judy Morrison also was?"

"I guess so."

"Were you surprised when Miss Harmon died?" asked Hanlon. That question startled Manders. Hanlon could see his inner struggle. Deck could too.

"No."

Hanlon waited. Deck waited. Manders took a deep breath and watched Hanlon. Hanlon was experienced at the quiet game; Manders was not.

"Cynthia had a way of making enemies. I don't think anyone who knew her could have been surprised."

"You did not mention this before, Mr. Manders."

"Why should I?" demanded Manders as he started to feel trapped. "Cynthia knew what she was doing."

"What was she doing?" Hanlon continued not giving Manders a rest.

"Nothing," muttered Manders. Silence greeted this remark. Manders looked up to see Hanlon and Deck calmly watching him yet again.

"Alright," snapped Manders. "You want to know about Cynthia Harmon? She was a bloodsucker, a leech. She would find someone who could give her what she thought she deserved and that was it. She fastened herself on and drained you of everything. Your pride, your money, your life, all of it, she took it all! She made my life hell! Then that wasn't enough. She destroyed it!"

You stupid bastard, thought Deck. You did it to yourself.

"What was she doing?" Manders continued. "She was asking to be killed!" More quietly he added, "Cynthia deserved to be killed. Judy Morrison didn't."

Manders looked exhausted and totally unraveled. Deck knew this was the best time to break a suspect, to get a confession. So he was surprised when Hanlon's next words were, "That will be all for right now, Mr. Manders. I'm sure we'll need to talk again. First we need to talk with the rest of your employees."

"Yes, yes of course," said Manders relieved to have the inquiry move away from him. "Will you use the staff room again?"

"That will be fine," said Hanlon. As they moved towards the staff room, Hanlon knew Deck had questions.

"So, Sergeant," said Hanlon. "You have a question?"

"You had him on the ropes, sir, why let him go?"

"Patience can be a valuable tool, Sergeant," said Hanlon. "Especially when you haven't yet got all the facts. We have some missing pieces and while we fill those in we will give Mr. Manders enough room to make a mistake or two. Patience, Deck, patience can be more unnerving than the direct approach for some people and in some situations."

Deck just nodded as they made their way through the bank to the back room.

"Home sweet home," Deck remarked upon entering the messy room.

The paramedic supplies had been removed but everything else looked the same or worse. Dishes were scattered on the table and all over the little kitchen area. More boxes blocked the exit. Pulled-apart newspapers were strewn over the couch. A few umbrellas were sitting open drying.

"God, it looks no better than the last time! If they look after the money the way they look after this room, I sure wouldn't want to bank here! This better not become a habit. I couldn't stand to spend part of every week here."

"I doubt it will be a regular thing," Hanlon calmly replied.

"I hope you're right; but if this new one was killed to make it look like the Harmon death wasn't a fluke or a one-off, then a whole series of deaths might occur."

"If this Judy Morrison was as forgettable as Manders implied," said Hanlon. "It is more likely that she saw something or someone she shouldn't have."

"Damn!"

Hanlon raised his eyebrows slightly but said nothing. Deck noticed his interest, subtle though it was.

"I thought for a minute we had a nice juicy maniac murderer!"

"Not this time, Sergeant," Hanlon replied with a smile.

"I guess not," answered Deck. After some thought he added, "It might explain why Manders is so angry. He didn't want to have to murder anyone but Cynthia."

The Inspector gave no reply. In fact, he showed no response at all. He slumped down into one of the chairs and appeared to be ready for a nap. Deck knew better. Hanlon, like Manders, was angered by this second death. There would be no more thought of retiring, of being too old. All thought would be used for his latest puzzle and the finding of its solution, the murderer of Cynthia Harmon and Judy Morrison.

15

LEAVING THE INSPECTOR alone with his thoughts, Deck went into the main body of the bank to check in with the EMS attendants who had been first on the scene and with Thomas. After hearing what was known so far, Deck collected a list of all staff on sight, pulled their files and started to organize an interview chart. This second poisoning had affected only the deceased so the entire staff was available. With less disruption, the branch had remained open. Customers and employees continued to transact business. The interviews would be fitted around that. This was going to be a slow and probably long day.

While Deck was getting things organized, Hanlon was replaying every conversation to date. What had he missed? What insignificant remark had been important? It had all been so clear with one death. Cynthia made an acceptable victim, if there was such a thing. No one had been eager to find her killer. Would it be the same with Judy Morrison? He would know very shortly.

As if on cue, Deck returned.

"Thomas left while we were with Manders," he said. "Left a message saying it's poison again. He'll call you later when he gets more details sorted out."

"Fine."

"You want to see the staff in any particular order?" Deck asked.

"Your choice, Sergeant. Also, send a couple uniforms to notify Judy Morrison's husband."

"Okay, will do," Deck replied as he left.

Pat was again the first person to be interviewed. Hanlon watched as with confident strides she came into the room at sat directly in front of him on the couch.

"As I tried to tell the other officer," Pat said, nodding towards to Deck, "I can't tell you anything about Judy's death."

"Really?" asked Hanlon sensing Deck's irritation.

"I wasn't in the room when it happened. I was at my desk."

"You weren't where exactly?" Hanlon persisted.

"Here!" Pat said gesturing around the lunchroom.

"So Judy Morrison died in this room?"

Pat's face said obviously and her body language said get on with it you're wasting my time.

"And you were not in the room at the time?" Hanlon said.

Deck watched knowing that Hanlon's reaction to Pat's impatience would be to go slower and slower, repeating every question and every answer.

"You're weren't here at the time?" Hanlon repeated and finally Pat answered.

"No, Inspector, as I said," Pat replied slowly and distinctly. "I was at my desk."

"Who was in the room at the time?"

"I have no idea."

"Wouldn't there be schedules?" Hanlon asked. "Timing of when people took breaks?"

"I don't work on that side. You'll have to ask someone else."

"And we will," Hanlon said. Pat attempted to rise but

Hanlon continued and she sat back down. "What can you tell us about Judy Morrison then?"

"Nothing," Pat replied. Into the silence that followed, she finally added, "She worked here. That's the only way I knew her and the only thing I knew about her."

"What about her personal life, her friends, who she had lunch with or her breaks with?" Hanlon insisted.

"Gossip again, Inspector," was Pat's only answer.

"We need to get to know the victim, Miss Martin," Hanlon said. "If we are going to find out what happened."

"I worked with her that is all and that is all I know about her," replied Pat as she again started to rise. This time Hanlon did not stop her.

"Man, does she have some attitude!" said Deck.

"Yes," agreed Hanlon. "But does it have anything to do with the case? That's the question."

"If they're all going to be like that, can I put that holiday request in again?" Deck asked as he went out to get the next person on the interview list.

Over the next few hours, the officers were able to conduct the majority of the interviews. With the entire staff available for questioning, there was greater opportunity for someone to have seen, heard or to know something. That was not, though, always the case. Having more people did not necessarily mean more information as the officers quickly discovered. It took very few questions to reach an understanding of the morning's events. More questions just provided repetition of that earlier information.

"Sounds familiar, doesn't it?" remarked Deck. "Mike Baker arrives and makes the coffee. This Judy Morrison arrived second. Everyone else was later. Everything was normal. No one noticed anything. Coffee break came. Everyone chatted and was normal. Judy Morrison didn't say much but she never did. Normal. It's all too bloody normal to end with a corpse!"

"Exactly," answered Hanlon. "What else do we have?"

"Deceased sitting quietly having a coffee on the break," read Deck from his notes. "She showed signs of discomfort. She collapsed and here we are. At least this time, nothing was moved. Maybe the lab will come up with something. One good thing about having a double murder, everyone knows the routine."

"Too much so," remarked Hanlon. "Our answers have all been too polished."

"They make sense," said Deck.

"Too much sense."

"For once in this nutty place," said an exasperated Deck, "we have been getting clear concise answers that sound reasonable. No one yet today has confessed and no one has blamed God. To me that's an improvement but not to you, I gather. Would you prefer the loony-tune answers?"

"What I would prefer," Hanlon said thoughtfully. "Are responses that do not seem to be given because they are expected. Everyone seems to be telling us what they think we want to hear. I'd like some individuality, some opinions, and some feelings. I'd like anything but the tidy paint-by-number death that has been described so far."

"Okay," said Deck. "Do you want to see Diana Hillis now?"

"No," Hanlon said shaking his head slightly. "We'll see her last if possible."

"Then we only have Shirley Foster and Doris Webster left. They probably won't give you routine answers," remarked Deck. "No sir, not those two!"

"Of course, Deck, Mrs. Foster is what we've been needing," answered Hanlon. Knowing Deck's lack of imagination, he added, "Why have you been hiding her?"

"You want to see her now then?" was Deck's only reply.

Hanlon gave no sign of having heard Deck. When the two men had started working together Deck had tried to figure out what Hanlon was dwelling on in his moments of silence. No longer. Decks now sat patiently with his own thoughts and seldom were they about a case. For Deck, life was uncomplicated and held many pleasures. He let his mind drift and realized tonight held great promise with a well-matched basketball game scheduled on channel 8. Deck glanced over at Hanlon. Nothing. The quiet contemplation of their own thoughts continued. Neither man would have been surprised to discover that those thoughts did not match

Hanlon was reviewing the original interview with Shirley Foster. She had been confident, very confident. There was no hesitation as she explained the method of poisoning nor as she had casually called it deliberate. No less impressive than her calmness was the fact that Shirley Foster had been accurate. Her guesses or her observations were correct. But were they guesses? Were they even observations? Hanlon kept hearing Shirley's voice repeating, "I told my husband I was going to kill her." She had said something else he should remember. Yes, that was it. She had said there would not be another death. No, those weren't her words.

"No one else will die from this morning's little drama," Hanlon repeated aloud.

"What?" asked Deck who had been absorbed in trying to figure out when he was going to be able to try out the new fishing gear he had bought last week.

"Something Shirley Foster said in our first interview," answered Hanlon.

"You want to see her now then?" Deck asked again.

"No," Hanlon decided. "Let's see Doris Webster first. Then we'll see Mrs. Foster and that should leave Diana Hillis."

"The lady who thinks God is our culprit," groaned Deck as the left the room.

While he was gone Hanlon ran through his previous conversation with Miss Doris Webster. Deck had a right to have apprehensions. Doris hadn't been the most coherent witness but she had known of Cynthia's argument with

Dave Manders. Had she known more? Possibly, possibly. She had been scared. Yes, there was definitely a possibility that she knew more.

Hanlon's conclusion did not seem valid as he watched Doris Webster enter the room with Sergeant Deck. He saw an older, sadder Miss Webster. She moved slowly, bowed she was. Had she slept since they last questioned her? It didn't look like it.

"Good morning, Miss Webster," Hanlon said. "How are you today?"

"No one tried to kill me," Doris said quietly.

"Why would anyone want to harm you?" Hanlon asked.

"I don't know," Doris muttered. "I don't know anything. I can't help you. I can't help anyone. I don't want to hurt anyone. I've never wanted to hurt anyone. Can't I go; can't I please go?"

"In a minute, Miss Webster," answered Hanlon. "We're trying to get an understanding of this morning's events. Did you see anything unusual? Or possibly you heard something that might be useful."

"No, no," muttered Doris. "I can't tell you anything."

"Okay, Miss Webster, don't worry," said Hanlon. "Tell us about Judy Morrison."

"She was young. She was young but you couldn't say pretty. It's a sad thing."

"What is?"

"To be young," sighed Doris. "And not pretty. It's sad."

"Was Judy sad?" Hanlon asked.

"Yes, she was sad and she was frightened."

"What was she afraid of, Doris?"

"When you are young and not pretty, you are always afraid."

"Was she afraid of Cynthia Harmon?"

"Everyone should have been afraid of Cynthia Harmon. She was evil. She deserved to die but not little Judy. She shouldn't have died. It has to be a mistake. I didn't want it to happen."

"What didn't you want to happen, Doris?" probed Hanlon.

"What, what?" a startled Doris replied. She looked full at Hanlon and he saw for the first time the eyes of a trapped animal. Doris wasn't simply confused, scattered, or even scared. She was cornered; she was caught in some kind of snare.

"You said it was a mistake. You didn't want it to happen." Hanlon repeated watching her even more closely. "What was a mistake, Doris. What didn't you want to happen?"

"Judy," Doris stammered.

"Judy's death was the mistake?" pushed Hanlon.

"I didn't do anything. Can't I go now? I can't tell you anything."

"What didn't you do, Miss Webster?" asked Hanlon.

"Nothing, nothing, oh no," Doris moaned as her eyes searching wildly around the room. "I didn't, I didn't. Please leave me alone."

"You said that Judy's death was a mistake," continued Hanlon. "Why is that?"

"I didn't want her to go away, not like Cynthia. I didn't. I don't understand. I didn't want it to happen. I don't know. I don't know. Can't I go? I can't help you. I didn't want it to happen."

What the hell is all this about, Deck wondered

"No one wanted it to happen," Hanlon finally said, giving a small nod to Deck. Taking his cue, Deck led Doris from the room.

Doris was worried about something. Was it important, Hanlon wondered? To Doris, obviously it was. But to the case? He didn't know. Was it something she'd seen? Was it something she's done? He didn't think so but he had to be sure. He was not going to get Doris to tell him by direct questions. He needed someone who knew Doris, someone who could talk to her.

Hanlon looked up as Shirley Foster entered the room and wondered if she was the suitable person. His indecision ended with Shirley's first words.

"Well, I didn't kill Judy I'll tell you that right now."

"Glad to hear it!" Deck said before he could stop himself.

"So who did?" demanded Shirley.

"You tell us," suggested Hanlon.

"Then it is murder?" Shirley asked. "Everyone I think assumed so, you know, being so soon after Cynthia. Besides Judy was so young, you'd think we'd know if she were sick enough to die. Mind you she never said much. We might not have known if she was seriously ill. She hadn't looked good since Cynthia's death. Just thought it was nerves. But really it can't be murder; why kill a mouse!"

"Is that how you saw her," asked Hanlon, "as a mouse?"

"That's what she was. Did you meet that husband of hers? Husband, my Aunt Fanny. Mean little bastard. If they were married, I'm Queen Elizabeth. He was her whole world; she talked of nothing else. When she talked, that is. Then again, she always looked like she wanted to say something but was afraid. I don't know. It doesn't make sense. She isn't a suitable victim. Now Cynthia was a suitable victim. Once she was dead that is. That's it, Inspector that's the key. Cynthia was a victim only after she was dead; Judy was a victim every moment of every day."

"Thank you, Mrs. Foster," said Hanlon.

"You are very welcome, Inspector," said Shirley graciously. "But I don't see that I've been much help. It happened right over there, you know," she continued, while waving her arm towards a chair beside the boxes hiding the rear exit. "Just sat there and died. Hardly a sound. Probably still trying to hide. Just as unnoticed when she died as when she was living. Like I said a mouse   harmless. She shouldn't have been killed. When I find your killer for you that's when you can thank me."

"I'd prefer you leave that to us," Hanlon said sharply. "We do not need a third corpse."

"The answers are not suitable, simply not suitable."

"Doesn't matter," Hanlon insisted. "We do not want you trying to do our work for us."

"No, Inspector, not that answer," explained Shirley. "The choices for our solution are not logical. One: Cynthia's death was an accident. Our murderer actually meant to kill Judy all along. It isn't probable. Cynthia was just too delicious a victim. Two: the murderer wants to create confusion as to who was the real victim. Killing Judy could be an attempt to make it look like a serial killer killing solely to kill. Then why use two poisons? Judy didn't die the same as Cynthia. I watched them both. No that's not it. Only thing left: Judy knew something about Cynthia's murder and so had to be killed to be kept quiet. But how could she know when I don't!"

"You've been very helpful," Hanlon started to say, ending the interview.

"Damn," said Shirley as she got up and walked out.

"It sounded like she wanted to be the second corpse just so she'd know what was going on," remarked Deck.

"She does like to be in on things," Hanlon agreed.

"Doris Webster, too, though," Deck continued. "She sounded like she thought she was meant to be killed not this Judy Morrison. Everyone was glad that Cynthia was killed. No one wanted to find her murderer. But this time, everyone...."

"Feels guilty," Diana Hillis said finishing his sentence as she entered the room. "My being your last interview is starting to feel like a bit of a tradition," she said with smiling eyes to Hanlon. Turning back to Deck, she continued, "You are correct, Sergeant, everyone does feel guilty. Cynthia was not liked. No one was sorry she was dead. You could even say they were a little glad. Now they're wondering if Judy's death is a punishment for how they felt after Cynthia's murder. I'm not saying that the staff believes in voodoo or even that they all believe in an angered God; I'm saying their consciences are bothering them."

"And you?" asked Hanlon watching and appreciating Diana's calm movements as she situated herself on the ugly orange couch.

"Me?" asked Diane. "Does it ever amaze you, Inspector, the number of choices we are faced with in our lives? They never end. Each time I think this must be it, I find my decision brings me to another question that requires another choice. When I travel on my road and reach an intersection A goes left and B goes right. I choose B only to be faced with another intersection. What if I had chosen A? Do you understand?"

"Yes," Hanlon said.

No, thought Deck.

"Good," said Diana laughing slightly. "I'm not sure I do."

"So what are you going to do?" asked Hanlon.

"You do understand," Diana said looking at him sharply. "I'll have to watch what I say. I'm used to talking and having no one know what I've said."

You're safe with me, thought Deck.

Hanlon and Diana sat quietly for a few moments watching each other. They smiled and Diana started to talk.

"Judy should not be dead. Cynthia was asking to be removed. She enjoyed trying, and often succeeding, to destroy others. Judy was harmless. She was what you'd call a professional victim. I hadn't decided if I wanted Cynthia's murderer found. I don't know if I would, even if I was sure the past would stay the past."

"I can't guarantee that," said Hanlon.

"I know."

Deck watched Hanlon and Diana who were oblivious to his presence. He thought about their wordless communication, and he remembered what Hanlon had said. If she did it, we have our work cut out for us.

"I can't," said Diana smiling. "deliberately permit Judy's killer to go undiscovered. You have my assistance, Inspector; although I don't know that it has any value."

16

THE OFFICERS FINISHED interviews shortly after noon. Neither of them mentioned, nor thought of, lunch. They returned to their car and slowly moved east on Cook Street back to the station. Silence weighed heavy between them.

Deck hadn't said much after the interview with Diana but Hanlon knew he was puzzled and not comfortable with Hanlon's approach. You didn't ask a civilian, a suspect, to become involved in an investigation. Hanlon and Deck had worked together for some time; there was trust there. There was trust and respect. Deck didn't always know where Hanlon was going with an investigation but he believed in him and he went along, usually learning something in the process. This time it was different. All Deck had said was "I guess you know what you're doing here, right?" But did Hanlon know?

Hanlon knew both Shirley and Doris had more they could tell him. And even perhaps Pat did.

Pat was controlled, openly uncooperative. Was it relevant or totally unrelated? Did she know something? Or was she simply one of the many people with a grudge against the police?

Shirley appeared to be open and willing to be helpful. Her deductions concerning the first death had been very accurate. Were they deductions? That question kept haunting him. For the second death, she had again assumed murder but not so definitely. But she had been definite about one point; what was that? Oh yes, Judy had not died the same as Cynthia. Anything there?

And then there was Doris. What about Doris? She was obviously afraid and guilt-ridden. Had she seen something? Had she heard something? Was it even possible she had done something?

He didn't know the answers. With Pat, he probably could get her to talk. With Shirley and Doris that was not such a certainty.

The officers pulled up into the parking garage and walked to the lobby of the station.

"I think I'll go out and have a smoke," said Hanlon.

"I'll see if there's any update from the coroner's office," Deck replied flatly.

"Both Shirley Foster and Doris Webster know more than they're saying. We need someone to get them to talk," Hanlon said. Was the old man explaining or, worse, apologizing? It wsn't like him.

"You're the one who taught me not to get involved especially with suspects," Deck replied. "You do know what you're doing, right?"

Hanlon didn't reply. He turned to go out the front door with all his focus on getting his pipe ready to light. Deck gave him one last glance and then headed upstairs to the detectives' area.

Hanlon walked out the front door where the Totem Pole of Unity greeted him, and stopped there to light his pipe. The quick short puffs, the steady flame, the whole act of getting the pipe going helped to slow down Hanlon's thinking. Some people meditated.

Hanlon liked the Totem Pole. It had come about through

cooperation between the Songhees Indians and the Victoria Police Historical Society. It supported unity. He walked to the end of block where he was faced with a second sculpture, if you could call a totem pole a sculpture, Trust and Harmony.

Trust, harmony, unity were all good words. The latest approach to how the police should fit with the community. He understand these latest changes, the need to be more accessible, to be seen as less combative and more participatory. He did believe that trust, harmony and unity were how people should treat each other, including police officers. However, when he saw the likes of Cynthia Harmon or Judy Morrison on the morgue table, it was hard to see where any of it fit in the world of his work.

He looked up and saw the Salvation Army building across the street. On the other corner was the Rotary House, and next to that a Funeral Home. What a corner – three of the buildings, Rotary House, Salvation Army and Police Headquarters, reflected the possibilities in life. The fourth, the funeral home, showed life's one certainty. With a sigh, Hanlon turned around and headed back to the station entrance.

In going back he found himself seeing nothing. Well not "nothing" exactly a parking lot, a chain link fence, cars and the back of memorial arena were all visible. This new station location was neither quiet and peaceful nor active and full of people. It was empty. How could a person think here?

At the old station, he could stroll through the courtyard between City Hall and the MacPherson theatre. He could sit by the fountain and share the sights and sounds with the tourists. When struggling with bigger puzzles, he could go down another block and wander through Chinatown and Fan Tan Alley. So what if the old station had been falling down while all around it the buildings were being refurbished. A man could think there.

He had to face what was happening and what the results could be. Diana Hillis. Diana was very attractive. She was a first class murder suspect. Is this the person he should have agreed to let assist him? He needed someone close to Doris Webster and Shirley Foster to fill in the gaps. Why not Diana? If she were the murderer sooner or later she would make a mistake. The closer she remains the easier for him to notice any slips. The closer she remains the easier for him to get emotionally involved. Deck was right you didn't get involved, especially with suspects. Did he know what he was doing? Hanlon repeated to himself. Yes, yes he did. Then what would happen if she were guilty?

Hanlon tapped the remaining ashes out of his pipe at the entrance of the station and straightened his back to go in. As he did, he saw there beside the entrance a lone bicycle. It was small, with training wheels. How rare to see and how sad, so forlorn and lonely. Hanlon had to stop this.

What would happen if Diana Hillis were guilty? He would face that question when and if it occurred. Now he needed Diana. Doris Webster and Shirley Foster would confide to her what they would not tell him. As he entered the detectives' room, Deck looked up and greeted him by waving a file folder at him.

"Well, Mrs. Foster was right again," Deck said. "As Thomas said at the inquest, Cynthia Harmon died from paraldehyde. Judy Morrison died from good-old arsenic. Thomas says probably your basic weed-killer."

"Arsenic," Hanlon repeated. "Good."

"Good?!" Deck responded amazed.

"That opens possibilities," Hanlon replied cautiously.

"It does?"

"Check the time of death," said Hanlon. "Then check the reaction time on arsenic."

"You think she didn't get it at the bank?"

"It's possible that she ingested the arsenic prior to arriving at the bank."

Was that relief again in the old man's voice?

"The husband," said Deck. "I knew he was no good!"

"You do jump to conclusions," remarked Hanlon. "Have the officers who went to inform him of the death returned yet?"

"Yeah, they said he was real broken-up."

"You are a cynic, Sergeant," Hanlon said. "We have no reason to assume he is guilty."

"Yes, sir."

"I think we should have a little chat with Mr. Morrison," Hanlon added. "Do we know where he is at this moment?"

"The notifying officers went to his place of business..."

"Place of business?" Hanlon said interrupting.

"A garage. Like I said, he was real broken-up," Hanlon continued without empathy, "and went home after he was notified."

"A place to start," said Hanlon. "And Deck..."

"Yes?"

" Let's have a fuller check run on him while we're out. CPIC, CNI, the whole nine yards."

"With pleasure," Deck smiled as Hanlon rose to join him in leaving the room. Neither officer had reached the door before Hanlon's phone started ringing. Hanlon and Deck look at each other, deciding whether to stop or not. Shrugging, Hanlon returned to his desk and picked up the receiver.

"Hanlon speaking."

"Inspector Hanlon, my name is Richard D'Angelo. I'm the Corporate Security Officer for the CIBC. I believe Mr. Manders from our Cook and Fairfield branch gave my number to you when you attended the incident there."

An ex-cop, thought Hanlon. Why do we all talk like we're being interviewed by the 6 o'clock news?

"Yes, certainly Mr. D'Angelo. I believe you've spoken with Sergeant Deck regarding the file. Has something come up since the last time the two of you talked?" Deck perked up at hearing his name and started listening to the half of the conversation he could hear.

"Please, my name is Dick, Inspector. I was a member of the RCMP for 15 years and that was long enough to learn that I didn't like being called anything other than my first name. The only Mr. D'Angelo I know is my father. And to answer your question, yes something has come up, it may be related, it may not. I think it probably is."

"Sergeant Deck is here with me Dick. Let me put you on the speaker phone so we can all be in on this." He motioned Deck to sit near the telephone, and pushed the button enabling the speaker function. "There we go. So, what do you have for us?"

"Well, it is standard practice after unusual incidents in a branch, to have our internal audit team conduct a review of the branch. Just to ensure that everything is in order, you understand?" D'Angelo stopped and waited. Hanlon filled the blank.

"I see, please continue."

"In fact the branch was scheduled for an annual review within a few months anyway, so we just accelerated the timing a bit."

"And....you found ......something," Hanlon filling in another pause.

"During the course of the review we discovered that there were some discrepancies in the inventory of engraved forms. That would be the bank drafts, money orders and travelers cheques in street terms."

Deck and Hanlon exchanged a quick glance.

"How much?"

"Well that's the thing. We can't really say for sure, not accurately, not yet."

There was another pause. This time Hanlon just waited.

"Potentially quite a bit," D'Angelo continued. "Umm, unlimited actually." Hanlon and Deck were both staring at one another. D'Angelo plunged ahead.

"You see, there is no limit on the value of a draft. It's filled out for whatever amount is requested. It can be virtually any amount, and with some of the drafts, any currency. I'm waiting to hear if any of the missing items have been negotiated. Until we know that we have nothing to go on. Hell, they might just be misplaced, or accidentally destroyed or something."

"You don't think so, do you?"

"No, no, I don't. Cynthia Harmon was known to run a pretty tight ship according to the audit reports I've seen. However the latest report shows that there has been some decline in the control at the branch. It looks like most of it is in the areas that her assistant Mike Baker has direct responsibility for, but as the CSM – that's Customer Service Manager – Mrs. Harmon was also personally responsible for these things. I would have expected her to be aware of any discrepancies like these. I am still waiting for the traveler's cheque company to advise us if any of the missing cheques have been negotiated. It can take some time to get this information because there is a delay between sale and negotiation so normally we don't get worried too quickly but with this situation...... I hope to know one way or the other within a couple of weeks."

"Have you ever had an internal theft situation that resulted in a murder, or rather murders in one of your branches?"

"Murders?!"

"There was a second incident this morning, Mr. D'Angelo," Hanlon replied.

"Dick, please. Who, what?"

"Then Mr. Manders has not been in touch with your office?"

"No, I'll correct that," D'Angelo replied firmly. "On the new incident, any details you can share?"

"Only one person was affected, is deceased Judy Morrison," replied Hanlon. "Cause of death was poisoning. To my question, Dick, have any internal thefts resulted in murder?"

"No way, this would be the first of its kind. If, and that's a big if, that turned out to be the case, you might be interested in something else the audit noticed. Aside from the missing negotiable items we also have some higher than usual cash shortages. Judy Morrison was the teller in particular with the most cash losses. Over the past 2 years we have written off over $10,000.00 in unexplained cash differences at that branch."

Deck whistled under his breath. A mental picture of the television, sound system and computer in the Morrisons' apartment flashed through his mind.

"Is Mr. Manders aware of these discrepancies, and does he know what your thoughts are in regard to them?" Inspector Hanlon asked the security officer.

"Oh yeh, he knows that there were problems identified in the audit report. He's known that for a few days actually. I was on vacation until this morning and this being a one ex-cop office... well, I would have preferred letting you guys know about this before Manders was told, but the bean-counters jumped the gun a bit I'm afraid. You really should have heard earlier, especially if it might have prevented the Judy Morrison thing. Can't go there, of course, a fool's game what ifs, should have dones, could have dones."

"Do you think that Manders may have confronted Mrs. Morrison about the missing cash and the other things?"

"The cash, yes. The drafts and that, maybe, maybe not. Hard to say. Yes it is possible that he did. His neck is on the line a bit because he is ultimately responsible for anything that happens between those four walls."

"Okay. Sergeant Deck and myself were on the way out the door when you called. We were intending to speak with Morrison as a matter of fact. We already have some ideas regarding Mrs. Morrison's death. Without going into details, what you have just told us further supports what we're already thinking. Does your bank do any background checks on your employees and their immediate families by any chance?"

"Some employees we do, most we do not. Historically it has only been done on people who are involved in high-risk parts of the business. We're starting to be more consistent around that but until recently it was quite sporadic. I doubt there would have been any done on the branch personnel over there. Why do you ask?"

Sergeant Deck leaned in closer to the speakerphone. "Morrison's husband, Jim. We've had an interesting talk with the boy. He looks like a junkie; he acts like a rat. Wouldn't trust him as far as I could throw him. I'll bet you know his type."

"Damn right I do. I worked drugs for several years."

"I think we know where your $10,000.00 is too. Some very nice toys in the Morrisons' apartment! Big screen television, complete DVD surround sound system, state of the art computer."

"Oh… most interesting. Mrs. Morrison would not be at a pay level that would support that kind of lifestyle. Any ideas what the 'husband' does for a living?"

"Works at a garage – mechanic we're told. Could be into other things," Deck made a sour face as he replied. Hanlon nodded in agreement.

"Okay, well I'll get out of your hair, you guys have much more important things to do than talk to me, I've run out of things to tell you for now anyway. Think I'll head out for a coffee and a doughnut." D'Angelo chuckled at his own joke. Hanlon and Deck did not.

"Thanks Dick. Please do let us know the results of your other inquiries as soon as possible." Hanlon pressed the disconnect button on the telephone.

The Inspector looked at his Sergeant, "I don't know about you, but I'm rather anxious to speak with Mr. Morrison. But first – Mr. Manders. He has not been telling us everything he knows and that does not make me happy."

17

HANLON PUNCHED HIS speakerphone on and quickly dialed the number Deck handed him from the file. "CIBC, Cook and Fairfield. How may I help you?"

"Mr. Manders, please."

"And who should I say is calling?"

"Inspector Hanlon, Victoria Police."

"Oh! Yes, yes sir. Just a moment please." The Inspector was always surprised at the reaction the use of his title could elicit. Sometimes it was useful; sometimes it was not. This was one of the times it was.

Manders' voice was strained and higher pitched than normal as he came onto the line.

"Inspector. I was just going to call you." Deck and Hanlon exchanged a glance that showed their disbelief at this statement.

"You are a step ahead of me," Manders continued. I certainly hope so, thought Deck.

"Mr. Manders, I just finished speaking with a Mr. Richard D'Angelo."

"Oh."

The Inspector grinned slightly but remained silent

allowing the bank manager to think about what this could mean.

"Are you still there Inspector?"

"Yes, I am Mr. Manders." Sargent Deck also allowed himself a small grin as he listened to the exchange. Much of the respect he had for his superior officer was a result of the manner in which Hanlon controlled interviews. This was promising to be a prime example of the Inspector's well developed skills.

"Yes,.... umm...well, I suppose that Mr. D'Angelo probably called you regarding the, aah....results of our audit." Manders' voice was quite thin now. There was a hint of a child's whine in the tone.

"Yes, that is correct Mr. Manders."

"I thought so. I was told I should let you know what they found and I was going to… but I'm not sure everything is as bad as they say. I haven't had time to double-check their findings, so I didn't want to waste your time. With everything else that's going on, I didn't want to confuse things. And it's been very busy around here. I've had some people quit, and we were already short staffed, what with, well you know."

"You should have told us, Mr. Manders." Deck was torn between impatience with Manders' avoidance of discussing the missing items, and amusement at the way that the Inspector was not allowing him off the hook.

" Well, since you talked to Mr. D'Angelo, you know everything anyway," Manders replied.

"We want to hear your side," Hanlon persisted.

"It isn't my fault. The audit claims that there are some things missing from our inventory. But Cynthia was responsible for those things. She kept track of them. I can't be personally aware of every piece of paper in this office. I have to look after the big picture. Keep the clients happy, bring in new business, do what the people in Vancouver tell me to do. Do what they say is important. And if I don't…"

"Yes. I understand that a bank manager has many responsibilities Mr. Manders. I'm sure that we all do," the Inspector said, attempting to cut off a very long-winded and uninformative whine.

"It's been even worse lately, what with all of this. And the auditors did not help any. They were in the way and it just added to the problems." Manders' voice was now at least a full octave above its normal tone. Deck was beginning to worry that Manders might just have a massive coronary if this lasted much longer. The Inspector seemed to share that thought.

"Mr. Manders, I want to hear about the missing cash and negotiable instruments. What is missing and what do you think happened?"

"I told you. I'm not convinced that there is anything really missing."

"I'm sure that your auditors have plenty of experience, Mr. Manders. I doubt that their reports are carelessly prepared especially under these circumstances. Wouldn't they have double or even triple checked their findings? Wouldn't they be very confident of what they're reporting?"

The detectives could literally hear the telephone handset being twisted in the bank manager's hand. The pause before he answered was just a couple of heartbeats too long.

"I guess so. I was very busy. I didn't see them do that. I didn't want to pass along something that might not be correct."

"Do you really doubt their findings Mr. Manders? Mr. D'Angelo certainly didn't seem to have any doubts."

"Yes. I mean no, I mean they probably would be careful. I just wanted to be sure it wasn't a mistake. Mistakes do happen, sometimes." It sounded to Deck like Manders had just recognized the light at the end of this tunnel. It was indeed a locomotive. It had his name on it.

"You've already said that a couple of times now. You have had time to review the records. Have you done that?"

A touch of irritation had entered the Inspectors voice. Deck was sure that it was more for show than real. Voicing disappointment in the answers being given was an old interrogation tool that was very useful in helping an evasive person abandon that course of action.

"No, no, I haven't."

"Then you don't really doubt their findings do you?" Hanlon got Manders to admit.

"It's just…."

"What is it, Mr. Manders?" demanded Hanlon.

"I wasn't trying to hide this from you, if that's what you're thinking," Manders answered. Hanlon and Deck's silence forced Manders to continue. "It's just with the other things, you know with the deaths, I didn't want you to get the wrong idea."

"The wrong idea?" Hanlon asked looking at Deck with amazement. Now how was Manders trying to squirm out of it, thought Deck? "Are you trying to tell me you don't think the missing money and items have anything to do with the deaths."

"I don't know, maybe."

"You are telling me that besides having two people dead, one definitely a murder you also have a thief? What is it you're not telling us, Mr. Manders?"

"I…I just… I just didn't wish to speak ill of the dead, so to speak." Now where is he going, thought Deck starting to get very frustrated with Manders' dance.

"In what way would you be speaking ill of the dead?"

"Well, it's obvious, isn't it? The person who had the ability to make cash and negotiable instruments, well you know, disappear, was Cynthia. All of those things are, or rather were her responsibility. You'd never know that from what the audit report says. Their report sounds like this is all my fault."

"And what about Judy Morrison?" asked Hanlon. "I understand some of the cash that is missing could be attributed to her?"

"Maybe. But Judy," Manders seemed to be feeling he was on more solid ground again. "Judy was, she just wasn't. Well, I just can't see her organizing and getting away with everything the audit says is missing."

"So you think Cynthia Harmon was responsible?"

"I don't know," Manders said returning to his confused state.

"And how do you think this fits with Miss Harmon and Mrs. Morrison's deaths?"

"I don't know," repeated Manders helplessly. "I don't know if the missing funds has something to do with the deaths or not. Cynthia is the only person who could have taken that much without it being noticed. Surely you don't think I stole from the bank? Maybe she was feeling guilty and, you know, couldn't go on. Yes, that might be what happened. She couldn't stand the guilt, so she... you know.... committed suicide. Imagine, all of this suspicion, and it turns out that there was no murder, it was a suicide." Manders actually sounded relieved as he said this.

"Do you really believe that, Mr. Manders? You knew Cynthia Harmon – well. Does that sound like something she would do?" Hanlon asked.

"God, I don't know, I tell you!" There was silence. "Do we really know anyone?" asked Manders hearing both Sybil and Cynthia's voices telling him the life he knew was over. "We had sex, Inspector, that's all. It doesn't mean I knew her."

Hanlon and Deck cringed in one motion. It was a common enough occurrence, it was even a natural enough occurrence in many ways. Certainly, individually and together, they had seen and heard much worse. However something in the cold and self-interested way Manders said those words made the officers' skin crawl.

" And how is Mrs. Morrison's death connected?" Hanlon asked, not getting distracted by Manders' theory or by his own disgust.

"God!" replied Manders unraveling again. "Does there

have to be a connection? Couldn't it be just, well just bad luck? Bad timing. Maybe she was so upset about Cynthia that she…" Manders voice faded out. He couldn't even convince himself that there was a grain of truth in that idea, and any relief he had been feeling was now completely gone.

"You don't really believe that do you?" This was more a statement than a question.

"No. I guess that is too much of a coincidence. Okay, okay, I didn't know what to think and I didn't know what you would think. I didn't want to tell you about the missing money because maybe you'd think I might have had… I didn't do anything. I don't know…"

Deck and Hanlon exchanged a glance, as the line stayed quiet for almost a full minute.

"Mr. Manders, we will want to see the report from your auditors. We'll also need to know everyone who had access to the missing items. Please have the report copied for us. And while you are doing that please also consider a more reasonable explanation for how these thefts may have occurred. Either Sargent Deck or myself will be in touch with you soon to arrange delivery of the report. And for your explanation."

Hanlon disconnected the speakerphone. He looked at Deck.

"He probably has no idea about the how or the who of any of it. I doubt he has any idea what happens in that office. What I'm not sure of is whether he is more afraid of us, or the bank people in Vancouver," the Inspector said as he rose from his chair and reached for his coat.

Deck stood up as well. Rubbing his chin, he reflected on the conversation with Manders.

"Frankly," he said. "I don't think he knows which end is up. Or he's one hell of an actor."

18

WITH THE DEPARTURE of the audit team, the branch should have returned to normal or at least relative normalcy given Cynthia's death. It didn't. With two deaths in two weeks, it didn't have a chance.

The trauma woman had promptly reappeared. This time there was little reaction, little discussion. The remaining employees were adapting to the continuous questions, the ongoing doubts and suspicions. They were adapting to the deaths. Cynthia's death had been a huge surprise with a large impact. Judy's, coming second, did not have a strong impact. Even if Judy's death had been first, though, it would not have generated the reaction Cynthia's death did. It had been Judy's lot in life to be invisible and it seemed that was to also be the case in death.

Things continued and started to form a new routine. Customers were served, money was made, and employees came to work most days. On the surface, things were functioning as before. However, it was quieter. There were fewer jokes, fewer casual conversations. People were retreating from each other and trying to focus only on the work. And behind closed doors, there were ongoing meetings between Mike Baker and Mr. Manders.

Mike never smiled now and was working late which never used to happen. During the day, all the cash and negotiable supplies were being checked and rechecked. After hours, he checked through files. The staff would come in and find things, even their things, had been moved. Nothing was said. Just as Manders had not told Hanlon and Deck about the audit findings, he had not yet told the staff. The tension was building from more than simply the two deaths. Suspicions were starting to rise and still nothing was said. That was until Shirley Foster did.

"So I wonder how much was stolen," she pondered aloud. "And I wonder if that's why Judy was killed?" It was afternoon coffee break and little did she know that Hanlon and Deck were at that time having a similar conversation with Mr. Manders. She was alone with Doris, Pat and Diana in the lunchroom and yet Doris still looked around to see if anyone had heard.

"Why do you say such things?" Doris wailed.

"I was around one other time when this happened. It was the same. Real hush, hush. It's as if it didn't actually happen unless someone said so out loud. 'Course no one died that time – just got fired, didn't even go to jail."

Diana sipped her juice and waited. She knew better than Inspector Hanlon how to get answers from Shirley. You had to appear disinterested.

"That's right, isn't it, Pat?" Shirley asked. Pat nodded and, like Diane, waited. She, too, knew Shirley well. "You were here then. Remember when that teller kept borrowing money from her cash drawer. I was really surprised! I mean really she was the dumbest teller we ever had! I had always assumed it took brains and planning to embezzle but I guess if you had any real smarts you'd know how easy it is to get caught. The dumb don't realize all the checks. So who do you suppose did it this time? Maybe we should look for the stupidest person we can find."

"Mrs. Foster!" Doris exclaimed interrupting Shirley's

laughter. "Two deaths and now more trouble and you think it's funny. It's not funny! It's horrible! How can you say such things? How can you make jokes?"

"Don't get in a dither, Miss Webster," Shirley said. "I don't think you did it."

Doris uttered a sound between a moan and a cry as she ran into the ladies' room.

"Miss Tactful has struck again," Diana remarked.

"She's just spinny."

"If anyone should know.....," Diana said not finishing the thought.

"Okay," Shirley said. "Maybe I get carried away; but she is even stranger than usual since Cynthia's death. You don't suppose she did it? Wow, what a thought! It is so annoying. I should be able to figure this out. It should be obvious, especially the stealing part."

"Why should you know more than anyone else?" Diana asked.

"Well, like I said, the stealing is just stupid. And I sat right across from Cynthia," Shirley said. "I saw everything and heard everything."

"Anything more than anyone else?" Diana asked doubtfully.

"Sure," Shirley insisted. "You take the day she died, I saw her with her coffee. I know her coffee cup was there. If I could only remember when she got it and what happened to it, then I'd know who killed her."

"Well let me know if you remember," Diana said, uninterested.

"Unless you're the murderess!" Shirley said, laughing at her own wit.

"One might say your obsession is to hide the fact that you are the guilty one," Pat interrupted seriously with a slight shaking of her head. She rose, moved to the sink, rinsed her cup and set it on the draining board. As she turned to go back to the front banking hall, she looked at Shirley and added, "Or you're trying to get yourself killed".

"Very good," Shirley laughed as she followed Pat out of the room..

Diana sat in silence for a few moments. Did Shirley know anything? Diana didn't think so. No, Shirley wanted to know something but Diana didn't think there was anything there. Would Hanlon be disappointed? Now why was she concerned about Hanlon's reaction? Two people were dead and she was worried about making a good impression. She had to admit that she found Hanlon attractive with his quiet authority, his loneliness. She recognized someone she thought would be a peaceful, comfortable companion. Companion? The lies we tell ourselves. She also recognized someone whose arms she wanted around her. It had been a long time, her sister regularly said it had been too long. It was hard not to remember the pain of relationships, were they ever worth it? Was it in her to risk, to be hurt again? What was she thinking – he was probably married with six kids. She didn't believe that. She did believe he considered her a suspect. The fact was two women were dead. Whatever was going to happen with Hanlon would happen. What was she going to do about the deaths?

Doris returned from the washroom and checked to see if anyone was still in the lunchroom. Seeing Diana alone, she entered.

"Feeling better, Doris?" Diana asked.

"What?" asked Doris startled by the question. "I'm fine."

"This has been very upsetting for you."

"How can Mrs. Foster laugh at the evil in this place?"

"It's her way," Diana said quietly. "She doesn't see it as good or bad; she sees it as a change, as exciting."

"It's not exciting. I don't like exciting. It's all not right. I know it isn't. I don't know what to do but I know the deaths and the guessing is wrong. If only we could stop it, go back to how it was."

"We can't do that."

"No, no," agreed Doris. "It's too late to stop it now."

Diana walked to the sink and rinsed her glass. Although she was facing the opposite direction, she was very conscious of Doris's confusion and suffering. She waited, hoping Doris would need to confide in her.

"Do you think anyone knows what happened?" asked Doris.

"No."

"Not even the police?"

"Not yet."

"Then you think they will?"

"Probably," said Diana, sensing Doris' inner turmoil as Hanlon had felt it earlier. "Is there something that is worrying you, Doris?"

"People dying," Doris exclaimed. "People who shouldn't be dying. Mrs. Foster's prying. The police."

"It isn't your fault, Doris," said Diana.

"Isn't it?" asked Doris. Diana watched her. She hadn't expected this. Was Doris actually responsible in some way?

"If you know anything," Diana said. "You should tell the police. Keeping it to yourself is only worrying you."

"I can't," Doris said. "What if I say too much? I don't know what I've done."

"If you don't want to talk to the police, talk to me," Diana coaxed. "I'll listen and help if I can."

Doris looked at Diana pleadingly. Diana saw a helpless child, a child longing to trust her. Hanlon's face flashed in Diana's mind and for a moment Diana wondered if she deserved that trust. Then Doris started to talk and it was too late to turn back.

"I didn't kill Judy," Doris stated flatly. "I know I didn't, but maybe she did."

"Who?" asked Diana.

"The one who gave me......the one," Doris started to say. "No, no I can't."

"That's alright, Doris," said Diana. "Remember I'm here if you decide to talk."

Diana waited, hoping Doris would continue. Instead, the next group of coffee goers pushed the door from the branch open and started into the room. Interrupted, Diana and Doris got up and returned to work without further discussion. Doris was obviously distraught and Diana was convinced she knew something. Or had she done something, that was the question.

19

HANGING UP FROM Manders, Hanlon and Deck again got up to leave the station. This time there was no ringing phone to call them back. They settled into their car and Deck pulled onto Caledonia going towards town towards Douglas Street. At Blanshard, they turned left and headed back to James Bay and Jim Morrison's apartment.

To drive in Victoria is to drive in circles. They matched the lights and quickly found themselves again heading to Beacon Hill Park. Going down the sharp dip before the final rise to the park entrance they passed the little motel that had achieved the aura of a landmark. It stood modestly alone in its corner slightly away from the waterfront, a little bit behind her majesty, The Empress Hotel. A small-understated affair, it was well suited to being on the highway outside a prairie town instead of here competing with the high raise, high priced hotel chains. Yet, here it stood and here it had stood for years and years and years.

It was such places, these familiar scenes, which caused Hanlon to like Victoria. There was a lot of history here and folks like Deck's wife were always learning more. To Hanlon, though, it wasn't about knowing facts, it was about things being constant, about having shared a past, about sharing a lifetime with surroundings that showed little change. It was these comfortable things that made Victoria not only his home but his family.

As Deck steered the car up the slight hill to join Douglas Street at the Beacon Hill Park entrance, he interrupted Hanlon's solitude to ask, "Do you really think Cynthia Harmon could be the thief?"

"It's possible," Hanlon answered.

"She liked money alright," Deck said. "But she also liked to have someone to torment."

A startled Hanlon looked at Deck. "Sometimes you surprise me, Sergeant," he said.

"Oh?" Deck replied not quite sure how the Inspector meant his remark. It was perfectly clear to Deck. Judy Morrison was stealing the money. Cynthia Harmon found out. So they had to get rid of her. The husband, who had been the instigator all along, then needed to close up loose ends and had killed Judy, his weak link. Simple. Too bad though, he had been sure Manders was guilty. Judy Morrison's husband was a good second choice. He was a bad one whose every word would probably be a lie.

Jim Morrison was indeed a liar. From his experience Hanlon knew it. No longer did he consider such reactions as unfair. In his first years, he tried to give everyone the benefit of the doubt. Slowly he started to trust less and less. Now he was prepared for everything to be a lie. Sometimes he wondered at his cynicism and wished he could once again believe without hesitation. This was not the case with Jim Morrison. Jim was a liar for no better reason than he didn't know how to tell the truth. Hanlon had known what was in Jim's file without even seeing it. There were petty crimes as a juvenile, bad credit as an adult. Nothing that would point to murder, but a steady escalation of offenses from petty property crimes to more personal things including an assault on an ex-girlfriend. Then he started getting bold with a few frauds and most recently a couple of weapons offenses. It was a common pattern that Hanlon knew all too well. As one gets away with little crimes the little crimes grow into bigger crimes. An air of invincibility begins to cocoon the maturing criminal, and even the occasional arrest is not seen as a failure, just a spot of bad luck. Crime becomes as much of a habit as heroin. Was it just as addicting, Hanlon wondered.

He wondered even more once they reached the apartment and Jim Morrison was pacing before him. Was this a person who death had just touched? Where was the flat grayness to the skin, the tautness around the mouth, the darkness under the eyes – where were these signs of grief, of sudden misfortune? This man looked almost excited.

"I shoulda known; I shoulda been able to stop her. Oh, my poor Judy," he moaned. Distraught, he definitely wanted them to see how distraught he was.

"So what do you think happened, Mr. Morrison," Hanlon asked watching Jim strut around the room. He was as cocky as on their previous visit. However this time it wasn't impotent aggression, it was confidence. Hanlon watched and let Jim continue.

"She was so afraid, so afraid of gettin' caught. It wasn't her fault. She couldn't help herself. I shoulda been here."

"What was she so afraid of, Mr. Morrison?" Hanlon pressed.

"Why Cynthia of course," answered Jim. "She kept saying Cynthia knows, Cynthia knows. She was afraid of Cynthia, of bein' fired. Losin' her job if Cynthia caught her. That place drove her to it. I shoulda been here. I coulda saved her."

"Are you telling me she committed suicide?"

"It wasn't her fault. She couldn't stop herself. All that pressure. That Cynthia bitch always on her back, waitin' for one little chance to fire her. And she didn't get a raise because of the bitch, so she had to do something 'cause that bank pays shit."

She also was afraid of you, Deck remembered. Deck has seen far too many Jim Morrisons, far too many situations where the Judys of the world ended dead or worse.

Deck was a strong man and knew his strength and somehow knew it came with responsibility. Responsibility to not use that strength against those weaker than him. While growing up, Deck and his brothers had endlessly heard "do not hit your sisters". Deck didn't need to be told. He had always innately understood that physical power could be misused and that the weak needed to be helped, to be protected from predators. Maybe that was why he had become a cop. It wasn't a hard decision. He was not one for soul searching. He was who he was and he became a cop. In that job he had met many people, been in many situations. Of all the types of people he had encountered none repulsed him more than those that lived off others, off the weakness of others. The users, the parasites, these were Deck's natural enemies and Deck saw such an enemy in Jim Morrison.

"What could Miss Harmon have known that would upset your wife to the point of suicide?" Hanlon asked.

"That's where I made my big mistake," Jim said. Hanlon raised his eyebrows slightly but said nothing. "Ya see Judy lied on her application. She said she'd worked in a bank. I thought that's what she was afraid of   ol' Cynthia finding out she lied. She was nosey that Cynthia. But now, you know, it looks like I was wrong. Oh, if only I'd known; if only I was here." Jim finished his speech with another elaborate moan.

"Why do you think you were wrong, Mr. Morrison?"

"Why because of the money and shit!" Jim seemed surprised with the policemen's lack of response.

"Well, I …..don't ya know….here, just a minute," Jim said as he left the room.

Hanlon and Deck shared a glance and a thought. What next?

"These," said Jim tossing money orders, travelers'

cheques and a little cash on the couch in front of the officers. "My poor Judy musta been in hell. So afraid, 'specially after Cynthia died. I guess she couldn't live with what she'd done."

"You never knew about all this?" Hanlon asked pointing at the money.

"No, nothing," Jim said with big blank eyes. "I thought it was about lying on her application."

Hanlon let Jim watch as he paid special attention to the new computer, the big screen TV, and the other proceeds of Judy's theft.

"I knew Judy was buying lots but she handled the money and we both, ya know, had jobs. I didn't think about it. If only I had, she might be alive."

"Who might be alive," Hanlon asked.

"Why Judy, of course."

"Not Cynthia?"

"Oh, yeh, I get it," Jim said slowly. "Maybe   maybe I shoulda seen there was too much money and then I coulda stopped her. She changed so after Cynthia's death. She was so desperate before and then…and then…I shoulda been here."

"When should you have been here?" Hanlon finally asked.

"When Judy killed herself," Jim answered.

"She died at the bank."

"Yeh, I know," Jim said. "But she must a taken the stuff before she left for work. Don't ya think? She wouldn't have hid it at the bank, would she?"

"So you weren't here when she left for work?"

"No, I never was. I always left for the garage, ya know where I work, before she ever got up. That's where I was when you cops told me about Judy. Oh, Judy!" Jim paused for a moment and then continued. "I would like to be alone now if you don't have any more questions."

"I understand, Mr. Morrison," replied Hanlon. Then

reaching towards the money and forms that Jim had dumped, Hanlon continued, "We'll just need to inventory and take all this with us. We'll also need a formal statement from you."

"Ya, ya sure whatever," Jim muttered.

The officers collected and documented the evidence, finished up with Jim and walked back to where they had left the car on Toronto Street.

"He sure wanted to tell us he had an alibi. Damn near booted us out once he did!" Deck said breaking the silence. "It makes sense. What a waste of time! Here we are running all over town, talking to all these...people and now it looks like it's sorted itself out without us." Maybe he'd get to use his new fishing gear sooner than he thought.

"You think he was telling the truth?" Hanlon asked cautiously.

"Except for the part about not knowing anything about the money," Deck said. "That was a crock but the rest fits."

"Yes, it fits," Hanlon agreed. "All that's missing is a suicide note."

Hanlon was right, but only until the next morning when there was yet another call from the CIBC. It was Manders.

"Yes, Mr. Manders?"

"Oh good, you're there," he said. "A funny thing happened this morning. I guess it really isn't funny. It's a letter, a letter from Judy. I think you would call it a suicide note."

"How did you get it?" Hanlon asked.

"It was in our envelope drop when we opened it this morning. You know, where customers can make deposits after hours. We only open it once a day, first thing in the morning. She must have put it in after we opened it yesterday and before she died. I mean, you know what I mean."

"How many people have handled it?"

"I have no idea," Manders answered somewhat annoyed. Then as he recognized what Hanlon's question meant, the bank manager slowly added, "Oh, you mean fingerprints?"

"Yes."

"We never thought you'd want to check it," Manders said somewhat flustered but still obviously relieved that it was all over. "It's quite clear about everything and it is her signature."

"Not her writing?"

"No, it's typed. Well, you know computer typed," Manders replied. "But it is her signature."

"You know her signature?" Hanlon persisted.

"No, not really, but the other girls do and they said it was Judy's."

"Okay, Mr. Manders, we'd still like it bagged up. Do you have any bags, vinyl preferably?"

"Sure, we have them for holding and shipping cash."

"Fine, please put the note in one of those. Try not to handle it any more than you need to and we'll be down to collect it later this morning."

"Don't you want to know what it says? Don't you want me to read it to you?"

"Certainly, Mr. Manders, go ahead."

"I can't go on." Manders read. "I took the money and Cynthia found out. I had to kill her. But now it's too awful. I'm sorry. Good-bye."

The letter said what Inspector Hanlon knew it would say and that is what he relayed to Deck. "Very predictable, Deck. We say everything fits except for a suicide note and now we have a suicide note which says just what we would expect."

"But in the envelope drop?" asked Deck. "She would have had to go back outside to put that in. No one mentioned her going outside. Why not leave it at home for the loving husband? She had to know it wouldn't be found until today."

"All good questions," Hanlon answered. "Not answered in the note. So it all fits."

"Right, it fits," said Deck. "It fit before and I thought it was over. Now, it fits too well." He looked at Hanlon and said, "If it's over why doesn't it feel like it's over?"

20

"IT'S BALONEY!" SHIRLEY exclaimed.

It was the end of the day, the same day that Judy's note had been found. The customers were gone, the doors closed and the cash put away. Everyone had been collected in the lunchroom, which also acted as a meeting room, for an announcement by Mr. Manders.

He hated these meetings. Every month it seemed head office sent some new thing out that had to be communicated by the manager in a staff meeting. In this case, though, he himself had decided he needed to talk to everyone together. He wanted these past few weeks closed off. He wasn't having much luck doing that in his own life but he was going to do it in his bank life. It was time to settle this. It was time to move on.

When everyone was present, Manders had repeated the information in Judy's suicide note although by that time no one was unaware of its contents. He positioned the contents of the note as the facts. It was the solution to the deaths and to the missing items. He meant his speech to be very professional, very black and white, nothing left for speculation. The formality of the moment was meant to put an end to the confusion and distress of the previous few days.

Shirley was having none of it.

"It's baloney!" she repeated. "There is no way Judy killed herself."

That's why Manders hated these meetings, they never went as planned. Someone, usually Shirley, said something! Fortunately for him, though, not everyone agreed with Shirley.

"Suicide is hard to understand at any time." Barbara said. Shirley's facial expression told Barbara that her words had had no effect. "No one can be sure what Judy was thinking. Not even you."

"She had been really upset since Cynthia died," Pat remarked.

"Yes, yes she was."

There was general rumbling of consent as the staff agreed. Everyone had noticed Judy's stress. No one mentioned the stealing, just her inner turmoil. They wanted it over. They wanted it settled. Shirley didn't.

"No way," she insisted. "I'm telling you she didn't kill herself and she probably didn't kill Cynthia."

"Calm down, Shirley," Diana said, trying to soothe the mood of the room. "We know you liked the excitement and were hoping to find a murderer but it's over."

"Diana is right," Mr. Manders said asserting his authority. "It is over and now it's time to start rebuilding the branch. I would like to express my appreciation for your professionalism during this unpleasant time. Now with some of the same effort I'm sure our branch will return to the level of good morale we previously enjoyed. Mike, I need to see you for a few moments in my office."

With that Manders turned and left the room. Mike followed closely behind. Taking this as an obvious signal that the meeting was over, some of the staff started to disburse. Others made no move to leave. Diana glanced over the ones that remained. Were they waiting to be convinced that it was in fact over? Did they want to talk? Perhaps they just weren't sure what to do now. What was she going to do?

"Diana," Shirley demanded. "Do you believe this nice neat letter that supposedly is from Judy?"

"It was her signature," Doris said.

"Big deal," Shirley said. "How hard is it to forge a signature? We see it done all the time. Wives sign their husbands' cheques. Children writing cheques on their parents account. You know it happens. You all know it happens. Can we tell the difference? Not usually. You know it and I know it. That signature means nothing."

"Okay, Shirley," Barbara said. "If that isn't what happened, what did? Tell us what you think you know."

"No, no," said Doris. "This isn't right. You will only make it worse."

"How can it get any worse?" Shirley demanded. "Besides, who said you have to stay? I'm not forcing you. All of you can go; who needs you! You want to be part of the whitewash of murder. You want to see a pitiful wimp of a girl blamed for Cynthia's death just because she was foolish enough to get herself killed. Fine. Leave. Who needs you?"

Her outburst was met with silence. No one moved. Did they feel the same doubts? It would be so much easier if what Mr. Manders had said was true. But Shirley seemed so sure of herself, so convinced. She was almost convincing.

"How do you know Judy didn't kill herself?" Diana finally asked.

"Because she was surprised!" Shirley exclaimed proudly.

"What?" was everyone's reaction.

"You saw her," Shirley exclaimed. "She was right here in front of us. Her face. She didn't know why she was ill and then down she went. If she had poisoned herself, she would not have been so surprised."

"That's it?" Barbara asked testily.

"Yes."

"Did it ever occur to you that she was surprised at the

pain? This has gotten quite as ridiculous as I am going to tolerate," Barbara said, rising to leave.

"Say whatever you want, but I know Judy didn't kill herself and I don't believe she killed Cynthia."

"We might not like the answer but that doesn't mean it's not the correct answer," Pat stated.

"She didn't do it I tell you!" Shirley insisted.

"C'mon, Ms. Holmes," Diana said lightly. "Tell us your solution. Tell us what really happened."

"I know who killed Cynthia or I will once I remember who brought her coffee that morning. Because she never left her desk, I remembered that, so someone had to have brought her the coffee. And when I remember who it was, I'll tell you what happened. I'll tell you who killed Cynthia and Judy, both!"

"No, don't say that," Doris wailed.

"Yes, I do say that," Shirley insisted. "Whoever gave her the coffee killed her. I know and I'm not giving up until I remember who it was."

"Aren't you afraid you'll be this phantom murderer's next victim?" Barbara asked scornfully as she left the room. Barbara shook her head over Shirley's obsession. Things were not going to return to normal. Her husband had been right. She would have to talk to Mr. Manders.

She crossed the banking hall, back to her offices next to Manders'. Mike was still in with Manders. The office door was open and as she reached Pat's desk, she could catch pieces of conversation. No one noticed her. She decided to wait where she was rather than continuing into her office.

"I'm sorry, Mike," Manders was saying. "But with the loss of, at this point, an unknown amount of money, Vancouver feels a new person is required for the position. They want someone stricter and with more of a risk background."

She couldn't hear Mike's response.

"No, I don't know who it is," Manders continued. "I know only what I've told you. You will be receiving an official letter of discipline. You will be required to improve your area substantially."

Mike again mumbled several words.

"No, you are not being made a scapegoat. This does nothing for my record either. The defalcation was by a person directly under your supervision. Don't let the deaths colour the issue. A member of the staff you were responsible for stole from this bank and you did not discover it. That is what your letter will say and I don't honestly know if your career will recover."

Mike's voice could again be heard slightly. But now the other women were leaving the lunchroom and the noise caused Manders to rise from his desk and close the office door.

"You still here?" Shirley's voice startled Barbara.

"Waiting to talk to Mr. Manders, but he's still with Mike," Barbara said by way of explanation.

"Probably getting canned," remarked Shirley. "Why do you want to talk to him? Going to give your notice?"

"Do you always say any asinine remark that comes into your tiny brain?

"Why so touchy?" Shirley said laughing. "Do you have something to hide? It's no secret that you've never really been here. You obviously don't have to work and I've never seen anyone who says less about herself. It will be no surprise to anyone that you aren't sticking around. It'll also be no loss."

There was a visible tension between the two women. Both sizing each other up, each knowing there was an instinctive competitiveness and wondering how far it would take them. Barbara chose not to play and did not rise to Shirley's bait. The women separated with Shirley leaving the bank.

Barbara decided to also leave and moved back towards the lunchroom area to get her coat from the closet. As she opened the door, she heard Doris confiding to Diana.

"I didn't mean to kill her. I didn't. It was a mistake. I did give her the coffee but I just did what I was told. I didn't...."

"Am I interrupting?" Barbara asked, since Doris had stopped talking upon seeing her.

"I have to go," Doris said almost running from the room.

"Now what was all that about?" Barbara asked.

"Nothing," Diana said and wondered if she was speaking the truth. Did Doris know what she was saying? If so, what to do, what to do? What was justice? Cynthia's death had looked like justice. Diana hadn't been sure she wanted Cynthia's murderer caught but now here was Doris confessing. Confessing to what though? Every part of Diana believed Doris needed to be protected not punished. She needed to do something, but what?

21

DETECTIVE INSPECTOR HANLON sat quietly looking out his office window. Those weren't the sights or sounds, though, that he saw. Like a private movie, all the conversations since Cynthia Harmon's death kept playing in his head. The faces, one by one, played on a continuously looping track. Doris: scared. Over the years, Hanlon had seen many sides of fear   fear from guilt, fear from threats, fear of what they knew, fear of what they didn't know and even fear of life. What was Doris' fear? Shirley: curious and confident. Should he listen to anything she said? Manders: falling apart. Mike: the martyr was how Deck had described him. Diana: forget Diana. And Judy: poor Judy. Even Manders looked at Judy as poor Judy. All the others, all the many others, round and round their pictures went. A movie he didn't want to watch and that he couldn't shut off.

The final reports of the CIBC deaths rested on his desk awaiting his signature. What was his delay? Cynthia's death was three weeks ago. The answer had been provided. It was time to close the file and move on. Soon the Chief would be demanding it. Something, though, was wrong; he could feel it. He didn't want to let it go. He was forgetting something.

The ringing phone did not fully interrupt his circling thoughts.

"It's for you," Deck said.

"Who is it?"

"I didn't ask," he replied. "It sounded personal."

Joseph Hanlon lived alone and spent the majority of his private life that way. He seldom received personal calls and was surprised Deck had made such an assumption.

"Hello...hello? Inspector Hanlon speaking," he finally announced.

"This is Diana Hillis," the voice said. "From the CIBC?"

"Yes, Miss Hillis, I remember," Hanlon said as Deck whistled softly. "I've been expecting your call. I've been waiting for an update and the thoughts you didn't share earlier."

There was a pause and then Diana replied, "I was hoping you'd be available to meet for lunch or for a coffee."

This wasn't what he had expected. Hanlon could feel Deck watching him and wished he would leave the room. Deck watched Hanlon's immobile face and wished he could hear what Diana Hillis was saying.

"Yes, we could have lunch," Hanlon said slowly and Deck became even more attentive. "Shall I come by about noon?"

"No, not here," she said quickly. "It's business, your business. I can't talk here and I'd rather no one sees us together."

"I see," Hanlon said flatly.

"I would prefer the people here think the police are finished. You understand?"

"Has something happened?" Hanlon asked without answering her question.

"Lunch?" she replied not answering his question either.

"Lunch," Hanlon agreed. They settled on meeting at the Oak Bay Beach hotel, the Snug restaurant, just after noon. Hanlon turned towards Deck knowing he was dying to speak.

"Well, have you got a hot one there or another cold corpse?"

"She wants to talk about the case."

"I've heard that before!" Deck said.

"You have?" Hanlon said in amazement. This ended Deck's exhibition of wit and Hanlon was able to relate the little that Diana had said.

"She's the same as you," Deck said with exasperation. "Won't let go. What is wrong with the simple explanation that we have? You are an old bachelor who can't remember what to say to a woman you want. You're both pretending it's this case that's bringing you together. There are other cases we should be working on."

"Fine," Hanlon said shortly. "You work on them until I get back."

"And the reports?"

"The reports stay where they are until I sign them, Sergeant."

"Yes, sir," Deck replied. He had overstepped his ground but he believed what he had said. The old man was in over his head. It would only be a couple of hours at the most. Who knew, maybe something would come of it for the Inspector. The old man with a woman, now that would be something different! Nothing would change with the case though, Deck was convinced. Judy's note had raised a couple of doubts, but hell it all fit. That was one good thing, at least they knew Diana wasn't a murderer.

Hanlon was not as convinced of that as Deck was. He headed out towards Oak Bay, taking residential back streets until Pandora ceased being one way. Turning onto Oak Bay Avenue, it didn't take Hanlon many minutes to reach Cynthia Harmon's building. Passing it and pulling into the hotel parking lot just a few feet away, he wondered at what made him and Diana select this place. No, he was not at all as sure of things as Deck was.

He sat opposite Diana and continued to wonder how

much of what Deck had said was true. It was true he had been alone a long time. It didn't matter; he had two dead people. That was why he was here. Hanlon knew something was wrong with the murder-suicide answer. He knew Diana could tell him more than she had. She was his only lead. Was she also his murderer? How far could he trust her? Was she here to give the update he'd requested? Or was it a game? He had known a lot of murderers who were caught simply because they could not leave it alone. Their egos had to continue the game of cat and mouse.

Hanlon raised his eyes and was surprised to see Diana looking at him, not at him   through him.

"You can't forget I could be your murderer, can you?" she asked. While he tried to form an answer she continued, "It doesn't matter. You don't need to trust me; you don't even need to like me. You just need to stay with Cynthia's death."

"Originally you wanted it left alone," Hanlon remarked.

"That was before I saw all the repercussions," Diana replied.

"Are you referring to Judy Morrison's suicide or something else?"

"Shirley doesn't think it was suicide," Diana said by way of an answer.

Before anything further could be said, their waitress stopped by to get their order. They had not looked at the menus, so quickly ordered a coffee for Hanlon, water for Diana and turned their attention to deciding on lunch.

The Snug had been a landmark for as long as either of them could remember. Heavy dark wood abounded. The walls, the tables, the odd assortment of sturdy, masculine chairs all were dark, solid and wood. No plastic or metal could be found here, no art deco, no latest fashion. This was a pub; this was a restaurant. This was the Snug, and in Victoria you need say nothing more.

A big traditional British bar, with the regulars' individual beer mugs hung above it, was the focal point of the main room. Past the bar, a raised area held additional seating. This section was framed with windows overlooking the water. Doors led out to a patio deck that was used only in the summer. This was October. It was closed.

Hanlon and Diana sat in the raised section at a corner table with the window to their back and the large fireplace, fire ablaze, to their right. The waitress returned with their drinks and took their orders – steak and kidney pie for Hanlon, seafood chowder for Diana.

With lunch underway, Diana started a new conversation. They chatted. They chatted like friends. One was the policeman who could not forget he was a policeman. The other was a woman who could not forget she was a suspect. They looked like friends.

Once the lunch was finished and the plates removed, Hanlon wistfully remembered the days of flashing up an after lunch pipe while Diana switched the conversation abruptly back to the murder.

"Shirley doesn't think it was suicide," she repeated. "Nor does she believe Judy killed Cynthia. Shirley is very logical and a pretty good read of people. Her deductions, which seem to come from left field, actually come from her logic. She is usually right."

"You think she's right now?" Hanlon asked.

"Yes," Diana said. "But what I think doesn't matter. If she is right, she could be in danger."

"Has something happened to cause this concern?" Hanlon asked.

Diana related Manders' meeting of the previous night. She told of Shirley's doubts, her solution and her intention to find the real killer.

"This was said in front of the entire staff?" Hanlon asked.

"Most of them," she answered. "Except Mike and Mr. Manders. They had left to go to Mr. Manders' office." The sat for a few moments quietly. Hanlon appeared to be falling asleep but Diana didn't believe it for a second.

"Do you believe that Judy killed Cynthia and then herself?" Diana bluntly asked. "Of course, you don't. You wouldn't look at me like I was your murderer if you did."

"We have evidence that Judy Morrison was responsible for the embezzlement," Hanlon replied flatly.

"I believe that," Diana agreed. "But she was so afraid of Cynthia, so afraid of everything. Shirley also made a good point; Judy did not know what was happening when she was dying."

"She might have been surprised by the actually dying. People who take poison think you just go to sleep. They don't expect the pain that comes first." Hanlon paused and then continued. "There is a motive. We have evidence that Miss Harmon was not above blackmail."

"The old witch kept records," Diana laughed. "I should have known! Was Judy listed as one of her victims?"

Hanlon tried to review Cynthia's records in his mind. That was what he was missing, Judy was not in the ledger. She should have been for the murder-suicide to be true.

"No," he answered. "No, she wasn't."

"She should be," said Diana. "Was anyone from the bank included?" She read his eyes and added, "Besides me. No need to be surprised. She emptied my life; I could only assume I would be shown and my husband would be listed as her trophy, no doubt. Anyone else?"

"I'll have to review it," Hanlon said making a mental note along side the one he had made to get a handwriting specialist to check the signature on the suicide note.

"If Judy was also murdered, it changes things," Diana said. "Do you think a person, who would kill Judy and frame her for Cynthia's murder, would have been worrying about poisoning extra people originally? Remember the first murder, two poisons were used. Maybe the two poisons were obvious to you but to the average person the symptoms might have been considered close enough – worth a shot at being taken for an accident. If two poisons hadn't been used, it would not have been so obvious that Cynthia's death was murder but then others would almost certainly have died. Would such a person concerned about additional deaths in the first case, frame and then kill Judy or kill and then frame her?"

"To cover their tracks maybe," Hanlon said. "The second poison – the poisoning of everyone else was an attempt to disguise Cynthia's murder. Framing Judy as you're suggesting could be for the same reason and so yes, could be the same person. That is if Judy was murdered."

Diana ignored his entire reply and continued to share her hypothesis.

"Suppose you wanted to kill Judy and decided to use Cynthia's murder to create the illusion of a guilt induced suicide. Even if the suicide wasn't believed, the two murders would be connected. When in fact they're not. "

"You are saying two murders," Hanlon said. "And two murderers?"

"Once separated they are easy to unravel," Diana remarked.

"You know who Judy Morrison's murderer is?" Hanlon asked.

"So do you," Diana said nodding. Hanlon waited for her to say more. She didn't. Was she right, were there two murders? Did he know who killed Judy? Why was she telling him this? Was it as Deck said, Hanlon and Diana were both the same and couldn't let go? Or was she saying she didn't kill Judy? What about Cynthia? Hanlon looked at Diana who was back lost in her own thoughts. Was he looking at a murderer?

"If we only knew why Cynthia was killed, it would truly be over," Diana remarked.

"Don't you mean who killed her?" Hanlon asked. Observing Diana's silence, a realization came upon him.

"You know who killed Cynthia?"

"I didn't say that."

"What are you saying?"

"I think I know how and that might also be who and it might not. A person can be an instrument you know."

Hanlon waited but he was only given silence. "Okay," he finally said. "What is the how?"

"I can't, I'm sorry, Inspector," said Diana. "You know the worse part of this? It's all the people who are innocent. They suffer, the guilty don't. All the while Cynthia's murder goes unsolved everyone is suspect, no one is trusted. I can't hurt the wrong person with guesses."

Hanlon waited but he knew no further information was to be forthcoming. They spent a few more moments together and then parted. Hanlon wondered what Diana hadn't told him. He wondered if she did know who the murderer was. He also still wondered if she was the killer.

Diana hadn't told Hanlon about Doris. She had planned to tell him but she couldn't. She had seen Doris's trusting eyes and hadn't been able to say that Doris had poisoned Cynthia. Not yet.

22

ANNA HAD NEVER seen her sister like this before. She was so silent and yet so determined. Diana was never a great talker and liked to take solitary walks around the park. Still, usually she was good company, peaceful company. Now all Anna could feel was Diana's restlessness, her intensity. Her walks had become obsessive, the silences deafening. When Anna asked what was going on, Diana just said it was getting closer. Closer to what? Anna did not like it. She was scared

"Do you know what you're doing?" Anna asked.

"What do you mean?" asked Diana.

"Miss Innocent," replied Anna. "You know what I mean. This murder you keep thinking about. The papers say it's been solved. A letter was left confessing to the whole thing."

"It's a phony," Diana said simply.

"How do you know?" Anna asked. When Diana gave no sign of answering, Anna continued. "Okay, I'll humour you. Say two people have been murdered; you could be the next. You're no Nancy Drew, you know."

"I'm not doing anything," Diana answered. "I'm listening to who wants to talk and watching who doesn't. Otherwise

I'm thinking. Nothing dangerous."

"Watching the wrong people can be dangerous," Anna insisted.

"Not compared to Shirley and her questions," Diana said. "She is amusing. She had the nerve or stupidity to ask Mike if he regretted killing Cynthia now that he didn't get her job."

"God," Anna sighed.

"Exactly," Diana agreed. More seriously she added, "She's only guessing right now but our murderer might not want to risk her guessing accurately."

"It would be a good cover if she were guilty," Anna said. "You did say she hated Cynthia. Of course, I don't see why she would have killed that other one. The one I found out about in the paper. Honestly, you could tell me what's happening. It might be the most excitement I ever see in my life, especially living with you."

"Ah yes, I know," Diana agreed smiling. "I'm simply too boring."

"Do you have to lay it on so thick?"

"Never mind," Diana said seriously once more. "The other one, as you put it, has no more to do with it. The police will finish that any time now." Before Anna could reply, Diana got up and left the room.

Diana was finished with the conversation and with sounding confident for Anna. She had her doubts, doubts that wouldn't leave. Mentally she continued to pace back and forth. What to do? What to say? She got up and left the room and within very few minutes she was outside pacing in her larger living room.

She headed slowly down Cook Street towards Victoria. She saw nothing. She walked away from Dallas Road and the scenic walks along the water. She liked to come upon the straits with the hazy shape of Washington in the distance, from the Douglas Street side of the park. So she took the long way. She headed past the backside of the park, past houses after houses and towards the shops in the little village part way up Cook Street. She noticed no gardens, no window displays. She walked by rote along the edge of the Park, left onto Park Blvd – a big name for a little jog of a street – along Heywood, up the little rise that was Southgate and then finally into the Park. Her thoughts continued to swirl and swirl driving her on step by step.

Just before she reached the entrance to the park, Diana left Southgate taking a little used path that lead up over a knoll of rocks and grass. Wild, there were no formal gardens here. Suddenly it was another world. Quiet and solitary, the arbutus trees and surrounding bushes comforted her.

Why was she struggling so? What she had expected to happen, had in fact happened. The police were continuing to investigate Judy's death. Wasn't it what she wanted? Hadn't she called Inspector Hanlon for that very reason? She had called not for lunch but to get the police to continue their investigation, to come back to the bank.

They had come back and Diana alone was not surprised. Nor was she surprised by their affect on the bank employees. She continued down the knoll and turned onto the path that leads around Goodacre Lake. Passing the few fellow October walkers, Diana did not notice their faces. She didn't see their dogs. She was seeing the staff's faces   their reactions to Hanlon and Deck's return.

Shirley had been delighted.

"I told you," she had gloated. "Didn't I tell you! It's not so cut and dried as that note or the papers or Mr. Manders would like us to think. Mr. Manders, I wonder   no, I guess not. If only I could remember, I would be able to solve the mystery."

"This is not a contest," Pat had reminded her.

"Maybe not for you," Shirley had replied. "But I intend to get as much fun from this as possible."

"You're impossible! Will you never grow up?" Barbara had demanded.

"Not if it means being as stuffy and scared as you," Shirley snapped. "Besides, you're all just jealous because I was obviously right."

Diana circled Goodacre Lake and crossed the main cement pathway to head towards Aviary circle. She felt rather than saw the aviary and wondered if there were ever, or if there ever had been birds in it. Doris' face flashed into Diana's mind.

Doris hadn't cared if Shirley was right or not. Doris was unnerved or maybe, more unnerved to be accurate since she had never recovered from Cynthia's death.

"Why are they here again?" she had cried to Diana. "You didn't say anything. I didn't. You know, I didn't do it."

"They're not here for you," Diana had said, hoping she was speaking the truth.

Diana continued along the path reaching the duck pond on Douglas Street side of the park. She could start to hear the traffic but didn't have to join that world quite yet. What was it about ducks that always made her want to smile? They are so in their own world, so simple somehow. Simple would be nice. It wasn't simple.

There was Mike. He had given no reaction to the police's return. He had been unresponsive since the night of the meeting. The new administration officer had not yet arrived but everyone knew he was coming. Mike was walking through the motions. Nothing touched him any longer. At least nothing at the bank touched him. If he was arrested for murder would it awaken him?

Diana continued along the pathway as it merged into Douglas Street's sidewalk and there she headed towards Dallas Road. Diana picked up speed now leaving the park and joining the world.

Barbara also had not been disturbed by the return of the police. After Cynthia's murder some of the part-time staff just never came back. A couple of other people had given their notice. A couple more resigned after Judy's death.

Barbara had joined their ranks and given notice as Shirley had guessed she would. Little was said by her. Nothing was asked by the staff. She had been a temporary visitor.

And Pat. Pat had worked at the bank for as long as Diana remembered and was a living example of cool, unaffected professionalism. Diana had known her for years upon years, but what did she know, very little really. Pat was someone who had always kept to herself now even more than usual.

Diana reached the edge of Beacon Hill Park and Dallas Road. She turned to the left and headed along the waterfront back towards the Fairfield side of the park. The air was always fresh here. One could feel space, could feel life. This was not a place for death.

Diana reached her front door refreshed once more. Another day gone. Tomorrow back to work and Manders. She wondered about Manders. He had been the most disturbed when the officers had returned. Diana had watched him struggle. He had obviously closed the incident in his mind and he had hoped in his staff's minds. That was not to be.

"Some minor points need to be clarified," Hanlon had told Manders. "Your cooperation will be noted."

Noted where, Manders' tired face had said, at my trial?

The police were different this time. Just a few very pointed questions were asked.

Hanlon and his sergeant were looking for something specific. The personnel files were taken away this time to be copied probably. Samples of everyone's handwriting were requested to be analyzed one assumed. Warrants were also provided authorizing the removal of the staff's personal bank statements. Did they find what they were looking for? Were they coming back? Days passed. Everyone wondered and no one knew.

No one, that is except for Detective Inspector Hanlon. He knew. The lunch with Diana Hillis had uncovered what he had instinctively known was wrong. There was no evidence that Judy was being blackmailed by Cynthia. They had assumed that was the case because it had been Cynthia's habit. She had kept records, good records. Hanlon had checked those records after his luncheon with Diana and confirmed what he had guessed. Judy had not been one of Cynthia's victims. Without blackmail, there was no motive for Judy to kill Cynthia.

Shirley Foster had been right again. She had also been correct about the suicide note. It was a fake. Shirley Foster had been very accurate with her guesses. Were they guesses? Was it logic? Was it knowing her fellow employees well as people? Or did she know these things because she was their killer?

Hanlon didn't know yet. It didn't matter he would soon. First he had to finish with the Judy Morrison murder. It would not be long now. He wanted one more piece. He waited patiently for the day that would supply the final detail. With the ringing of his phone, the expected element had arrived.

"He's here," Diana said. "Asking for his insurance money."

23

"**S**o we're back where we started," Deck said with regret.

With these words, he echoed the feelings of everyone involved except Diana and Hanlon. They had been prepared for this. They alone had deduced that Jim Morrison had arranged the artificial suicide.

Upon Diana's call, Hanlon had said, "Let's go". First to Deck and then within very few minutes of arriving at the bank, he said it again to Jim Morrison. It had seemed that Jim was expecting them. He was at his strutting rooster best. Shouting for what he was due, he wanted his poor dead wife's money. Yet at the same time, it was clearly a performance. Hanlon saw that and gave him little opportunity to talk at the bank. He wanted Jim at the station. Jim showed neither surprise nor even concern upon the suggestion of moving their conversation to police headquarters. In fact, he looked like he welcomed it. Bursting he was to tell someone how smart he was.

Once Hanlon and Deck had Jim somewhat comfortably set in one of the smaller, duller interview rooms, it took little to get Jim talking. He took complete credit for all of Judy's stealing. He was proud of it. He bragged.

"She'd never woulda thought of it," he said. "Stupid. She was stupid, real stupid. She comes home talkin' about all this money and shit. It was all wow, wow, wow to her. Couldn't shut her up, she kept goin' on and on, never seen so much stuff before. Not like me, I'd been around, you know."

"We could tell," Hanlon said in agreement.

"The stuff was a gift," Jim continued. "It was just sittin' there, waitin' to be taken. No one cared. It was goin' great and then the little bitch started gettin' scared. I told her we could fix it but she panicked. Then ol' Cynthia got bumped off. I didn't do that. Don't try pinnin' that on me! I didn't do no killin'."

"We know you killed Judy," Hanlon said patiently.

"Ya don't know nothin'," Jim laughed.

"We know you signed the suicide note; we know Judy wouldn't steal for you any longer; we know you expected to get her insurance money. Plenty of motive."

"I have an alibi," Jim stated smugly.

"Yes, that was quite clever," Hanlon said flattering Jim.

"Yeah, it was, wasn't it?" Jim agreed. No lawyer could have silenced his vanity. Hanlon sat and watched him and waited. Jim watched Hanlon and Deck watching him and then started to laugh.

"Okay, what the hell; it was good while it lasted. She wasn't nothin'. She did anythin' I told her. It was so easy. I woke her up before I left said 'Drink this' and she did. Stupid."

"Let's talk about Cynthia Harmon now," Hanlon said redirecting the conversation.

"I didn't kill that bitch," Jim yelled. "I could have but I didn't. So forget it, I'm not going down for that!"

The interview went on and on, over and over but Jim never changed his position about Cynthia. He insisted he hadn't killed her. Finally, Hanlon let him be lead away to one of the holding cells.

Hanlon and Deck stayed sitting in the stillness of the interview room. What now? Hanlon seemed to believe Jim. Deck did as well.

"So we're back where we started," Deck said more to himself than to Hanlon.

Yes, they believed Jim. Deck didn't want to but it didn't appear possible for Jim to have killed Cynthia. He had no key to the bank. Whoever had murdered Cynthia Harmon had been able to get into the bank before anyone else.

"Read me that list of people who hold keys to the bank," Hanlon said.

"Yes, sir," Deck said startled by the similarity of their thought. "Here we are: Dave Manders, Cynthia Harmon, Mike Baker, Diana Hillis, Shirley Foster, Barbara Scott and Lester Souch."

"Lester Souch?" Hanlon asked.

"The janitor," Deck replied.

"Right," Hanlon recalled. "Everything was as it should have been when he left the previous night."

"Doesn't narrow it down much," Deck mused. "We can eliminate Cynthia Harmon and, I guess, Lester Souch. Still leaves us with Manders, Baker, Hillis, Foster and Scott."

"Don't forget to include anyone who had access to those keys," Hanlon said.

"You mean husbands and wives?" Deck asked. "What about motives?"

"Yes, motives," Hanlon repeated absently.

The officers went step-by-step through their list of suspects.

Dave Manders had a key to the bank. He had a motive. According to the argument Doris Webster overheard, Manders had wanted to end his affair with Cynthia. Should they believe Doris Webster? Everyone said Manders hadn't left his office. How did he get the poison to Cynthia Harmon?

Sybil Manders could have entered the bank prior to

anyone's arrival. Everyone assumed she had. Motive? The affair with Cynthia might have disturbed her more than she let on in their interview. Neither of the officers put much faith in that supposition. The same stumbling block, how did she get the poison to Cynthia?

Mike Baker was an excellent suspect. He had plenty of both opportunity and motive. He was the one responsible for making the coffee. His word alone said he didn't make it that day. He had been sick from the arsenic but that didn't change anything. It would have been easy to fake. It would have been easy to allow himself to be poisoned slightly. He was a prime suspect. He had needed Cynthia's job. He needed more money. He had been a candidate for the defalcation. He had not been guilty of that, but was he guilty of murder?

What of his wife, could she be their murderer? It seemed unlikely. It was agreed that she had access to a key and she shared her husband's motive. Now, the officers knew that was stretching it. It did not seem possible that Linda Baker could have arranged Cynthia's death without her husband's involvement. Hanlon and Deck decided to put Linda Baker low on their list of suspects and her husband high on that same list.

"Diana Hillis is the next name," Deck said.

There was no response from Hanlon.

"She holds a bank key," Deck continued. "And she holds an old grudge against Cynthia Harmon."

"Who's next?" Hanlon asked.

"Shirley Foster," Deck answered, showing no surprise at Hanlon's reluctance to discuss Diana Hillis.

Shirley Foster had confessed to wanting Cynthia Harmon dead. She had known how Cynthia had been killed, she had known there were two poisons, she had known almost every detail of the entire investigation. She had the desire to kill; she had the opportunity to kill. For once, someone had the opportunity. Shirley sat directly opposite Cynthia. It would have been easy to administer poison to Cynthia.

It also would have been very easy to destroy the cup afterwards. The cup, Shirley had made everyone aware was missing. Shirley Foster, who would not let the murder rest, was looking better and better as a suspect. Yes, if Shirley Foster didn't get herself killed being an amateur sleuth, she would be a most promising name on their list.

Was there anyone related to Shirley the officers should consider? Shirley's motive did not appear to be substantial enough to spill over to anyone else. It was the weakest point in the case against Shirley Foster, no real motive. No, they need not consider anyone else at this point.

Next was Barbara Scott. Barbara was a shadow. It was as if she didn't exist. She had not been at the bank long enough to want to kill someone. She only had a key because of her role. A role that required sometimes meeting clients outside regular banking hours. In fact, she only had the key on a temporary basis as it was shared with the other financial advisors. It was just coincidence that she was the holder of it on the day of Cynthia's death. Was anything really a coincidence? She didn't know the routine of the branch, didn't know the staff all that well. She certainly didn't know them well enough to kill anyone. Unless she had known Cynthia from before, that is. And Cynthia had known her.

"Didn't Diana Hillis say she thought Barbara and Cynthia had known each other before?" asked Hanlon.

Deck checked his notes before replying, " Her sister did. While we were waiting for Miss Hillis, her sister related an earlier conversation in which Diana Hillis had listed a bunch of people who might want to kill Cynthia."

"Nothing really to go on there," Hanlon decided.

"No," Deck agreed. "If Cynthia Harmon did know Barbara before though and knew something from Barbara's past," Deck continued thinking out loud. "It would become public or it would be used for blackmail."

"This is too much guessing and too much stretching," Hanlon said. "We have nothing."

What about her husband, could he be their killer? Doctor Scott had not wanted his wife working. Murder was an extreme way of getting her to quit. He would have had access to Barbara's key. He also would have had access to the cause of death, to the paraldehyde – a hypnotic with a major effect on the respiratory system; even small therapeutic amounts can result in rapid, shallow breathing, coughing, and coma. It was fast acting and addictive and was now seldom used in North America. Paraldehyde was another of the many medical poisons.

"Doesn't that sound like an oxymoron," Deck had asked. "Medical poisons!"

Doctor Scott would definitely have access to the poison used to kill Cynthia. By extension, Barbara Scott probably could. Who else had a means of getting paraldehyde? It wasn't that common. That gave the officers little comfort. When it came to murder they had learnt the unattainable could always be attained.

"That's the list," Deck said. "Except for Diana Hillis." He waited for a response from Hanlon but none was forthcoming. Deck got up and left the interview room, leaving Hanlon alone with his silence and his thoughts.

That was their list, their list except for Diana, Hanlon thought. Diana. There was no denying it. Deck was right. Diana Hillis had a key to the bank. She knew the routine and the people of the bank perhaps better than anyone. She not only knew all the procedures; she also knew everyone's routines and their likely reactions. She knew everything it would have taken to poison the coffee and kill Cynthia and not be noticed. Motive could not be denied. She had made that clear. From the beginning she had been uncooperative, uninterested in finding Cynthia's killer. What had she said? She wasn't sure she wanted Cynthia's murderer found? Diana had changed when Judy had died. She had offered her assistance in finding Judy's killer. That she had done. Now what? Diana had not been able to let Judy take the blame for a murder she had not committed. Even though Judy was dead, Diana had been concerned about her. What had Diana said about a concerned killer? If Cynthia's murderer had not been so concerned only one poison would have been used. More people would have died but it would not so blatantly be murder. Diana Hillis. Detective Inspector Hanlon might not want to say it aloud but he wondered about Diana Hillis. He wondered. Had he found his killer?

24

THE ARREST OF Jim Morrison just reinforced the fact that Cynthia's assassin was still amongst them. That one thought never left the bank's staff. One could sense it; one could see it. A wariness was in everyone's eyes. Trust was a forgotten feeling. Suspicions were in everyone's minds though Shirley was still the only one who voiced them and she voiced them everywhere.

"I knew all along that husband was the one," she told her spouse upon hearing of Jim's arrest. "It had to be. He couldn't have killed Cynthia, though. No, no, he couldn't no access. Sounds like a road sign, doesn't it? Where was I? Oh yes, Jim Morrison. No, he couldn't have killed Cynthia. If he could get Judy to steal for him, maybe he got her to kill for him. Now there's an idea. Not much fun though. We would never know for sure. It would never be finished. No, it's got to be finished. What do you think? Do you suppose he had Judy do it after all? Stephen, Stephen; are you listening to me?"

No he wasn't and neither was anyone else lately except Diana. Diana listened to everyone. Shirley she heard from endlessly. But now Shirley was not the only one who wanted to talk. Many of the employees did. Some chose to talk about Cynthia. Some chose to talk about themselves, others about their families. Doris was an exception. She chose not to talk. Since the evening when she confided in Diana, Doris had been avoiding her. It had been subtle. No one but Diana had seemed to notice. Diana had noticed more than that. Doris was scared. Was it possible she was scared of Diana? Did she regret her confession? Didn't she know Diana wouldn't, couldn't, hurt her? How could she? Did Diana know it definitely herself? With these doubts, Diana decided not to pressure Doris to return to their conversation. In time Doris would again turn to her. Where else was there for Doris to go?

"Did you hear, Diana?" shouted Shirley. "Miss Webster has confessed. Can you believe it? Dizzy Doris killed Cynthia!"

"How do you know?"

"I told you," Shirley replied. "She confessed. She walked right into Mr. Manders' office and said right out that she had given Cynthia her coffee. Just like that, if you please. After having hysterics while doing the mail, she was as calm as anything. I did it, she says. Isn't it great! I didn't get to solve it but still who would have thought of our Miss Webster?"

"Were you in his office at the time?" Diana asked.

"As a matter of fact, no. I was in Barbara's and heard it all. You know how close the offices are. With the doors open, you can hear everything!" Shirley said without embarrassment. "I should have known, probably did and couldn't believe it. That's it. I knew but didn't believe it, so dismissed it from my mind. That must be it. This is something! Can you believe it?"

"No," answered Diana.

"I don't think Mr. Manders does either," Shirley said slowing down slightly. "At least, he's not being very careful with a confessed murderer."

"What, he hasn't put Doris in shackles?" Diana asked sarcastically.

"No," Shirley answered in all seriousness. "He hasn't even kept her in his office. He's letting her go anywhere she likes in the office. Wandering around the bank like she's anyone. He did phone the police. I bet they'll be impressed with his handling of a criminal."

"Doris is no criminal," Diana said. "And if you weren't enjoying the drama so much, you would realize Doris didn't kill Cynthia any more than you did."

"I know no such thing," Shirley retorted. "And if Doris didn't do it, maybe I did!" Shirley stamped off to tell someone else her news since Diana had been so disappointing. Shirley ran into a problem, however, finding anyone who hadn't heard by this time.

Everyone had heard and everyone was avoiding Doris. Shirley was correct in that Dave Manders had not known what to do with Doris. No better did Doris know what to do with Doris. She had spent many tortured days and nights in doubt and now that she had spoken she was deflated. The worry was gone; the indecision was gone. Things could return to normal. The rest of the staff did not feel that way. She could sense their discomfort. There was nothing she could do about that. She had always been an outcast. She was used to it. For her, things were going to return to normal. First, though, she had to speak to the police. Doris decided to wait in the coffee room. She would be alone. She wouldn't be bothering anyone. She hoped the police would not be long.

She need not have worried. Upon receiving Manders call Hanlon and Deck practically sprinted to their car and travelling with lights and siren they pulled into the bank's parking lot in record time.

"So God did make her do it," Deck said as soon as Hanlon relayed the details of Manders call.

"It would seem so," was all that Hanlon said. He didn't like it. Did he believe Doris was his murderer? Something felt wrong, contrived. Or was his discomfort because he felt sorry for Doris? Or was it his pride, should he have figured this out without needing this out-of-blue confession? He didn't know but he didn't like it. Poor Doris, he knew what she was in for and he knew she could never cope.

"And she wasn't even on the list as having a key, so how did she get in before the others to make the coffee?" Deck was asking.

"Maybe she didn't," replied Hanlon.

"I get it," Deck said. "She put it in afterwards. So who did made it? Mike Baker lied to avoid suspicion! I hate liars and especially liars who just lie cause they're cowards."

"We don't know any of that yet, Deck," reminded Hanlon. "It's all guess work until we can get it clarified with Manders."

But, sitting in front of Dave Manders, he wondered if they were going to get anything clarified. Manders had visibly aged since their first visit, even since their last visit. The hair was no longer smooth and tidy, the clothes hung baggy against his frame. The illusion of success and youth was gone and Manders didn't look like he noticed or like he cared.

"I didn't know what to do," Manders was saying. "It is so improbable. Miss Webster is…well she isn't…. I would never have believed she was capable of…capable of….any of this. She had trouble with filing. How could she know about the poisons? Where would she get them?"

"I believe her parents had been ill for several years before they died," Hanlon said.

"What's that got to do with this?" Manders asked.

"Doris Webster was involved with their nursing," replied Hanlon. "The knowledge of drugs often is a result of such circumstances."

"If you say so," said Manders doubtfully. "What will happen to her?"

"That will be for the courts, Mr. Manders."

"Yes, yes I know," Manders said. "It doesn't seem fair

somehow. It could have been any one of us. Cynthia was…
It could have been any of us."

"You mean it could have been you?" Hanlon asked.

"Yes, damn it, it could have been!"

"But it wasn't," Hanlon said.

Manders watched Hanlon for a moment before replying.
"She tried to destroy my life," he finally said. "I don't know
yet but she might still succeed. If you had heard her that last
night. I could have killed her!"

"That was the argument that was overheard?" Hanlon
asked.

"Yes," Manders said, finally acknowledging the dis-
agreement. "If you had heard Cynthia, I could have killed
her. Maybe I should have. It's not right that Doris should be
punished for this."

"That's rather noble, Mr. Manders."

"Noble?" Manders said laughing bitterly. "No one,
Inspector, no one would believe that."

Manders walked to his doorway and sent Pat to get
Doris from the staff room.

The scream could well have woken the dead.

It resembled Pat's voice. It paralyzed the office. For a
short moment there was not a sound or movement anywhere in the bank. Then the scream was repeated. Even
louder this time. As the second scream reached its full pitch
both Deck and Hanlon were out of their chairs, guns in hand,
and at a dead run towards the lunchroom. The bankers they
passed enroute remained frozen in place, wide eyed.

A third scream began as Deck entered the lunchroom,
Hanlon on his heels.

25

ECK PUSHED OPEN the lunchroom door and almost crashed to the floor. The reason was twofold, he was trying to avoid a full force collision with Pat, and he had placed one foot squarely into a pool of blood that was spreading across the linoleum floor. The blood was coming from the throat of Doris Webster. Or rather the last few gushes of blood were coming from an open wound that had been the throat of Doris Webster. When she was alive.

Inspector Hanlon followed Deck into the room trying to avoid the thickening blood. He immediately placed his hands on the shoulders of Pat to calm and to steer her. She wasn't screaming now, actually she was gagging and began to vomit as he turned her away from the body and right into several other staff members who were trying to get a look at the body on the floor. Many of the new arrivals then screamed themselves, and Pat was ready to join in.

"Get these people out of here," Hanlon said to no one in particular. He pushed Pat in the direction of one of her co-workers and continued his orders. "Here, look after this woman, and all of you get away from the door. Somebody call 911 for an ambulance. Now!"

Turning away from the doorway and the spectators,

Hanlon carefully made his way over to Deck who was kneeling next to Doris. Deck held one of her blood-drenched arms, and was feeling the wrist for a pulse. There wasn't one. There couldn't possibly be since all Doris' blood was on the floor. She had not been dead long – minutes perhaps. Was she killed while they were with Manders? Deck and Hanlon, saying nothing, both asked the same question.

Deck looked up from his place next to the body. So much blood. As evidence it was useful, but he and Hanlon had contaminated the scene, accidentally of course, when they rushed into the room. They hadn't disturbed the body though. Perhaps Thomas would be able to find something from it. He sure hoped so. He saw a spray pattern of blood on the refrigerator that continued another foot or so along the wall. The forensic boys will be able to tell a lot from that he thought. God, this was a bad one!

Hanlon turned back towards the door. Two of the bank staff were craning their neck around the doorjamb to get a look.

"I said go back into the main office. Go wait for the ambulance or something. Get away from here."

Hanlon often wondered at the attraction that violence, ugliness, and death held for so many people. It was always the same. No one could stand to look but no one had it in their power to turn away. Hanlon did. He had seen too much devastation in his time. It had long ago lost the fascination that attracted civilians.

In spite of his quick instructions to leave the area, most of the staff had seen enough. Enough to keep them awake for many nights. Enough, he knew, that it would stay with them for the rest of their lives. Just as the first gruesome death he had seen still followed him each and every day. These people had seen a lot in the past few weeks. They had been changed the day of Cynthia's death but only with this violence would they realize that. It would be years perhaps before they realized how changed, before they realized the truth   the truth that he had come to realize with all the ugliness of his work.

The violence of unplanned death, the cruelty of one person to another, the baser side of human nature changed everyone involved. Once changed, no one could go back. Hanlon looked at the few faces still in the door and felt a kind of sorrow for them.

"Deck, go and look after the rest of the staff."

Deck stood up, slipping again in the blood. He stepped onto a clear section of the floor nearer Hanlon, leaving behind well-defined shoeprints in blood with each step. As he passed Hanlon to leave the room, he came face to face with Diana and Manders who were finally entering. The four of them stood still and silent.

"Sergeant, the ambulance should be here soon. Please meet the crew at the door. By the way," he interrupted turning to Manders. "Has the door been locked? The bank closed?" Manders just nodded.

"Fine," Hanlon continued, turning back to Deck. "The ambulance crew won't be able to help this poor woman, but they will want to take a quick look for themselves. Then, they'll need to look after the rest of the staff members who've had quite a shock. And call for Thomas too."

"Yes sir." Deck looked relieved to have something to do away from the carnage in the lunchroom. This was nothing like the first visit to this room. Did he ever imagine that first morning that the poisoning of Cynthia Harmon would lead them here? But it had to have. This could not be unrelated. It just couldn't. As he moved towards the main office Hanlon's voice stopped him.

"Sergeant, I think you'll want to clean your shoes and hands a bit before you go out there."

Deck looked down at his hands and saw blood. He saw a lot of blood. He stepped across the hall and into the Men's room. The sound of a tap running at full volume filled the room as Hanlon, Diana and Manders stood facing each other in silence.

26

HANLON TURNED AND squarely faced Diana. He
waited. She said nothing with words but her eyes
slowly made mention of Manders' presence.

"Perhaps you should check that the rest of your staff remain in the office, Mr. Manders," Hanlon said. "See how
everyone is doing from the shock and get them ready for
the ambulance crew."

"Yes," Manders agreed quickly. "Yes, of course."

Once Manders had left the room, the detective and
Diana were alone. Diana looked around for a chair not splat-
tered with Doris' blood, sat down and quietly started to talk.
Hanlon remained standing. He was perfectly still, not moving a muscle or giving a clue to his inner thoughts.

"I'm responsible for this," she said slowly. Diana got up
and tried to pace but the room had little space not covered
in blood and she returned to the chair and to needing to
look up at Hanlon. Raising her eyes to Hanlon's, she read
his reaction   .

"No, Inspector, this is not a confession. I almost wish it
were so this could end. I thought she was safe. I honestly
did. I was watching Shirley."

"Shirley?" Hanlon asked interrupting.

"With her snooping and her questions," Diana answered. "I worried for her safety. I didn't think Doris was in danger. I was a fool and I cost her her life."

"I see," said Hanlon professionally almost coldly.

"No, you don't see," Diana said shortly. Bouncing out the chair she stood to face him as an equal. "Doris was worried, scared. She had started to confide in me but we were interrupted. We were interrupted." She repeated these words slowly to herself and sat back down. "She had started to talk to me and then became scared and avoided me. I left her alone. I thought she was safe. I was wrong, so very wrong."

Diana stopped and disappeared into her own thoughts. Hanlon waited. Taking a deep breath, Diana steeled herself to continue her confession.

"Do you want to hear the rest, the ironic part?" Diana asked. Hanlon knew it was a rhetorical question and made no reply.

"I didn't tell you," Diana continued. "I was protecting her."

"From what?" asked Hanlon although he knew the answer. He had heard it many times.

"From you," Diana replied.

Diana waited for a response from Hanlon but none was forthcoming. How could she tell him all she had to say? Would he even believe her? He hid it as best as he could but she saw his mistrust. He doubted her every word. Could she have done anything different that would have changed where they were now? It was a pointless question. They couldn't go back. Judy and Doris were now gone; gone while she and he danced around each other. It was too late to change the story. What had to be done would be done as best as she could do it. Somehow she had to convince him.

"Doris told me who killed Cynthia," Diana said.

"Really," Hanlon said sharply. "And this is the information you kept from me."

"Yes."

"You thought she would need protection from me if I knew this?"

"Yes."

"I see," said Hanlon trying to hide the anger that was more personal than he cared to admit.

"You don't see," Diana said desperately. "Doris killed Cynthia!"

"So what is this?" Hanlon asked impatiently waving his hand at Doris's pitiful body. He couldn't let this happen; he was a professional. He had to remain calm and alert. There was no room for his personal feelings   none at all. Three people were dead and he was dealing with murder.

"Doris killed Cynthia," Diana repeated. "Doris gave Cynthia that cup of poisoned coffee but she was just an instrument in the murder. She was used. If you would quit thinking of me as your only suspect," she continued, rising once more to her feet, "I could tell you who killed Cynthia and Doris. I've told you how. I could tell you who. I didn't do it. Damn it, I swear I didn't!"

Deck returned just as Diana finished speaking and was met with an unnerving silence. The room was full of anger. He couldn't miss that. Diana slowly returned to her chair primly sitting with her head down looking at nothing but her hands. Hanlon's anger Deck could feel from the doorway. The Inspector seldom showed anger or even felt it. Deck had seen it only once or twice before and each time he hoped he would never have to see it again.

"Yes, Sergeant," Hanlon barked.

"The coroner is on his way," Deck said. Glancing at Diana, he didn't know if he should say anything further.

"You can say whatever is on your mind, Sergeant," Hanlon said with more control.

"Yes, sir," Deck answered. "I've taken Mr. Manders' official statement. He didn't have much more to say than what he told us on the phone. I understand Doris Webster didn't elaborate on her confession while with him. She said that she gave Cynthia Harmon the poisoned coffee and that she wanted to talk to the police. That was all. He then called us. Doris Webster left his office to wait for us to arrive. He never left his office and never saw her again."

"Thank you, Sergeant," Hanlon said slowly. "I want you to remain here until the coroner is finished and the body is removed. Continue on with the interviews. I will meet you back at the station. I'm taking Miss Hillis there now."

Both Deck and Diana had surprise in their faces but neither said anything. Neither of them knew where to look. They couldn't look at each other with their questions nor at Hanlon with their doubts.

"She has an idea," Hanlon continued, "I'd like to check out further. I'm going to have her look at what we've got so far. With knowing the deceased so well, she might see something we missed."

Did this mean he believed her, Diana wondered? No, she didn't think so. Looking at him, she saw many things. She saw an intense man, an attractive man, but first, she saw a policeman. No, she didn't think he believed her. Why should he?

"Yes, Sir," Deck said. This was not a time to disagree.

Diana rose and headed towards the door. Hanlon followed behind her. Deck moved to let them pass. Turning back towards Doris, he almost whistled. What was Hanlon doing? What was his plan? Did he have one? This was one nutty case.

27

DIANA FOLLOWED HANLON out to the squad car. What was this about, she asked herself but said nothing out loud. Neither did Hanlon. Silently they got in the car and pulled away from the bank.

Hanlon did not turn onto Cook Street heading towards the police station. Instead he headed the car up Fairfield towards Oak Bay. Diana sensed more than watched Hanlon. He was still angry but even so his movements were smooth, controlled. He was restful. This man who wanted to arrest her, she found restful?! What had she got herself into? She refused to ask where they were going and settled into watching the sights that were passing by her window.

There was little traffic as they rolled first past houses, then a few shops and the back of a school. Gently curving up a small hill they came upon a neighbourhood shopping mall on the left and the Ross Bay Cemetery on the right. She had lived in this area for a short time in a modest rented house. That was after her husband's death and before she and Anna bought the one they now lived in. Life did have a way of changing.

Hanlon turned off of Fairfield and onto Richmond heading for Oak Bay, little knowing this was the exact route that Cynthia had taken each and every day to work. That's where they were going. Hanlon was taking Diana to Cynthia Harmon's condominium. Why? He didn't really know. There was something. The relationship of these two women was intertwined throughout this case. It had been there before Cynthia Harmon's death. Had it driven the events that followed? In some ways he felt it had driven his investigation. That was over.

Hanlon turned onto Oak Bay Avenue still with no words. With most suspects silence was more unnerving than questions. He felt no such uneasiness in Diana. She sat quietly beside him and seemed to him, serenely confident. Good company to Hanlon was someone you could sit in silence with comfortably. Hanlon saw Diana scanning the shops they passed as they went through Oak Bay village. It was peaceful driving with someone who didn't need to talk the whole time. He was finding Diana good company. He also still found her a good suspect.

Maybe the silence was just Diana's reluctance to slip and say something that could ensnare her. Maybe the serene confidence was because she felt no guilt. Hanlon had to stop this. He would drive himself nuts and not be able to see the truth when it appeared. Diana knew Cynthia, she knew all the suspects and she herself was a suspect. He would give her every opportunity to either screw up and show herself as the killer or to help expose the real killer. He told himself it didn't matter which happened, he just wanted the case solved. He knew that wasn't true.

"This is where Cynthia Harmon lived," he said pulling in front of the building.

"Nice," Diana said getting out of the car. "Very nice," she remarked after they had entered the building and she stood looking out the picture window.

Hanlon let Diana wander throughout the apartment watching what she noticed, what she picked up, what she ignored.

"Our Cynthia did all right for herself," Diana said. "I never gave it much thought how or where Cynthia lived but this would suit her. It's all money and style but no life and no warmth. You know, for the first time, I believe she's dead. It's funny but I can almost feel sorry for her. I'm glad you brought me here, Inspector. I don't know why you did, but I'm glad."

"I brought you here to look at these," Hanlon said walking towards the dining room table. On it were all of Cynthia's photo albums and her records. "We need to know more about the people in Miss Harmon's life."

"Her victims you mean," replied Diana.

Hanlon didn't directly answer. Opening the first album, he continued, "You said you knew who killed Cynthia and how. The why might be in these records. Then you can tell me your theory." Diana said nothing. Hanlon continued, "We believe these people contributed to Miss Harmon's life-style over the years. Some might not have been voluntary."

"Oh, I think you can be sure of that, Inspector," Diana said. Sitting down at the table, Diana started going through the books one by one. Hanlon wandered around the apartment trying not to hover over Diana. Finally he settled on the couch watching her and waiting.

"Many of these are old," Diana mused. "Surely these people would have moved on with their lives. Cynthia would no longer be a threat."

"Had you?" asked Hanlon. "And why did you say threat?"

"Because of the style of killings, I guess," Diana said ignoring his first question. "They both seem like something that had to be done. There was almost desperation especially with poor Doris. Like killing was to protect something rather than gain something. Oh, I don't know. I'm just rambling."

"No, what you say makes some sense," Hanlon said, watching as Diana stopped at a particular picture. She frowned and moved on to another then turned back to it. She handed it to Hanlon.

"Do you know who any of these people are?" Diana asked. Hanlon shook his head.

"It's a long time ago," Diana said continuing. "Looks like from when she was in Vancouver – you know the group home. Most of the other pictures are just one or two people. This is a group shot. It's funny and there's something familiar about it. I'm not sure what though." She reached for the picture and Hanlon returned it. She continued on through the albums and came across the more current ones including one of Mr. Manders with his wife, Sybil.

"You know, Inspector," Diana said. "We may be making this more complicated than it is."

*   *   *   *   *

Deck had returned to the station only to discover Hanlon and Diana were not there. Neither was there any message from Hanlon. Deck set about completing the reports on Doris's death. He was not overly surprised to find Hanlon was not at the station. This case from the beginning had not been predictable.

Deck liked things simple. Most things were, he found. Some people's human nature just had to complicate things. It wasn't his. At first, Cynthia Harmon's death had seemed obvious. She had been having an affair with Manders; it was getting ugly. It was his only way out. It would have been tidy and easy, except for Cynthia Harmon. She had made so many enemies. There were too many suspects and they were good suspects. Doris Webster's death was different though. Deck went back over the morning's events.

It was a rushed affair. And risky. Thomas had said she was likely killed not long before they had arrived. Someone had walked up to her and killed as quickly as they could. Someone who Doris knew was a killer. Why had she let that person get so close to her? He answered his own question – she was Doris.

There was so much blood. Thomas said with the angle of the cut and the apparent speed of the act, the killer could have avoided getting much or any of Doris's blood on themselves. Deck didn't believe that. The perpetrator had to have got some on them. That's what Deck believed. Yet he hadn't found anyone with blood on their clothing and he had looked hard. Pat's shoes had a little blood on them. That was understandable, she'd been the one to find Doris. Of course, she also could have killed Doris then stepped away and started the screaming. Pat hadn't shown up as a real suspect in any of their investigation. Yet she too had not been upset by Cynthia's death. Deck wondered. He wondered just how much they knew about Pat.

The interviews with the staff had yielded nothing. No one admitted to going into the backroom after Doris had talked to Manders. Three people admitted to being in the washroom at the time of the screams. Any one of them could have been washing away the blood. No one admitted seeing anyone doing so. No one remembered seeing anyone coming or going or doing anything. It was nothing, nothing, nothing.

Deck finished his report just as Hanlon and Diana entered the detectives' room. Deck watched them as they headed towards him. There weren't any handcuffs on Diana. The anger seemed to be gone. They had brought some of Cynthia's belongings back with them. Deck watched as they unloaded the photo albums, the bank records. Had Hanlon's idea worked? Had they found something? Were they finally going to solve this case? Deck had a ton of questions and hoped Hanlon was about to answer them. Hanlon looked at him and smiled. They were close.

28

As Diana and Hanlon had come out of the lunchroom into the main banking hall, all noise ceased. The employees, who worked in the open counter area, stopped and silently watched Diana and Hanlon cross the banking hall to the front entrance. Those employees who were in their offices looked up and watched intently. Hanlon and Diana stopped just outside Manders' office waiting to be let out and the bank door locked behind them.

Manders looked up from his office desk but did not rise or say anything. Neither Hanlon nor Diana glanced in his direction. Pat who sat right outside Manders office got up from her desk and let them out the bank's front door. She looked directly into Diana's eyes and then turned away.

After locking the door, Pat turned back towards the inner part of the bank and found all her colleagues' eyes upon her. They looked like frozen statues that were slowly starting to thaw. Their faces reflected apprehension, bewilderment and then understanding. Even without handcuffs the common conclusion was obvious: Diana was guilty.

Everyone remembered the little clashes between the two women. The staff had remained much the same over the last three years. They all had grown to know Cynthia and Diana well, well enough to know the friction between them. Was it hate?

"She always did hate Cynthia," Pat said to the group at large. There it was, out in the open. Some nodded; some mumbled; no one disagreed. Little more was said and everyone slowly went back to work with little energy and little interest.

The ambulance, the forensic team and finally the coroner arrived. They went through their business yet again and Deck went through another round of interviews. The staff was getting used to the intrusion. It was starting to be even more familiar than the audits.

The medical and investigation teams finally left and with Doris's death happening early in the day, the bank reopened. To what extent possible, activity returned to normal. So did the conversations, all of which centered on Diana's guilt.

"Diana could never hurt Doris," Shirley said, contradicting the common opinion.

"Maybe she had to," Mike suggested. "To protect herself."

Shirley shook her head with a sadness she had never felt before. The game was no longer interesting. There had never really been any excitement. Diana would never and could never hurt Doris. Sooner or later the police would probably realize that. She knew that for a fact now, didn't she? What could she do? This wasn't right. She needed to think. Mike and the others were insisting it was all over. There was almost rejoicing with those words. Shirley for once had nothing to say. She wasn't listening and no longer heard Mike and the others. Later, at home, she still wasn't listening and didn't hear Stephen.

Stephen had heard his wife come in their front door and had moved from the kitchen to greet her. Shirley walked as if in a trance as Steve called to her. She wandered up the steps towards him and slowly followed him into the kitchen where he had been preparing dinner. Stephen continued talking as he turned back to the counter where he had been working. Shirley slid onto a barstool across from him and finally awoke to his words.

"Shirley," Stephen was saying slowly. "The radio said there was another death at the bank and that the police have a suspect." He watched his wife with a seriousness that denied the stillness of his voice.

"Doris," Shirley said quietly. "And Diana."

"Doris and Diana, what?" Stephen asked.

"Doris is dead and I think Diana's arrested."

Stephen turned his attention back to peeling the vegetables and waited for his wife to continue, as he knew she would.

"It's all mixed up, it's a mess," she said. "Doris went into Mr. Manders' office and confessed to Cynthia's murder. I heard her. The police came and when they went to talk to her, she was dead – her throat was cut and there was blood all over the lunchroom. Then Diana left with the police. Everyone was interviewed again. No one saw anything, no one knows anything but everyone is saying that Diana's guilty, that she's been arrested for the murders."

"Which murders?" Stephen asked. "I thought Jim Morrison was already arrested for Judy's murder?"

"For the others, for Cynthia and Doris," she replied. "But it's wrong, she didn't do it. It shouldn't have turned out this way. Doris shouldn't have had to die."

Stephen watched his wife with concern. This pensive woman was not the Shirley he knew. Stephen moved around to Shirley's side of the counter.

"It's for the best," he tried to explain putting his arm around his wife's shoulder. "This can't go on. I know she was your friend but if she's guilty, she's guilty and it's better this comes to an end."

"It's not right," Shirley said sadly. "And it won't really be finished if the wrong person goes to jail."

Further discussion was halted by the ringing of their

phone. As Shirley showed no sign of hearing it, Stephen walked over to the far wall of the kitchen and lifted the phone off its hook.

"It's for you," he said holding the receiver out for his wife. Shirley walked over to his side and took the phone.

"Yes?" she said without interest.

"Hello, Shirley," the voice said. "This is Diana."

*   *   *   *   *

As soon as Mike opened the front door to the Bakers' townhouse a similar conversation started. He took off his coat, hung it up and gave his wife a quick kiss. In between those movements, he recapped the day's events. However the focus and concern here was not for Diana, it was all for Mike.

"I'm not in any danger," Mike insisted.

"Not in any danger," Linda shouted hysterically. "Three people are dead! Three people! It's never going to stop, never."

Mike held his wife close against him as he guided her into their living area. Stepping around the toys, he picked up the remote and muted the TV. When he reached their couch, he moved the throw rug and pillows and sat down. Taking his wife's hand he gently pulled her down beside him. He held her in the crook of his arm soothing her as best as he could. She cried softly into his shoulder for several moments.

"Please, please," she whined. "Can't you leave that place?"

"Be serious, darling," Mike said. "We need the money."

Linda began to cry again from the latest in a long line of stresses and Mike held her close.

"It'll be alright," he said. "Trust me. Nothing will happen to me. It's over, I think. The police took Diana away with them. Everyone knows she has always hated Cynthia.

It looks like she's going to be charged with the murders. There's nothing to worry about. There won't be any more deaths and the police won't be coming by again. Trust me, haven't I always taken care of us? We'll be fine."

"Really?" she asked wanting to be reassured. Mike tightened his arms around her and whispered softly into her ear. Slowly amid the whispers and kisses Linda's tears stopped and a little smile returned to her lips.

"It's so horrible," Linda said returning to the original subject. "How could she do that to that poor old lady? How could anyone?"

"There probably wasn't any choice," Mike explained. "Sometimes things happen that make you do things you don't really want to." They sat quietly and after several minutes Mike, believing things were settled, rose.

"What's for dinner?" he asked moving towards the kitchen. "And where's my girl Erica?"

"Do you think Diana did it?" she asked, rising to follow him into the kitchen but not quite ready to follow him in his change of conversation.

Mike shrugged as he turned back to the living room to pick up the ringing phone.

*   *   *   *   *

Alone in the dining room of their Rockland home, there was little sign that Sybil and Dave Manders had ever shared the same state of affectation that Mike and Linda did. They sat at opposite ends of the formal dining room table separated by more than the floral centerpiece.

Dave had come home early, wanting to talk to Sybil. His world was unraveling. With Diana's departure and probable arrest, he was hoping things could get back on track. However his early arrival had not spurred Sybil into conversation. Instead she had had the dinner accelerated and here they sat. Dave picked at the food on his plate and wondered how to start. Here too there was no concern for Diana or Doris or even Cynthia. It was all about Dave.

"Couldn't you change your mind about going away?" Dave asked finally to break the silence. His wife looked up at him but didn't answer. Instead she continued with apparent enjoyment to eat her evening meal. "Could you at least delay it a bit? It's going to be hard enough getting things back together after all this. I still could lose my job and you want to leave me without a home, without friends, without any money. Okay, I made a mistake, one mistake. Why can't you forgive me? I would forgive you. I love you. That's what people who love each other do – forgive. Don't I mean anything to you? Didn't I ever?"

"You can ask me that?" Sybil said by way of an answer. "Never mind. It was a long time ago and I was another person. Young, I was very young and looking back now, I can only feel very foolish. Every time I look at you I am reminded of what a fool I was." She folded her napkin and laid it beside her plate before she continued.

"One mistake you say," she remarked. "Which one would that be?"

"Why, Cynthia, of course," Dave replied surprised.

"I see," his wife said with controlled calm. "Not the woman you were with the night before our wedding, not the woman you tried to seduce during our honeymoon, not the whole list of others?"

"What are you talking about?" asked her husband stunned.

"You know exactly what I'm talking about," Sybil continued. "I told you I have known all along what you were like and what you were doing. There was always someone very happy to tell me all the details of all your little pastimes."

Dave did not welcome this information. Their life had been very happy in his mind. They never argued; theirs was a calm dignified marriage. He had married for money and position and he had found more. He had found a marriage he never dreamed was possible and now it was all slipping away.

"All these years," he asked. "Was it all a fraud?"

"It was on your side," his wife said not bending. "Why shouldn't it be on my side."

"We were happy," Dave insisted. "We were. Please can't we go back? Can't we try? I need you."

"You need my money," Sybil replied. "That's all you ever needed and all you ever wanted." She rose from the table and left the room, assuming the conversation was over. She had been in control of their home for so long she was not prepared for her husband as he followed her into the front parlour area. Sybil took a seat in her favourite wing chair and picked up the book she had been reading earlier. Dave came and stood directly in front refusing to let the discussion die.

"Not any more," he continued. "Maybe in the beginning. But now I need you and I want you. If you want to go away, we can go away. If you want to stay, I'll stay. I have nothing without you."

"This thing with Cynthia has totally unnerved you, hasn't it?" Sybil said looking up at him with more curiosity than real interest.

"It was a mistake," Dave said flatly.

"What was," Sybil refusing to let it end there. "Getting caught with her in your little affair? Or that she had to be killed?"

"Her death has nothing to do with us," Dave insisted. Sybil stood up and Dave backed up slightly. She stood solid before him and waited.

"I told you the police took Diana away," Dave said. "It's over."

"You said that before," Sybil replied moving away from him and towards the hallway.

"This time it is," Dave said disheartened. "Please don't go."

"I told you I wouldn't leave before things were settled," Sybil finally admitted. "I hope this time it really is finished."

"It is," Dave said as the phone started to ring.

*   *   *   *   *

Dr. Scott came up behind his wife as she stood looking in the antique mirror that hung in their entrance hall. She had been late home and arrived only a few moments before. She had taken off her coat, hung it properly in the front closet. She was tired. She showed no sign of seeing what was in the mirror. She showed no sign of seeing her husband.

"Not getting vain, are we, darling?" he asked.

A startled Barbara jumped and spun around. Her husband laughed and took her hands.

"Now what is occupying your precious thoughts?" he asked. His wife smiled and shook her head slightly. "I don't like seeing you worry like this. It's not good. Remember, Barbara, you do not have to work there any longer if it's too much for you."

"No," Barbara said quietly. "I'm alright."

"If it starts to affect your health, you can quit this instant."

"It's nothing," Barbara insisted. "Besides I have already given my notice. What's a couple more weeks?"

Robert Scott put his hand under his wife's elbow and led her firmly the few steps needed to reach the start of the oak staircase.

"These unpleasant events have upset you, I'm afraid more than you want to admit. I suggest you rest for a few minutes before dinner. If what I heard on the radio is correct, these last weeks should be uneventful. If not, if this suspect doesn't get charged, I still may have you leave sooner."

"I can't Robert," Barbara insisted.

"If you say so, darling," her husband said patronizing

her. "We will see." Then more firmly he added, "You know I don't like problems in my life and there is always a way to eliminate them."

"There won't be any more problems," Barbara said as her husband turned away from her and moved towards his study's desk and its ringing phone.

29

ANNA HILLIS DROVE her blue Honda Civic into her driveway and walked in through her front door to find Diana hanging up the hallway phone.

"Who are you talking to?" she asked. "And what's going on? The radio said there was another death at the Bank and the police finally have a suspect."

"That's three questions. And you can only have one," Diane replied.

"Stop it, Diana," Anna said. "This isn't funny. People are dying."

"Yes, I know," Diana said. Sadly, she then added, "It was Doris today."

"Doris!" Anna repeated in amazement. "Why would someone kill Doris? She was killed wasn't she?" But Diana had walked away and was no longer in the hallway. Anna followed her in through the house to the kitchen and repeated her question.

"Was she killed?"

"Yes," Diana replied closing the fridge door. She put the cheese from the fridge on the counter and reached for a large knife. Anna watched in shocked silence as Diana started cutting the cheese and arranging it on a large platter.

She stopped and looked at the knife and then her sister.

"She had her throat cut," Diana said.

"I don't like this," Anna stated emphatically. "Talk to me! What is going on? I don't understand any of this and I don't understand you. You're scaring me."

This brought Diana back from wherever her mind had taken her and for the first time she seemed to notice how upset Anna was.

"It's alright, Anna," Diana said reassuringly. "It's almost over. In fact I'm going to end it tonight."

"What are you talking about," Anna demanded.

"Sit down and let me finish this. I'll tell you while I get ready." Diana turned back to the cutting board and Anna sat at the kitchen table. "While you can't believe everything you hear on the news, in this case they are mostly right," Diana continued reaching back into the fridge for pickles to add to the platter. "There was another death, Doris. And I think most people believe someone was or will be arrested, me."

"You!"

"I'm not," Diana said. "But I think I'm still suspected. Anyway that doesn't matter."

"Doesn't matter!"

"If you keep repeating everything, this will take a long time." Diana stated matter-of-factly.

"Okay continue, but could you try and do it in some order so it makes sense."

"Doris went into to Mr. Manders' office this morning and confessed to giving Cynthia the poisoned coffee."

"What?!" Anna interrupted and received a quick frown from Diana. "Sorry," she added and waited for Diana to continue.

"Mr. Manders phoned the police and by the time they arrived someone had slit her throat in the staff room. She was dead." Diana paused for a moment before proceeding. "Doris had confided in me and because of that and for other reasons, the Inspector had me leave the bank with him. I imagine most people thought we were going to the police station and that I was being arrested. We did go to the police station but first the Inspector took me to Cynthia's apartment. It's very nice by the way."

"I don't care how nice Cynthia's apartment is, was, whatever!" an exasperated Anna snapped.

"Anyway," Diana continued. "The Inspector had me look through a lot of Cynthia's stuff. We then went to the police station and he showed me the files. We talked a bit. Then he let me go. He didn't arrest me or charge me or whatever. He just let me go. He didn't even really say anything. He still thinks I might be a murderer, the murderer."

"I can't believe that," argued Anna. "You couldn't kill anyone. He must know that. He liked you and you liked him. I could tell. He couldn't think you could kill someone."

"You don't think other murderers have people who like them?" Diana teased. "It doesn't matter," she continued. "He can't let himself trust me. I can see it in his eyes. And why should he? I could have killed Cynthia. No," she said silencing her sister. "I could have killed Cynthia a hundred times over but not Doris. For Doris this has to stop. So I have invited a few people over to bring this to a conclusion. One way or another it stops here tonight."

"You've invited them here? To unmask a murderer? You're asking to be killed yourself!"

"If that's what it takes." Diana replied taking the cheese and pickle tray with the knife into the living room and leaving Anna confused and alone.

*　　*　　*　　*　　*

Linda continued on towards the kitchen as her husband picked up the phone. Upon hearing him say, "Hi, Diana" she turned around and went to stand right beside him. She listened to every word of Mike's side of the conversation.

As soon as he up, Mike relayed everything Diana had said. Linda didn't like it.

"But what does she want?" Linda asked her husband. "I thought you said she was arrested?"

"We thought she was," Mike answered. "She left with the police. Now, I don't know. That's why I have to go."

"What did she say?" asked his wife once more.

"Nothing more than I told you," Mike replied trying to appear calm but Linda could see the nervousness. He moved back to the front door he so recently had walked through and once again reached for his coat. "She said that the killings had to stop, that she had some ideas she wanted to discuss with me and that I should come over to her place tonight."

"Don't go," Linda begged.

"I have to," Mike replied. "What would it look like if I didn't. I won't be long, promise." With those words Mike left to see what Diana knew or thought she knew.

*   *   *   *   *

Dr. Scott handed the receiver to his wife without moving. He listened closely to every word and when Barbara hung up, he questioned her until the whole conversation had been repeated.

"Well you are not going alone," Dr. Robert Scott said to his wife. "I have had enough of this whole thing."

"I know, Robert," Barbara replied. "I'm sorry any of this happened. I know how upsetting it is for you."

"Now, now," Robert said condescendingly. "It's not your fault. Even though we wouldn't have been involved if you hadn't insisted on going to work. Oh well, it's over now or will be once we finish with tonight. Then things can go back to the way we like them."

"Yes, Robert," Barbara agreed. "After tonight it will be finished. At least that's what she said. But really you don't need to come, I'm fine by myself."

"No, my dear," Robert insisted. "This is going to be finished and will no longer to be a disruption in our lives. I'm coming if nothing else to make sure this Diana Hillis understands that. Now get your coat and I'll bring the car around."

*   *   *   *   *

The Manders were having a similar conversation as they walked up to Diana's door. It was a conversation that had started the moment Dave had hung up the phone from Diana's call.

"You didn't have to come," Dave was saying to Sybil.

"Didn't she ask for me specifically?" Sybil replied.

"Well, yes," Dave said hesitantly. "But I don't know that it was important."

"Not important," Sybil replied with scorn. "Three people are dead, Dave."

"Yes, yes, I know." Dave said. "You just won't understand me. What I'm trying to say. You need not be bothered by all this."

"You are still my property and I take care of my property," Sybil replied. Then quickly added as she saw her husband start to preen, "Don't get any ideas, nothing has changed. I just don't want you to do anything else that's stupid."

Dave wilted and Sybil continued, "Oh don't pout, Dave. Besides I've always thought Diana was very bright so I want to see what kind of show she's arranged."

"How can you talk like that? I've never seen you like this."

"You never have seen me. At least not in a very long time," replied Sybil looking straight into her husband eyes. "Ring the doorbell, Dave."

30

SHIRLEY BURST INTO Diana's crowded living room with her husband Stephen in tow. "Am I too late? Did I miss anything?" Diana's phone call had rejuvenated Shirley. All her energy and interest was back. Looking around, she saw a collection of somber, sullen faces. "Well, nothing's happening! Why are you all just sitting there like that?" she exclaimed.

"We were waiting for you," Diana replied. Shirley was right, Diana thought looking around the room. Everyone was seated and silent. There was a tenseness in the room. There was no talking, no movement.

Diana stood near her fireplace in front of her guests like a teacher in front of her classroom. The floor cushions that usually filled this area had been removed to make more room. Directly opposite her was a large window through which one could see the front garden and watch the traffic on the street. In front of the window was a small couch with reading lamps on small tables at both ends. Here Dave Manders sat, obviously stressed. No longer was he the man who had everything. Now he looked tired and lost. Sybil Manders sat beside him on the couch looked as calm and gracious as always. Well maybe not quite as always, she was discretely watching everyone very carefully.

To Diana's left, beside the fireplace was the door to the kitchen. Across the left wall, a slightly larger couch sat in front of a wall full of books. Here Barbara Scott sat waiting and, like Sybil, watching. Her husband sat beside her annoyed and arrogant. He kept reaching towards the cheese and pickle tray, which had been placed on the center coffee table.

To Diana's right were two armchairs. Mike sat on the front edge of one trying to look relaxed. He was not succeeding. Behind Mike was the doorway to the front hall and the front entrance. It was here that Shirley stood with her husband.

"Well I'm here," she declared. "Let's get the show on the road."

Shirley moved across the room and sat down beside Barbara Scott on the large couch. Rather than take the remaining empty chair, Stephen followed her and perched himself beside his wife on the couch's arm.

At that moment, Pat appeared in the hall doorway.

"What are you doing here?" Manders demanded.

"Diana invited me," Pat responded neutrally. There was no answer to that as each one of them was there for that same reason. Pat took the empty chair beside Mike.

Diana offered refreshments to the new arrivals. Robert Scott continued to be the only one eating. Everyone had accepted drinks.

Anna brought in the final refreshments. She left the room giving her sister a look that said, "I want no part of this."

Diana looked around the room and slowly started to walk back and forth in front of the fireplace as she talked.

"I have known Cynthia Harmon a long time. Before she was Cynthia Harmon in fact. She was always like you knew her, greedy, mean. She liked to hurt people and she did hurt a lot of them. When she died, I wasn't sorry. I don't think any of us were." She stopped and looked at the faces watching her. No one disagreed. Diana continued, "It seemed like a kind of justice. It wasn't. Even so if it had stopped there, I don't know what I would have done. Would I have left it like that?" She asked this last question more to herself than her audience. No one moved.

"But it didn't," stated Shirley prodding her along.

"No it didn't," resumed Diana turning back towards the group. "And two more people died. Innocent people died. Would Jim Morrison have tried to kill Judy if Cynthia hadn't been murdered? I don't think so. And then Doris. Doris had to die, I understand that. She knew how Cynthia was killed. She knew who had killed her. She, in fact, had killed her. But being Doris she was still searching for another answer. I'm not Doris, I'm not searching, and I will not let Doris' murderer go free,"

Diana stopped and looked from one face to another. "I am also not going to let the shadow of guilt fall over all of us any longer."

"What's all this melodrama, Diana," asked Mike. Leaning to put his glass on the coffee table, he made motion towards rising as he continued, "Do you know something or not?"

"I know that you had plenty of means, opportunity and a motive to kill Cynthia," she replied. "And Doris' death was an act of desperation. And you, Mike, are a desperate man. Have been for some time. We all have seen that."

"We sure have," chimed in Shirley.

"You're not without suspicion yourself, Shirley," Mike said diverting the attention from himself. "Maybe all this insistence that you were going to find the killer was to keep anyone including the police from suspecting you! And who had a better opportunity to kill Cynthia than the person who sat right across from her?"

"Aw, come on," Stephen said rising slowly. "You know that is nonsense. You know Shirley wouldn't do something like that."

"Like what, Stephen," replied Diana. "Poison Cynthia or

slit Doris' throat?" Stephen stood still and silent. Slowly he sat back down with his arm over Shirley's shoulder. Diana continued, "Do we ever really know what another person will do? What about it, Dr. Robert Scott? Can you say definitely what your wife will and will not do?"

"Of course I can," Robert answered. "And right now she is leaving as I see no reason why we should stay."

"No?" asked Diana. "How easy is it to get paraldehyde, Doctor? Pretty easy for you, maybe pretty easy for a doctor's wife?"

"He didn't even know her," Barbara stated. "Neither of us did. I didn't meet any of these people or you until I started working there. It's not like I knew Cynthia like you did," she said to Diana and then turning to Manders. "Or you did."

"What are you looking at me for," Dave Manders sputtered. "I didn't kill her."

"Never mind, darling," Sybil said. "Diana is just stirring things up to see what we'll say, to see if someone will let something slip. Aren't you, Diana?"

Diana shrugged. Turning back to the fireplace, she waited for a moment and then started to talk once again. "Doris is dead. She did not deserve to die. Maybe Cynthia didn't either. I don't know. But Doris' death I can't and won't let go unpunished. Regardless of what the police think, I didn't kill either of them and I'm not going to be the scapegoat. Nor am I going to let anyone, except the guilty one, be blamed or suspected. We need this closed so we can get on with our lives. I brought you all here to show you," she paused and turned back to face the group, "what you are doing to people who have done you no harm. You were compassionate enough to use two poisons so only Cynthia would die. Are you really willing to leave us all under the shadow of guilt, to have an innocent bystander be blamed for your crime? Or are you willing to go on killing? That's your choices. Don't you want all this to stop?"

"Who exactly are you talking to, Diana?" Pat demanded.

"Diana is just making a point, my dear," answered Sybil. "She's talking to whoever killed Cynthia or Doris. She is saying one of us killed them." Pausing Sybil stared straight into Diana's eyes. Diana stayed perfectly still seeing no one but Sybil. There was silence until Sybil continued. "Maybe she's right. Not one of us is sorry Cynthia is dead and any one of us could probably have killed her. We all know it. But not everyone needed or wanted Doris dead and we all didn't have the opportunity to kill Doris, isn't that right, Diana?"

"Yes," Diana said. Looking full at Sybil, she added, "But it doesn't mean that the same person killed Doris."

"Really, Diana," she laughed. "You expect us to believe in 3 killers!"

"Any one of us could have killed Cynthia," Diana said, repeating Sybil's words.

"I protest," Robert started to say.

"Protest all you want, but it's true," Diana continued turning to step directly in front of him. "But only someone who works at the bank could have killed Doris. Doris died to protect whoever killed Cynthia. Dave could have been protecting you, Sybil." Diana said as she wheeled around directly facing Sybil.

"Good God," Dave exclaimed. "What are you saying?"

"She's not saying anything, darling," Sybil said never, taking her eyes off Diana. "Are you, Diana?" The two women faced each other like two fighters ready, willing and able to go the distance. A hush went over the rest of the group. After a few moments the sounds of stirring could be heard. This seemed to reawaken Diana. She broke off from Sybil, turned around and walked back towards the fireplace.

"What is this, Diana?" asked Shirley. She was sitting very still holding onto her husband's hand.

"I thought you wanted to find the killer, Shirley?" asked Diana rhetorically. "That's what this is about. So what precisely am I saying?" Diana paused and looked around the room before settling on Shirley's face. "I'm saying you could have killed Cynthia and Doris. Who had a better opportunity? You were sitting right across the desk from Cynthia. It would be easy to slip something into her coffee. But maybe you considered that would be too obvious so you used Doris. Did you have to use Doris? You said you were going to kill Cynthia and maybe you did. You were first to hear Doris was going to talk to the police. You could easily have got Doris alone. You've known everything about the deaths, even about Judy. Did you really figure it out or did you know because you are the killer?

"You're crazy," Shirley said, less sure of herself and of Diana.

"Am I?" asked Diana.

"Why would I kill her?"

"That is a question," admitted Diana. "Maybe all the losses weren't by Judy. Maybe some of the monies that's missing went into your pocket. Maybe Cynthia found out or found out something else you didn't want her to know."

"That's nonsense. You're making this all up. Grasping at straws, that's what you're doing! And I wasn't the first one to hear Doris confess. Barbara was there too," Shirley said. Pointing at Pat she added, "And Pat could have heard everything from her desk!"

"Now wait just a minute," Pat said indignantly.

"And what about Mr. Manders?" Shirley continued. "He was the real first person to hear.

"Yes, there's Dave," Diana said thoughtfully turning to face Dave and Sybil. "An untidy affair would not have fit well in your world, would it, Sybil? A husband over his head with a parasite, is that how you saw the situation? Is that why you decided something needed to be done?"

"She didn't....." Dave started to say.

"Don't say anything, Dave," Sybil said, never taking her eyes from Diana's face. "She is only guessing."

"Yes, I'm guessing," Diana said smiling. "I'm guessing Dave is too weak and too cowardly to have planned and committed Cynthia's murder. But I'm guessing if you were in it together, he would be just desperate enough to kill Doris." Sybil just smiled. Dave Manders squirmed in his seat and couldn't continue to be silent.

"She didn't do anything!" Dave stated finally. "And I called the police right away when Doris confessed. Why would I do that if I were guilty? And why would Doris confess to me if she knew I had killed Cynthia? None of your suggestions make any sense." Dave visibly relaxed feeling he cleared himself cleanly.

"Who says you gave the coffee directly to Cynthia?" Diana asked. Turning towards Pat, "Who says you didn't give it to someone, someone who you're always giving instructions to and who is constantly doing things for you?" Dave jaw dropped and Pat's body stiffened.

"What are your implying now, Diana?" asked Pat.

"What do we know about you?" Diana remarked, relaxing her aggressive stance and returning to the front of the room. "You sit there by yourself outside Dave's office. You come and go and no one really knows what you're doing. Who knows, maybe Cynthia wasn't the first person in the branch Dave had an affair with? Maybe you didn't like her taking your place?" Diana paused and smiled unkindly at Pat before continuing. "One thing we do know about you is how often you go to the gym. You, of anyone, had the strength to grab Doris, hold her and slice her throat."

"And she was the first one to find Doris's body," Shirley added.

"Yes, she was," Diana said, waiting for a reaction from Pat.

"When she was pointing you out as the killer," Pat said calmly to Shirley, "she was making it up, and now when she's doing the same with me, you believe her?" Pat sat comfortably in her chair showing no nervousness or tension. She slowly crossed one long leg over the other and continued, "If you are waiting for me to break down and confess, Diana, you will be waiting a long time. If this is all you have you are pretty desperate."

"And speaking of desperate," Diana continued turning to Mike. "We come back to you. Money is right up there as a motive for murder. And who had better opportunity? Who says you didn't make, and poison, the coffee? Only you. And you wouldn't have been able to give Cynthia her coffee yourself. She would have smelt a rat. You had to use Doris but did you have to kill her?"

"You don't know what you're talking about," retorted Mike.

"Are you sure?" Diana said calmly. Mike sat stone still not responding. Turning to the Scotts, Diana continued, "And so what about you two?" Talking to Barbara alone, she said, "You have made it clear, too clear, that you're not interested, not part of this. But you are part of this. You keep saying you didn't know Cynthia but I don't believe you. So what was it? Something from long ago you want to keep buried? I've known Cynthia a long time, a long long time. I can fill in lots of gaps for the police about Cynthia's past. If there's a link that you're trying to hide, they will find it. I will make sure they find it. You, as easily as anyone else, could have asked Doris to give Cynthia some coffee. She would have done it for you and not thought a thing about it." Turning to face Robert Scott, she added, "And you, Doctor, where do you fit in all this? Because I know that you do."

"You know nothing," said Robert. "You're just going around and around in circles stretching your imagination and wasting our time. You know nothing."

"Maybe I don't know who did kill Cynthia but I know it was someone in this room. Doris knew," Diana continued. "Doris knew that the coffee she gave Cynthia was what killed her. She also knew who asked her to give it to Cynthia. She gave me some clues. It shouldn't take long, with a little digging, for the police to figure it out, once I tell them everything. And I'm prepared to tell them everything. Every little thing I can remember and," turning to face Robert, "everything I can imagine. It will be better all around to get this settled quickly." Turning back to face the whole group, she continued, "To settle this for yourself, whoever you are. So here's the thing. You have 24 hours to go to Inspector Hanlon or I do."

"There isn't anything you can tell the police," Robert stated with conviction. "They're not interested in the rambling of a fool. They're more likely to arrest you than listen to you. You know nothing," Robert concluded. "And you've had all of my time you're going to get. Come on, Barbara. I have had enough of this charade. We're leaving. Play your games, all of you, but we will not participate any further. Manders, my wife will no longer be coming to work at your bank. Send any outstanding pay and anything else due her to our home." With that the two of them left the room.

"I think we will follow their example," Sybil said rising and beckoning Dave to join her. "Good night, Diana, always interesting."

"You don't really think I killed them, do you?" asked Shirley. "I thought we were friends." Diana didn't answer and Stephen took his wife's hand and together they followed Sybil and Dave out of the room.

Pat rose, nodded to Diana and left the room.

31

MIKE ALONE REMAINED. He sat like a stone, his eyes unfocussed. Diana waited for him to say something or for him to do something. Finally, he rose and reached for the knife from the cheese platter. Toying with it, he wandered the room still not acknowledging Diana or where he was. He walked past the front couch and stood in front of the wall of books. He finally turned and moved back towards the center of the room, towards Diana. Now he was looking at her. She could see him struggling to say something, but what?

"I don't know what to do," Mike muttered. Diana waited and slowly Mike continued. "You don't understand, you can't understand. I felt so trapped. So many things, so many problems, and Cynthia – everywhere Cynthia nagging, threatening. It was too much. It still is. I don't know what to do."

"Don't do anything stupid, Mike," Diana said sharply,, looking down at the knife. Mike followed her eyes and seemed to be startled to see what his hand held. He jerked and in doing so tossed the knife on the table. He stood in shock, then turned and almost ran from the room.

Diana turned back to the fireplace feeling tired and

drained. She prodded the fire though it didn't need it, and in her mind's eye replayed the evening. It was as she had planned and as she expected. So it was done. Would it work? Did they now believe she wasn't the killer? Did they believe it was one of them? What next? Was she ready? Her question was answered by a voice.

"Did you mean what you said?" Dave Manders asked.

"Yes," Diana said turning. He was standing much too close. "Where's Sybil?"

"In the car," he replied. "I said I forgot my wallet in here. Sybil didn't kill Cynthia. So I wouldn't have needed to kill Doris to protect her." His voice was flat and for once his body looked alert and firm. Diana stepped away.

"Unless you killed Cynthia," Diana said. There was silence from Dave Manders. He started to fumble in his pockets, his eyes searching the room. He was looking for something. His eyes stopped at the table where Mike had thrown the knife.

"I do understand what it must have been like, Dave," Diana said trying to break into his concentration. "Cynthia could be charming."

"She was so beautiful," Manders replied withdrawing into himself. "She was so alive and had such an appetite – for everything." He turned to look at Diana then added, "She made me feel young." Diana watched Manders deflate in front of her.

"Go home, Mr. Manders, you have things to do and so do I." She walked towards him and slowly turned back to watching the fire. She did not hear him leave nor did she hear the next person enter the room.

"He didn't kill her," the voice said. "And you know it, don't you? You said you didn't know who did it but you do, don't you? "

"Yes," Diana said turning to face the other woman. The veil was lifted and before Diana stood someone she had never encountered. A street fighter had replaced the elegant

Oak Bay wife. The knife from the coffee table had replaced the designer handbag. "And now me, Barbara? When does it stop?"

Barbara kept walking towards Diana as Diana tried to back away. Well, this was it. Her plan had worked – recreate the desperation that drove Doris' killing, provide an accessible weapon, drive for the boiling point in a controlled environment. That had been the plan. It had worked. Now what? Diana hadn't thought any further. Barbara had seemed small, fragile almost. Diana hadn't been afraid of her. She had been wrong.

"I knew she'd never leave me alone," Barbara said marching towards her. "And now you!"

Diana kept moving away from her but for every step she took, Barbara stayed with her, pushing furniture out of the way when necessary. It wasn't a big room. Diana had to think of something. She had expected to be able to talk to Barbara, overpower her if necessary but first just talk. She watched the wide-eyed animal stalk her. Where was Barbara? Maybe if Diana could get her to talk.

"But why, Barbara," Diana said. "What did Cynthia know?"

"You want to know, you want to know," screeched Barbara spinning around to find something to destroy. "You do all this and you know NOTHING!" she continued screaming. "You're all the same, so superior, so perfect. Ruin other people's lives without knowing a THING!"

"Then tell me, Barbara," said Diana, as soothingly as she could. "Explain it to me. Why Cynthia?"

"She would never have left me alone," Barbara's voice now had taken on a mournful whine. "I had to. She would never have left me alone. She'd have continued questioning, poking, and prying until she had remembered. And then she would have ruined everything." Noticing Diana again, Barbara raised the knife and once more started towards her prey.

"Ruin what, Barbara?" asked Diana beseechingly. "Tell me, I want to understand. I knew Cynthia too. I don't blame you."

Barbara looked at Diana like she was a new specimen in biology class. Cocking her head to the side, she continued to watch Diana, watch for a change, a movement, any movement. "Robert," she finally said letting the knife hand fall to her side. "She would have ruined Robert. He would have left me." Diana waited, not daring to interrupt Barbara. "It was so long ago but she would have brought it all back, all back. Robert would have found out. Robert. I didn't do anything wrong. I was young." A little lost child looked to Diana for approval.

"No, of course not, Barbara," Diana said the scripted lines. "I'm sure Robert would understand. Why don't we just tell him? Get it over with."

"Oh, it's going to be over alright!" Barbara screamed. Diana had triggered the fear and Barbara's turmoil was back. She again started moving towards Diana, blind to any obstacles. "No, no. Robert would never understand. His mother would not have approved. They are above all that. No moral weakness. None. I was 15!"

"That's all in the past," Diana said trying to bring Barbara back to sanity.

"No, it's not," Barbara raved. "It's not. My baby, my poor baby. Gone   I let my baby go and I worked and worked. It took me so long to get here, to get Robert, to get my life. The life I get from Robert. I gave up my baby. I won't go back. Cynthia would have remembered. She would have ruined everything, I couldn't let her ruin everything. I can't let you. Why couldn't you leave it alone?"

"Doris." Diana said, trying to distract her knowing there wasn't much time left.

"I didn't want to hurt her but she was going to talk. I had to stop her – she left me no choice – like you."

Diana had no room left. She was in the corner of the bookshelf. The tipped over end table blocked her exit. Barbara now only had one purpose. All the energy in the room came from Barbara. Her left hand whipped out and grasped a clump of Diana's hair. Pulling her head back to expose the neck, Barbara raised her right hand and brought point of the knife to under Diana's right ear.

"This is what she must have done to Doris," Diana thought, believing it to be her last.

"Hey, what's going on?" It was Mike's voice. Barbara turned and gave just enough room for Diana to break free of her grasp. The knife nicked the edge of her neck. Too close, too close. Barbara was struggling to understand this latest development. Now there were two but Diana was still closest.

"It's over, Barbara" said Diana. "Can't you see that. You can't get away from both of us."

"I have to, I have to," she cried as she struck at Diana. Mike dove over the couch and pinned Barbara to the bookshelf pulling her arm away from Diana at the last moment.

"Hold it right there," Hanlon ordered.

Diana turned and saw him and Deck rushing through the doorway, guns drawn. "What are you doing here?" she asked.

"I called him," Anna piped up triumphantly now entering the room.

"We were on our way to Barbara's when we got your sister's call," Hanlon said as Deck handcuffed Barbara. "You couldn't give us a couple of hours? Had to do it all alone, trying to get yourself killed?"

Smiling, Diana gave him a little shrug.

32

ALL THE STATEMENTS had been given, all the questions answered, and everyone finally left. Anna and Diana sat companionably together in front of the fireplace. Diana watched the flames, sipped a drink and thought about days long past.

"So when are you going to tell me what this was all about?" Anna asked interrupting Diana's remembering.

"I thought you had it all worked out," Diana teased. "Calling in the cavalry like that."

"I had it worked out that you were crazy," Anna countered. "And needed protection."

"Yes, well, thanks."

"You're welcome," Anna replied. "Now quit stalling."

"There isn't much," Diana said. "And it's so sad that such an insignificant event could have caused all this." Seeing her sister's puzzled face, Diana continued. "It was back when Sam and I were married. Cynthia went after Sam and I guess she won."

"You don't have to go over that again, Diana."

"It's alright," Diana replied. "It's over. In a funny way, this whole thing with Cynthia and Barbara has made me realize it really is over and it's okay. Anyway, it was at that time that Cynthia became pregnant. She said it was Sam's. I didn't believe she was even pregnant but there is a birth certificate so I guess she was. She went to a group home in Vancouver to have the baby. She said it died. She kept the birth certificate but there's no death certificate. So the baby was probably adopted. Sam's son, it's odd to think about. In that group home, there was another girl struggling to change her life the same as Cynthia."

"Barbara?" asked Anna.

"Barbara," Diana answered. "They both had moved a long way from that time and neither would have wanted to go back or have it come out. Barbara's new life was built around her husband and he is very, very precise about what is and is not acceptable. I think we're safe in assuming she never shared that part of her life with him. Tolerance and acceptance do not seem to be his strong suit. She probably didn't think he would marry her if he knew about her past and she was probably right. Then with not telling him before they married, she sure couldn't tell him after." Diana paused and sipped more of her amaretto before continuing. "It must have been quite a surprise for Barbara when Cynthia came back from holidays. She recognized Cynthia right off and definitely did not want their time together in Vancouver to become known. So to Barbara, Cynthia was a threat. She used Doris to kill Cynthia by getting her to give Cynthia the poisoned coffee. I don't really understand the mass poisoning in the coffeepot. That was pretty feeble. Then again, there was desperation in everything Barbara did. Doris realized pretty quickly what had happened and started to come unglued. So then she became a threat. Now that murder was very desperate. Barbara heard Doris confess when Shirley did. So, she followed Doris into the lunchroom. With everyone around and the police arriving any second, she slashed Doris's throat, rinsed the knife and tossed it in with the other dirty dishes, cleaned herself up and then went back to work." Describing Barbara's actions out loud silenced both the sisters.

"And this was the person you decided to set a trap for?" Anna asked. "To make yourself a threat to?"

"I wanted her to think I was a threat, yes," Diana explained. "I needed her to show herself. I needed to be sure it was Barbara. To be sure that I hadn't figured it out wrong."

"I thought Doris told you who had done it?" Anna asked.

"Not exactly," Diana confessed. "Doris told me that it was a 'she' who told her to give the coffee to Cynthia but then we were interrupted before she could say more. We were interrupted by Barbara. That might or might not have been important. Doris was pretty nervous so I couldn't really tell if it was Barbara or if it was simply the interruption that caused her to stop talking. Then when Shirley told me about Doris' confession, she said she had heard it from Barbara's office. So obviously Barbara could also have heard it. Of course, if it was that easy to overhear from Barbara's office, Pat could just as easily have heard it from her desk. Just guessing, all circumstantial."

"Then Hanlon took me to Cynthia's," she continued. "I looked through her stuff and in some old pictures there was one with a group of women. It looked like it would have been about the time Cynthia supposedly was in the Vancouver group home having Sam's baby. Everyone's name was marked with the picture. None of them matched directly anyone at the bank. Not the full names, there were some first names that did. There was a Barbara. There also was a Patricia and a couple of other common names. I didn't recognize any faces. Neither did Hanlon. Actually it was pretty hard even to recognize Cynthia. The clothes, the hair, everything. Everyone had changed so much."

"So did you really not know who was the killer when you brought all these people together tonight?" asked Anna, as Diana paused to stir the fire.

"The thing I kept coming back to was, why now?" Diana

answered. "Most of us have been working with Cynthia for years. So what changed to make it necessary to kill her now? That brought me back to Barbara and her being new. Everything kept bringing me back to Barbara. It had to be her but I needed to be sure."

"Well, now you can be sure!" Anna said. The sisters sat with their own thoughts for a few moments and then Anna voiced hers, "To think all this was just to keep a thousand year old secret from your husband   the person who is supposed to love you."

"You want the really sad part?" Diana said, nodding.

"What?"

"I don't think Cynthia had any idea who Barbara was. She just knew Barbara wanted to avoid her and that piqued her curiosity. Cynthia was so interested in herself I don't think she'd have recognized her own mother any more even if she had walked right up to her."

"Nuts! They were both nuts. I'm glad it's over!" said Anna with finality. "So then what about this policeman?"

Across town a very different pair had reached the same point in the conversation.

"So what about this Diana Hillis?" Deck asked Hanlon.

"I don't know what you're referring to, Sergeant."

"You're the one who taught me not to ignore my instincts," Deck replied. "And there you were knowing she was innocent and determined to think she was guilty just because you wanted her. So what's the excuse now? The case is over and she's not a murderer. Never thought she was personally."

"You didn't," repeated Hanlon. "You didn't happen to mention it before."

"You weren't ready to hear it before. All in turmoil trying to avoid admitting you liked her. Well you can call now. You've wanted to all along," Deck said handing him the phone.

"And when did you get to be so observant," Hanlon

replied taking the phone.

"Well, I learned from the best, sir," Deck said, smiling.

THE END

ISBN 142510664-1